The Wildest One

USA TODAY BESTSELLING AUTHOR
MARNI MANN

Copyright © 2025 by Marni Mann
All rights reserved.

Visit my website at: www.MarniSMann.com
Cover Designer: Hang Le, By Hang Le
Editor: Jovana Shirley, Unforeseen Editing, www.unforeseenediting.com
Proofreaders: Judy Zweifel of Judy's Proofreading, Christine Estevez, and Vicki Valente
Photographer and Cover Image: PaperbackModel, Daniel Jaems

No part of this book may be reproduced or transmitted in any form or by any means, electronic or mechanical, including photocopying, recording, or by any information storage and retrieval system without the written permission of the author, except for the use of brief quotations in a book review.

This book is a work of fiction. Names, characters, places, and incidents either are products of the author's imagination or are used fictitiously. Any resemblance to actual persons, living or dead, events, or locales is entirely coincidental.

ISBN-13: 979-8-9894377-7-1

When a man who once felt there was no greater life than playing hockey meets his forever love and she proves there's far more off the ice than on it ... except during the moments when the two collide and create spice on the ice.
Get ready, ladies.

PLAYLIST

"I Hope It Hurts"—Jessie Murph
"Joy Ride"—Hueston
"High Heels"—Hueston
"Nick Cage 93"—Hueston
"Different Kind of Pain"—Sam Barber
"Jolene"—Dolly Parton
"Fight & Fuck"—G-Eazy
"Champagne in the Morning"—Redferrin
"Meet the Devil in Oklahoma"—Josh Meloy
"Wildcard"—Coey Redd
"Dreams"—Fleetwood Mac
"Tall Boy"—Shaboozey

Click here to check out the Spotify playlist.

ONE

Beck

There was only one thing that smelled as good as pussy, and that was the scent of victory.

At the end of a long game, when I could stand in the middle of a bar and hold my beer in the air, shouting to my team, "To another win for the Whales," that was the most indescribable feeling.

The air thickened as my teammates moved in closer, huddling around me, repeating the words I'd just voiced.

Which I followed up with, "And to fucking destroying Boston—for the second time this season."

"Five to one," my left defenseman called out. "I'd say that's a shutout."

"Almost a shutout," I countered. "But I'll take it." I looked at each of their faces. "I'm proud of you guys!"

"And to our captain, for getting us a long-needed break," my right wing declared.

"Use it wisely," I ordered. "Cheers!"

"Cheers," they all repeated.

I kept my beer high, booze sloshing over the sides of most glasses while we attempted to clink them together. Once they hit, I took a long sip, and the huddle loosened around me, giving me just enough space to move out and position myself along the front of the bar. I was placing my back against the bar top, getting a full view of the room, when my goalie joined me.

Landon clasped my shoulder. "You know, you've got some balls to give a toast like that while you're in a bar in the center of Beantown."

I shook my head, laughing. "You know I give zero fucks." I moved to the right and left, as if we were in a boxing match and I was dodging his punches. "What, is someone going to fight me? Here? In front of my entire team? Come on, man. There isn't a single motherfucker in this bar who could even lay a finger on me."

Landon had transferred to LA a season ago after spending two seasons in Boston. So, when I'd taken it upon myself to encourage our coach and manager to switch up our travel schedule to spend tonight and the next two evenings here, rather than Washington, DC,—the team we were playing next —Landon was all for it. I'd noticed that when the East Coast fellas came to play on the West Coast, they never entirely gave up their love for home.

I wouldn't know.

Aside from attending Michigan State, I'd spent my whole life in California.

"Beck, you don't know this city like I do." He released my shoulder and held his beer with both hands. "The dudes around here will fight at the drop of a hat—even less. If you give zero fucks, I assure you, they give even less. Shit, they look for reasons to raise their fists."

I dragged out my exhale longer than I needed to. "I fight for a living. I train for hours every day, just like you. I'd like to see them try to beat my ass." I gave him a smile. "Hell, I'd welcome it."

"You're a fucking animal."

"That's why they call me the wildest one." I wrapped an arm around my chest. "Enough about that. You played a good game tonight, buddy." I unraveled that arm to pound his fist.

When he pulled his fingers back from bumping mine, he ran them over the top of his blond hair, which hadn't been cut all season, his strands popping off in every direction, like one of those spiky plants. Our team, like most, was superstitious—some didn't cut their hair, some didn't shave, and some didn't do either. When I was home, my barber came to my house every week to trim me up, but my face was an entirely different story. My beard had been growing since preseason.

"The game started off a little shaky." He pulled at his open collar. "I didn't think we were going to get the win."

"Our defensemen just needed to get their bearings. That's why I pushed to stay here. I can't fucking stand flying cross-country and playing the same night, and I know we had no choice with our schedule, but tonight, we had an option to either crash here or fly out, so I put my foot down." I gripped the back of my neck, working out a deep ache in the muscle, feeling the ends of my hair that were still the slightest bit wet from my postgame shower. "We're tired. We're sore. We need a rest."

"Ain't that the truth?" He rubbed his thumb over his mouth. "I didn't think Coach was going to change his mind"—he laughed—"but I should know better. When it comes to you, Captain, he always listens."

"Not always"—I punched his arm before my hand dropped—"but I put up a solid argument. He knows we need a minute. We've already been on the road for four days. After the next few games, it'll be close to two weeks. That's a long-ass time to be away. When we have a small break, like this one, I want to capitalize on it. Come the DC game, we'll be ready to play."

He hit his beer against mine. "A-fucking-men to that." He pointed at several of our teammates standing on the other side of the bar. "Except something tells me they're going to do anything but rest while we're here."

The group, our second line, was pouring back shots of something clear—tequila, vodka, whatever.

"I got them the break," I huffed. "What they decide to do with it is on them."

Once he took a drink, he ran his fingers through his beard, the scratching of his whiskers drowned out by the music. "Do you know how I'm going to spend it?"

"There's no question in my mind." I smiled at my friend. "How many women do you have lined up? One for each night we're here?" When he said nothing, I laughed. "More?"

"Just one—and that one is more than enough."

"She's an ex?"

He rubbed his lips together. "Not quite that. Just someone I used to mess around with." He dipped his head. "How are you going to spend these three nights?"

Considering it was after midnight, technically, there were only two left.

And my mind had already mapped out every hour that I didn't have to spend on the ice or in the weight room.

"I'm going to finish this beer, jump in an Uber, go back to the hotel, and sleep until tomorrow's practice."

His head fell back as he laughed. "I don't believe that."

"Why?"

"Because she can't take her fucking eyes off you."

I glanced forward, assuming that was where *she* was located. "She—" My voice cut off as a flash of black and gold came across my vision. "Oh fuck, yes." But it wasn't those colors keeping my attention locked.

It was the red of her hair.

Long strands that framed the most beautiful face I'd ever seen. The sexiest lips puckered around a straw as she sipped her pink drink, silver nails sparkling as she held the glass. Creamy skin and a small, sloped nose, eyes of an unknown color because they weren't on me. They were on the woman she was standing next to. The redhead's black-and-gold sweatshirt hung open, a tight shirt beneath—showing off the most perfect-sized tits and a narrow waist—tucked into her jeans, which were a little too baggy to show her legs, but I was sure those were just as fucking delicious as the rest of her.

"Sounds like you've suddenly changed your mind. Attaboy. We both know there's nothing better than having sex after a game to let out that pent-up aggression." He nudged my arm. "And by the way she's eye-fucking you, I don't think that's going to be hard."

"What are you talking about? She's not even looking at me."

She was still gazing at her friend, unaware that I was visually feasting on her, which gave my stare all the freedom to sweep up and down, devouring her body.

"Huh? She's staring at nothing *but you.*" He paused. "How do you not see what I'm seeing?"

I blinked several times, making sure my vision wasn't messing with me, and when I was sure it wasn't, I said, "Who are you talking about, Landon?"

His eyes widened as I looked at him. "How do you *not* know who I'm talking about? The blonde at three o'clock."

Three o'clock.

I shifted my gaze until I found the short-haired blonde who was doing just as he'd said—eye-fucking every square inch of me—and I immediately looked away. "Nah, man. She's not for me."

"You were looking at someone, practically fucking drooling. Who was it, then?"

"If I was going after anyone, it would be her." I nodded toward the redhead. "Twelve o'clock." I let out a moan. "Tell me you've seen a woman more gorgeous ... I dare you."

"Damn. She's hot as hell." He leaned in closer. "I was with a redhead once—it was a night I'll never forget. What I'm saying is, get your ass over there and buy her a drink."

I chuckled. "If I go over there, that's just how things will turn out—a night I'll never forget. I told you, I'm getting the fuck out of here and going to my hotel room. Alone."

A grin spread across his face. "Are you sure about that?"

"I'm positive."

"Why don't you look at her again and then repeat those words to me?"

Twelve o'clock was where my stare shifted, and the second it did, I realized why Landon had wanted me to take this second glance.

The redhead was finally looking at me.

And those eyes—*fuck*. I could see the blueness from here. Along with a hint of the most beautiful smile.

She had an unassuming style and a kind of softness I craved in a woman, but never got because most were like the short-haired blonde—overdone and edgy.

Two blinks. That was all the time the redhead gave me before her stare returned to her friend.

But it was a long enough span to make my goddamn dick hard. To make my hand clench my beer as though it were her waist. To make the need in my body grow like the puck was in my possession and I'd just passed the blue line on my way to the goal.

"Now I dare you to tell me you're not going to go over there and at least talk to her."

I ground my teeth. "Stop using my words, asshole."

"But notice you didn't disagree."

I slowly filled my lungs, using the same speed to let the air out. "You're killing me, Landon."

"No, brother. I'm saving you."

"From what?"

"If you leave Boston without knowing what she tastes like, you'll never forgive yourself."

I laughed.

"What, you think I'm kidding?" he pressed. "I know you. The second we get on that plane to fly to DC in a couple of days, you're going to bitch and moan about how you passed up the chance of a lifetime and—"

"How do you know she'd even say yes?"

"The only person who can get her to do that is you." He shook his head at me, grinning like a fucking fool. "I think she'd be all yours." His brows rose. "Are you going to prove that to me? Or are you going to go back to your hotel room, alone, and make one of the biggest mistakes of your life?"

TWO

Jolie

Little jitters of anxiousness fluttered inside my chest as we stood near the front section of the bar, the room getting fuller by the minute. I bit my straw, flicking my tongue across the end of the hard plastic.

"Tell me again why we're here," I said to my best friend and roommate, sipping a pink lady—a cocktail I never normally ordered, but it had sounded fun when the bartender mentioned it.

"Because our fake IDs didn't work at the arena—they're too strict there—and I needed a drink before we headed back to campus," Ginger said. "You dragged me to the game tonight, so I dragged you here."

"I didn't exactly drag you." I fisted several bunches of her dark curls, running my fingers through them. The long-standing joke in our friendship was that she should have been named Jolie, and given my hair color, I should have been called

Ginger. "The second the word *hockey* came out of my mouth, you were more than in."

"Ugh, true. You got me there." She suddenly had heart eyes. "The thought of those sweaty, bearded men with endless chiseled muscles does everything to me."

I shook my head, laughing. "We need to find you a hockey player to date. I mean, we have a whole team of them at Boston University. Why don't we start going to hockey parties so we can score you a boyfriend? Or two?"

Once an athlete reached his junior year at our school, he tended to move off campus, living in a house with a slew of other teammates. Ginger and I made our way around the party scene, but we almost always ended up at a frat house rather than the football, baseball, basketball, lacrosse, swim, or hockey house.

She snorted. "Jolie, we need to change that immediately and focus solely on hockey parties. Tomorrow night, we're rounding up the girls and going to the hockey house."

"Except they have an away game."

"Only my luck."

"Don't worry, they're home next weekend." I curled my arm around her shoulders and pressed our cheeks together. "We're going to make that dream of yours come true—mark my words."

When I released her, she replied, "I sound like the biggest nut, don't I?"

"What? No." I squeezed her arm. "I get why you have a love for hockey dudes, trust me."

"So, that means we need to find you one too."

My head shook so fast that my long red hair whipped into my face. "Hard no."

"Why?"

My cheeks puffed out as I took a deep breath. "I'm just ... I don't know."

"You're just, *what*?"

The straw returned to my mouth as I thought about her question. "I'm in my distraction-free era."

"What are you even talking about?"

"I'm talking about time." I leaned against the back of a chair. "The last thing I need is someone who's going to take up more of it when I hardly have any to begin with. Between classes and work, I'm swamped, girl."

She pointed her finger at me and smiled. "Your ass needs to make time."

I knew Ginger better than anyone—we'd been roommates since the first day of our freshman year; therefore, I knew where this conversation was headed. So, I sucked down the rest of my drink, hoping the gin would make this talk a little less painful, and set the empty on the table in front of the chair.

"But there aren't enough hours in a day to make that happen. You know I'm drowning as it is."

She looked away, and I could tell she was annoyed, which was what happened every time we talked about my lack of a dating life, but when her stare returned, it appeared like her entire attitude had changed. In fact, it was like the lotto had just put the fattest check in her hands, and she was gawking at all the zeros.

"Don't look. But, *oh my God*, Beck Weston is literally staring you down."

"Beck Weston?" That name needed no explanation. Hockey had been a part of my life since my earliest childhood memories. But I still said, "As in the captain of the LA Whales," because I needed extra confirmation.

"Uh-huh."

My heart was pounding. "We're talking about the guy who slaughtered Boston tonight, scoring four out of their five goals?"

"Mmhmm." Her eyes were as big as they could get. "And he's, like, *staring*, staring at you. Not just looking. I'm talking full-on ogling."

The nervousness that had been in my chest—the feeling that came whenever I had more work than I knew what to do with and I was trying to figure out how to balance fun and school and my job and failing miserably at all of it—moved to my stomach. "Why?"

She held on to my shoulder and shook it. "What do you mean, why? Because you're the hottest thing to ever walk the planet. That's why."

"Stop."

"You know it's true—wait, I take that back. You don't know it's true." Her hand stilled. "My mission in life is to make you one day realize it's true."

"Ginger," I groaned.

"We can fight about this later. The important thing right now is Beck." She waved her hand in front of her face. "I can't even believe we're breathing the same air as him. I'm trying to keep my cool, but I'm fangirling so hard that I can't stop talking." She jumped a little. "And he's still looking at you, girl. Like, he hasn't even noticed me checking him out because he's too focused on you."

The truth was, I couldn't believe Beck Weston—a multiple Stanley Cup winner, highest-scoring left wing in the league—was in this bar either.

But my reaction to things was much different from my best friend's.

"Where is he?" I asked.

"It doesn't matter where he is. You can't look at him. You have to keep your eyes on me and play it cool."

"Why? It's not like anything is going to happen. For one, he may be staring, but he'd never be interested, not when he could get any woman in this state—or New England, for that matter—to have sex with him. And two, even if he were interested—which, let me emphasize again, would be so far-fetched—I'd never do it. I'm not the *sleeping around* type—you know that. I'm practically allergic to the whole concept."

"Hold on a second. You're telling me you wouldn't?" First, she raised her brows, and as they lowered, she snorted. "Girl, are you high? I don't care what you say, you so would."

I couldn't even put my brain there. The idea was that incomprehensible.

But for just a few seconds, I tried to envision what it would be like—the fantasy of Beck Weston slowly lifting through the thick clouds. It was like I was standing straight under the sun—that was the level of heat that washed over my entire body. But it wasn't just a wave of scorching rays that hit me; it was a deep, consuming pulsing too.

What's even happening right now?

"You might be right." I nodded overaggressively. "I'd probably die for that chance."

She smirked. "Just like I thought."

"Not that it even matters. I'm sure he's already gotten bored with looking at me—"

My voice cut off after I turned my head, instantly connecting eyes with him.

Although I'd been to many games when Boston played LA—my father had had season tickets for as long as I could remember and I always went with him—and I'd seen pictures of Beck on gossip sites and on Celebrity Alerts, admiring him in person was something far different.

In all those pics, he was a super-good-looking guy, of course.

But as I stood less than ten feet away from him—where he was positioned by the bar top, next to the goalie of the Whales—I was absolutely certain he was the hottest man I'd ever seen in my life.

He had chestnut-brown hair that was long on the top, the sides shaved to the start of his beard, which was bushy and overgrown and so sexy in this alpha, unhinged sort of way. He had hazel eyes that were hooded as they focused on me, thin lips, a thick neck that had veins running down both sides.

And then there was his body.

He had to be around six-three and was extra broad. The first two buttons of his shirt were undone, showing a small dusting of hair and a gold chain, and the rest of the fabric hugged his bulging biceps and what I assumed was a set of chiseled abs.

I was positive I'd stopped breathing.

And thinking.

I blinked.

And then I blinked again, doing everything I could to remind myself that I was here, in a bar, beside Ginger, looking at one of the most famous NHL players to ever exist.

As each of those points processed through my head—the latter being the most dominant—I forced my stare upon Ginger. "I ... can't breathe."

"Neither can I—and he's not even looking at me."

I needed to get my thoughts straight. Right now, they were bouncing like a dribbling basketball. And I needed to get out of this spot. I felt claustrophobic even though we were in the center of a bar and there was plenty of air around me. There was something about being under his stare that was making me feel cemented.

"I'm going to go get another drink," I told her.

"You're going to do what?"

"I need one more drink, and then I need to go home and finish the paper that's due on Monday because at some point tomorrow, I need to go into work and get that to-do list cleared before I get too far behind."

"Babe, do I need to check your temperature?" She put her hand on my forehead. "Are you all right—"

I didn't let her finish her sentence before I turned away and walked the short distance to the bar, squeezing my way between two people, hailing down a bartender.

"Can I get a whiskey sour, please? Make it a double and go light on the sour."

"That's too tart for me. I'll just take the whiskey—also make mine a double. And put her drink on my tab."

My back stiffened at the voice that had come from beside me. I'd felt the shift and exchange of people as I was speaking my order to the bartender and sensed someone new was next to me, but it couldn't be Beck Weston. There was no way he'd followed me to the other side of the bar from where he'd been standing.

I took a quick glance.

Shit.

It was most definitely him.

"Hi." That was the only word that dared to come out of my mouth. All the others were locked on top of my tongue, the key nowhere to be found.

He let out a small chuckle—a sound that was better than any song I'd ever heard—and he smiled. "Hello." He wasn't just looking at me. He was looking through me. Those big hazel eyes, rimmed with long lashes, felt as though they were covering my entire body, not just connecting with my gaze. "I can tell you need a drink. I want to be the one who buys it for you."

Talk, Jolie. Use your words.

You've been around plenty of handsome men before, just not this delicious. But that shouldn't matter. At the end of the day, he's just another guy.

Who am I kidding? Beck Weston isn't just another guy. He's *the* guy.

I cleared my throat. "You think I need a drink?"

His tongue skimmed the inside of his bottom lip. "Yes."

"And what gave you that impression?"

"We'll call it a hunch."

My voice was soft as I said, "You don't have to buy it. I can pay for my own. But that's really nice of you to offer."

"I want to." He continued to look at me with those smoldering eyes. "Let me."

I found myself smiling, and then I found myself nodding.

As he leaned over the edge of the bar—our shoulders basically pressed together within the tight, narrow space we'd squeezed into—he extended his hand. "I'm Beck."

"I know. I ..."

I went to the game? I know all about your career? I'm the most avid hockey fan? I bit my lip instead of saying any of that and watched his stare move to my mouth.

His hand was so large as it clasped mine; I suddenly felt child-sized.

"I'm Jolie."

As he gripped me harder, my body reacted. This wasn't just a simple shaking of my hand. He was setting me on fire, and instead of using a match, he was using a flamethrower.

"Jolie ... that's different. I like it."

My throat was threatening to close in. "I'm named after 'Jolene.' You know, the Dolly Parton song. The lyrics don't exactly fit the way my parents met or their love story, but since it's the first song they ever danced to, it's meaningful to them."

Why had I gone from locked up to word-vomit mode? I was

starting to sound like Ginger, and no one in this world talked as much as my best friend.

"Jolene is your real name, then?"

I nodded, my fingers falling from his, and I immediately linked both of my hands together. "I shorten it, depending on my mood and who I'm meeting. But Jolie is what my friends call me."

"Jolie, what's your mood right now?"

I laughed. I didn't know how else to react.

"I guess you're considering me part of that friend circle," he continued.

While he waited for a response, my face blushed.

"A whiskey sour, light on the sour," the bartender said, placing a glass in front of me, saving me from replying. "And just whiskey." A tumbler was set in front of Beck.

I unlinked my fingers and wrapped them around the cold glass. "Thank you," I said to the bartender. "And thank you," I voiced to Beck, still staring at him as I added, "Tell me why, out of all the people in this bar, you want to buy *me* a drink."

He let out another laugh. "Why ... well, there are two reasons. The first, it gives me a chance to talk to you. As soon as I saw you, that's all I could think about. How badly I wanted to chat with the gorgeous redhead." His stare slowly dipped down my face.

Since I still couldn't breathe, my body a tornado of tingles, I lifted a hand from my drink and gripped a chunk of hair, hoping I could let go of some of this energy.

But the longer he looked at me, the more it built.

There was no release.

There was just this steady increase of the most relentless throbbing.

"And the second?" I asked.

His teeth nipped his lip, the same one he'd licked. "That

was one hell of a loss you guys suffered tonight. Thought a little booze might help ease the sting." He clinked his glass against mine.

"I'm not going to lie—tonight was a real doozy." I exhaled. "I was at the game."

"I figured."

"How did you figure?"

His stare moved again, this time down the front of me. "You're wearing your team's sweatshirt."

"Oh. Right."

I assumed his eyes would meet mine as I spoke, but they didn't. They stayed on my body, and as they gradually lifted, I felt myself inhale.

"Jolie, I won't hold it against you that you're a Boston fan."

"I won't hold it against you that you play for LA." I didn't have a Boston accent. I'd somehow spent the last twenty years pronouncing all my *R*'s correctly, but for my response, I imitated the way my mom—a born and raised Bostonian—would say it.

"You're funny." He smiled and pushed down the hairs that framed his beard. "You fit and sound the part perfectly."

"I've spent my whole life here. I even stayed for college. I know my city better than anyone."

Of course, there were reasons I had stayed, none of which I would get into with him.

"Where did you go to school?"

"You mean, where do I currently go?"

His brows rose, and he leaned back from the bar, taking his drink with him. "You're still in college?"

"I'm a sophomore at BU."

"Jesus." He paused. "What are you, nineteen?"

"Twenty."

"I'd guessed you were young. I didn't think you were *that* young."

"Young heart with an old soul."

His gaze narrowed. "I get that sense."

Since I was sure we'd reached the end of our conversation—there was absolutely no way this man wanted to continue talking to me—I wiggled the glass in the air. "Thanks again for the drink."

The section in which we were standing was highly desirable, given that the bar was becoming packed, so I stepped away, walking toward Ginger, catching eyes with her, which earned me the biggest grin. But when I was halfway to her, I sensed someone following me, and I turned around. Beck was only a few steps away, and this time, his stare was about level with my ass.

"What are you doing, Beck?" I focused on his eyes as they rose, my cheeks heating in response.

"What am I doing right now? Or what do I want to do?"

"Right now."

"I'm chasing you like a puck."

I laughed. "Why?"

"Because I want more."

"Of what?"

"You."

A reply that rocked me so hard.

"But you know nothing about me."

"What you've told me, which has only been a little, is nothing more than a fucking tease. That's why I'm saying, I want more. Your name, what inspired it, your age, birthplace, college—it's not enough, Jolie."

I brought the drink up to my lips, my hand not stable, so I added my other hand too. "I find that so funny."

"You do?"

"This bar is filled with women—"

"And not a single one interests me. Before I saw you, my plan was to finish my beer and leave. You changed that. I told you, as soon as my eyes landed on you, all I wanted was to talk to you."

I couldn't believe a word of what I was hearing. Not that he was lying, but that he was saying these things to me.

Regardless of how mind-boggling this was, the more he spoke, the longer I could look at him—and that was something I wanted more of.

"All right, Beck. What do you want to know?"

He crossed an arm over his chest. "You'll tell me anything?"

"I'll welcome the questions. Whether I answer them? That's up for debate."

He huffed out some air as he smiled. "Are you single?"

"Wow." I glanced around us. People were moving so fast; no one was listening or even paying attention to us. "You're going right in ..."

"If I was going right in, my hands would be on your body, and my lips would be on yours. This is nothing more than a conversation."

He had a kind of charm I'd never experienced before.

I attempted to swallow. "I'm beyond single."

"You say that like there are different levels."

"There's the desire to date, but doing nothing about it." I held up a finger, signaling this was level one. "There's actively seeking out dates." I added a second finger. "And there's wanting nothing to do with dating." A third finger joined, and I waved the bunch in the air. "I'm in the *wanting nothing to do with dating* phase."

"Why?"

I sighed. This topic was rearing its ugly head again, but this time, it was in front of an audience that filled me with the most nervous energy. "Time."

"As someone who spends a lot of that on the road, I can appreciate your stance."

"Are you single?"

"Beyond." He winked.

"Because of time?"

"Time is a factor, yes. Travel is another." He rubbed his lips together, and when he released them, they weren't as thin as I'd originally thought. They were still on the small side, but a little bit girthier. "Plus, I just haven't found someone I want to commit to."

"I get it. You have multiple games a week from preseason in September all the way through April, and then the playoffs start. That's a short window of downtime."

He slowly nodded. "You know hockey?"

"I grew up watching it. My dad has season tickets. If he wasn't traveling for work, we never missed a home game." I turned quiet. "That's how I knew who you were."

"Considering you're from Boston, I'm surprised you don't want to fight me."

I laughed, and it felt so good to just loosen up for a second. "As a hockey fan, I'm in awe of your talent. As a diehard Boston fan ... let's just say, you're skating on thin ice."

His tongue tapped the center of his top lip, edging the line of hair around his mustache. "How thin?"

I took another drink. "Why are you asking?"

He took a step closer, and I caught a whiff of his scent. It was a combination—a hint of a shower that he'd probably taken after the game plus a dash of something spicy, like the most perfect cologne.

"Can I be honest?" he asked.

"Yes."

"How honest, Jolie?"

"What's the worst that can happen? I walk away? Never talk to you again?" I shrugged since I assumed we were going to part in the next few minutes anyway. "Try me."

He reached forward, and I thought he was going to cup my face, but he was only moving a piece of hair off my lip.

But still ... that touch.

It was electric.

And I could feel it, even after his hand was gone.

"I'm here for three nights, and then the team is flying out to DC for our next game. I want to spend those three nights with you."

My eyes bulged. "You ... *what*?"

"I told you I was going to be honest."

I couldn't control what was happening in my body. The feeling, at this point, was indescribable.

"Define exactly what you're asking for. I want to make sure I understand you correctly."

"I want you to show me Boston. Show it to me your way. Someone who's from here, who knows the secrets of the city. Secrets a newbie wouldn't know."

I held on to my stomach, my arm pushing tightly against it so my insides wouldn't burst through my outsides. "You're saying you want me to take you to the dive bar Ginger, my best friend, and I go to because they don't card? And to the overlook in Beacon Hill that has the very best views of the skyline? And to my favorite running path in Cambridge because I love being next to the Charles River?"

"Yes."

I laughed—like really laughed. "You're Beck Weston. The most famous player in the NHL and, at this moment, the most disliked man in the city of Boston." I winced, apologizing. "Do you think I can just bring you anywhere? You're a celebrity. You're going to draw a crowd."

"I haven't in here."

"That's because everyone is too hammered to see you. But you *will* get noticed, trust me."

He smiled. "I have a baseball hat."

I shook my head, trying to make sense of this. "Boston tour, check. What else does this three-night excursion include?"

"I want you to stay with me. In my hotel room. The entire time."

I turned my head, needing a break from his stare. And when I had the courage to say, "That's all you want? Me to sleep in your bed," I finally looked at him.

His chuckle was deep. "No." He gripped the back of his head.

"Then, what?"

His gaze took a dive down my body again. "I want to fuck the Boston off you."

THREE

Beck

"**I** *want to fuck the Boston off you.*"
Those words hung between Jolie and me like they were dangling on a fishing line. And while I waited for her to respond—to just say something—I could see the different stages of her thoughts.

The amusement from the idea that I wanted her to take me around Boston. The hint of desire at spending the next three nights in my bed. The shock that I'd so bluntly told her I wanted to fuck her.

I finished off my whiskey, and after I licked the wetness from my lips, I broke the silence with, "I told you, time is something I don't have. Therefore, I don't waste any when it comes to going after what I want. And right now, what I want is you."

"Me ..." She said the word as though she didn't believe it.

That was where her unassuming style and softness came in, making her different from the short-haired blonde who had been eye-fucking me earlier, along with most of the other women I'd been with.

Jolie had absolutely no idea how beautiful she was.

But by the time I got on my flight to DC, she would know.

Because I had every intention of telling her.

"Yes." I focused on her eyes, slowly gazing down toward her lips. "You."

I couldn't stop myself from touching her. If she didn't want it, all she had to do was step away. But she didn't do that when I put my empty glass down on a table and slipped my fingers around the back of her neck and tilted her face up. What she did instead was lean into me.

"We're beyond single. We live on opposite sides of the country—you're in school, and I travel for a living—so things start and end here." I took another step closer, leaving very little room between us. "But while I'm here and when I'm not at practice, I want you to show me why you love this city. And at night, I want to spend the evenings inside you. Tasting you. Fucking devouring you." I let her process that before I said, "The question is, do you want to spend this time with me?"

Her thoughts hadn't calmed. I could still see them clear as day in her eyes. Eyes that were barely blinking as she looked at me.

"I ..." Her lips stayed parted, her chest rising and falling so quickly.

"You what, Jolie?"

I swore a whole fucking minute passed before she answered, "I want that."

"Then let's get the hell out of here."

She put her hand on my chest. "I just need to tell Ginger that I'm going. Give me a second."

"I have to close out my tab. Meet me at the bar."

My hand dropped from her neck, and I watched her go

over to her friend, taking in the full view of that perfect fucking ass. While the two of them exchanged words, I went to the bar, catching the bartender's attention to request my bill and signing the bottom of the receipt once he gave it to me.

Jolie was behind me when I turned around.

"Ready," she said.

I moved our bodies together. "You don't have a car, do you?"

She laughed. "I live in the city. I take public transit everywhere I go."

"Yeah, I figured."

I pulled out my phone, hit the screen several times, making sure the locations were correct, and said, "A car will be here in two minutes."

As I shoved my cell in my pocket, I took her by the hand and led her outside, the cold winter air instantly causing her to shiver. I wrapped my arm around her while she zipped up her sweatshirt.

I tugged on the sleeve, rolling my goddamn eyes as I took in the black-and-gold colors—hopefully for the last time. "I can't fucking wait to get this off you."

"Because it's my team's sweatshirt?"

"That, yes. And because I really just want you naked."

Her eyes widened, and I pulled her against the front of me, my hands going to her face.

I stared at her for several seconds before I spoke. "You're surprised to hear me say that, aren't you?"

"Yes."

"Why?"

"Why?" She sounded hesitant. "Beck, I'm honestly the simplest gal there is. I go to class, I work, I study, I go to dive bars, and I party with my friends when time allows it. I have absolutely no idea why you want to spend these next three nights with me."

The softness was growing—not hardening, but spreading across every facet of her. All that did was make my dick harder since there was nothing hotter to me than a woman who didn't know her beauty.

"You don't see what I see ..." I whispered.

"Not at all."

"There isn't a part of you that doesn't scream how fucking gorgeous you are." I dived my hands into her wild web of red curls. "Starting with this hair, your face—"

"My entire childhood, I was picked on for having this hair. I begged my parents to let me dye it so I could feel like the blondes and brunettes in my grade—hair color that didn't make them stand out like mine did. But my parents never allowed me to, they thought I should love the red. So, I endured years and years of endless bullying."

I tightened my grip. "And now those same women would kill to have hair like yours."

She gave me a half smile. "Who knows?"

"What about your face? You can't tell me anyone had anything to say about it, aside from how jealous they were that they didn't look like you."

"In ninth grade, I got called out by a classmate because I had come to school with barbeque sauce on my cheek. She thought it was from dinner the night before and I was this grimy kid who didn't shower in the mornings—or ever. But my mom made the very best barbeque ribs, and I had some for breakfast, and I missed a spot when I was wiping my mouth." She let out a shuddering breath. "From that point forward, my face wasn't of interest to anyone. I became the grimy kid who never washed."

She was so fucking adorable.

"Can I tell you something?" I leaned in, my lips inches from hers. "Hearing that only makes me want you more."

Her eyes narrowed. "Are you telling me you're the kind of guy who isn't afraid of real moments?" I felt her take in some air. "Because that would make you a unicorn."

"Why would you think real moments would bother me?"

She shrugged. "You're Beck Weston."

"And?"

"I don't know ... again, you're Beck Weston."

"And you think I'm a man who only seeks perfection?" I shook my head. "Shit, I'm far from that, Jolie. Listen to me. We all have real moments. Athletes especially. We're under a microscope, and some of our most vulnerable experiences are caught on camera and blasted all over the internet."

"You mean like the meme that exploded last week, showing you stretching on the ice?" She smiled.

I whistled out some air. "Like that, yeah."

"You know the ladies were dying over that meme, right?"

"That's what I heard."

She moved her face back as though she wanted a better look at me. "How many hundreds of thousands of new followers did you gain from that?"

"I wouldn't know. I don't manage my social media. I stay far away from those apps. If someone wants to say something to me, they can come say it to my face. I don't need to see their comments—not when they wouldn't have the balls to voice any of that unless they were behind a screen of protection, like their phone or computer."

"The comments weren't bad—at least not the ones I saw. They were quite the opposite actually. That one move you made turned on thousands and thousands of women." She giggled.

"I get that some could find it hot. It does look like I'm trying to fuck the ice when I stretch. But what those women don't see or understand is the pain we get in our hips and groin and how those stretches are necessary—and while we look like we're fucking, we're actually groaning at how badly it hurts."

She lifted her shoulders. "I think I'd rather have that than throwing up on the bench, or having a bat in the cave, or having a questionable crumb on your cheek during a conference. Those are shiver-worthy situations."

"But instances like those have happened too, I promise. They just haven't gotten airtime."

And hers had while she was in school, the bullying causing her to stay in her head, her thoughts eating away at her.

My sister, Eden, was the same way for entirely different reasons.

"Tell me something, Jolie. Were you one of those women who got turned on while you watched me stretch?"

Her face instantly became red.

I brought my mouth closer to hers, but I didn't kiss her. "Answer me."

"Yes, I was."

I chuckled. "What did you think about when you saw that meme?"

Her shyness was showing. Her innocence.

I liked that.

"The same thing everyone else was thinking..."

Generic.

I needed her to use her words.

"Which was?" I pressed.

She bit her lip while she stared at me. "What it would feel like to be beneath you while you were doing that."

I smiled. "You're about to find out." I turned my head toward the curb, seeing that the SUV had pulled up. "But that's not the only answer you're going to get. After these three nights, you're going to know just what my body is capable of." My fingers, now on her sides, stretched toward the top of her ribs, her back arching from my touch. "And how I'm going to make your body feel and all the different ways I'm going to make you scream—ways that will go far beyond ice-humping."

Her chest rose.

"Are you ready for that?"

She nodded. "Yes."

"You're sure?"

Her chest didn't lower, which told me she was holding her breath. "Beck, I'm so ready."

"Good. The car is here."

My hand moved to her lower back, and I walked her toward our ride, opening the door, where she climbed in first before I got in behind her.

As she was moving toward the other side of the back seat, I stopped her, positioning her in the middle so she wouldn't be far. "I want you close."

My arm slipped around her shoulders as the driver took off toward my hotel.

"What part of the city are you staying in?"

I took out my phone and showed her the screen where the name of the hotel was listed. "Whatever one this is."

"Fancy."

"You know the place?"

I wished I could see more of her face, not just the random parts that got lit from the passing cars and the streetlamps.

"Of course. It's one of the nicest hotels here. It's close to the arena. You'll be able to walk there."

"We did this afternoon after we checked in. I'll be going there every morning for practice."

She made the air in here smell so fucking good.

"Tell me, is the hotel in your favorite section of the city?"

"No. My favorite is South Boston."

"Why?"

She shrugged. "It's a whole vibe with water views and a wild nightlife and a cool mix of everything and anything you'd want to do." She went quiet for a moment. "It's too bad you can't have a couple of days with no practice."

I chuckled. "My body would fucking love that. But midseason, Coach is never going to let that happen. So, every day we're here, we'll use Boston's arena and weight room and work around their schedule."

One thing I could see—and I was fucking obsessed with—was her smile.

"Oh, I'm sure Boston is going to love that. The enemy on their territory—I bet they want nothing more."

"We've shared our facility with other teams before. We know the unwritten rules. We'll be respectful."

"Will that even matter?" She turned her body more toward me. "You hockey players live to fight. Whether it's on or off the ice."

My arm lowered from her shoulders to her waist. "Fights find us."

She laughed. "Right."

"They do."

"I grew up less than five minutes from here. Most of my guy friends who played hockey were hotheaded with a raging New England temper. I know how they think, how they react, and what sets them off. They don't just stumble upon arguments. They welcome them. And I'm not being stereotypical, but I'm being stereotypical. Hockey has a type, and submissive, nonconfrontational, and relaxed aren't it." She paused. "Unless you're going to tell me the West Coast is different from the East Coast?"

I rubbed up and down her sides, enjoying this conversation

more than she probably realized. "I think both coasts are equally angry."

"Just like I thought." She tapped my chest. "Is that where you're from? The West Coast?"

"LA."

"Wow, it must be nice to play at home and be close to your family—if your family still lives there."

My family.

Who were as well known in the food space as I was in the hockey scene. Most of the people I spoke to knew me from both avenues. It was refreshing to talk with someone who wasn't drilling me about where our next restaurant was opening, or if we were looking at venturing into any new cuisines, or even inquiring about some dirt on my teammates—shit I wouldn't talk about. Ever.

And maybe Jolie did know that my family and I owned The Weston Group—a collection of hundreds of restaurants and a few clubs—and that just didn't matter to her. Or maybe she had no fucking idea.

Either way, I dug it.

"My whole family—my four siblings and my parents—all live in LA."

"Hold on a second." Her hand went to my shoulder. "You have four siblings?"

I laughed. "Three brothers and a sister."

"Whoa." Her fingers squeezed. "I only say it like that because I'm an only child. To think about growing up with four siblings is completely wild to me."

"So is being an only child. What was all that quiet like?"

Her body returned to its previous position, her back resting along the seat cushion. "It gave me a lot of time to think."

"I can imagine."

"What was it like to live in a house that was super loud?"

I stilled my fingers as they were stroking her waist. "It gave me little time to think."

"Ha! Do they come to your games?"

"Most of my home games, yeah."

"I love that they're there to support you."

The SUV came to a stop outside the hotel. I opened the door, getting out first, and I helped Jolie to the ground. I thanked the driver and shut the door, walking her toward the entrance.

"I'm just warning you now, if we run into any of my teammates, there will be a comment. They can't help themselves. We're a bunch of inappropriate bastards with way too much shit to say."

She smiled, the lights by the hotel's overhang allowing me to see the shine of her teeth and the light blue of her eyes and the hint of flushness in her cheeks. "If it happens, I'll try not to internally die."

"Don't do that. My team's relationship is fifty percent hockey, fifty percent razzing each other. It's me they'd be picking on, not you."

My hand left her lower back and found her fingers as the doorman opened the lobby door for us. We went inside, immediately heading for the elevator. I hit the button, and as we waited, I watched her look around the large space.

"My home for these next three nights, which is nuts. I never thought ..." As her voice drifted off, her gaze locked with mine. "You do know I have nothing with me except for this purse." She lifted her wrist, where the small bag dangled. "No toothbrush. No change of clothes. Nothing."

"Whatever you need, I'll have delivered to the hotel."

The elevator doors opened, and we stepped inside, where I hit the button for the top floor.

"Even clothes?" she asked.

I moved her toward the back, leaning her against it. My arms lifted, and my hands pressed against the mirrored wall on a spot above her head. And what that did was create a cage, Jolie in the center.

"I'd prefer if you didn't wear any."

Her brows lifted. "The whole time I'm with you?"

"Yes."

"What about when I take you around Boston? You'd like me naked then too?" She smiled.

My face went to her neck. Given her age, I expected a scent that was light, fruity, even extra sweet.

Scents that did fucking nothing for me.

But what I inhaled off her skin was a sexy aroma, filled with vanilla and amber. My eyes closed while I took another breath of her, and when I felt like it was enough—even though it wasn't even close to enough—I placed my lips in front of hers. This new position caused her to take a quick intake of air.

"Naked when we go out, no. I wouldn't share what's mine —and that's what you will be over these next couple of days."

"Yours. *Huh*." She rubbed her tongue over the inside of her top teeth. "Does that mean we'll be stopping by my dorm to grab clothes?"

"Your dorm," I echoed. A seven-year age gap wasn't an eternity, but if I considered the amount of life I'd experienced between twenty and now, it was. Still, a fucking twenty-year-old? *Jesus Christ*. "If you need clothes, I'll have those delivered too. You'll want or need for nothing while I'm with you—I give you my word."

"I believe you."

My hand went to her neck, and I tilted her face up at me. "You just need to make me one promise."

"What?"

I rubbed my thumb over her bottom lip. "Over these next

three nights, you hold nothing in. If you want something, say it. If you need something, tell me. If you want to scream, I want you to let it out."

Her lips parted with my thumb still on them. "If I want something ..."

"Let's say ... if you want me to lick your pussy while you're taking a shower. If you want to know what it tastes like to drink champagne off my dick. If you're coming so hard that you can't hold in the moans, but you're worried someone in the next room will hear you—those are the kinds of things I'm talking about. Hold nothing back."

"God, you're dirty."

I let out a small moan. "Is that a promise?"

She nodded. "Yes."

"Now fucking kiss me."

I waited for her to close the distance between us, to put her lips on mine before I went in for a real kiss. And once I did, I slid in my tongue, deepening what she was lightly giving to me, and that confirmed every question I'd been wondering—how she'd taste, how her mouth was going to feel, and how she'd react the second my tongue touched hers.

As I devoured her, her body went completely limp, and I held her weight against the mirrored wall. Her taste was even more incredible than I'd thought it would be, the feel of her exactly what I was looking for, her softness reaching a level of innocence.

But everything I was learning—like the fact that she knew how to move her lips, but didn't seem overly experienced—told me she wouldn't ever take charge.

That would be on me.

And that was just what I wanted.

I pulled back as the doors behind us opened, a quiet ding

signaling that we'd reached my floor, and her eyelids slowly lifted, her hand instantly going to her lips.

Not to wipe them.

More like she couldn't fucking believe what had just happened.

"Come with me." I reached for her other hand and led her out of the elevator and down the hallway to my suite at the end. I waved the plastic key card in front of the reader, allowing her to enter before I moved in behind her, wrapping my arms around her waist and turning her toward me. "That wasn't enough."

Her hands went to my shoulders. "Our kiss?"

"The taste of you—I need more." I picked her up, wrapping her around me, her body weighing nothing compared to the weights I lifted. I carried her through the living room area, past the balcony, and into the bedroom, setting her on top of the dresser.

"Looks like you're wasting no time."

"Do you remember what I said to you at the bar about time?" I gripped the wooden ledge on either side of her.

"It's something you don't have. Therefore, you don't waste any when it comes to going after what you want. And right now, what you want is me."

"Every word of that." I put a finger under her chin. "Unless you don't want me to ravage you ..."

Her legs were still circled around me, and she tightened them. "That's not the case at all."

"What is the case, then?"

She moved her hair off her shoulders. "Do you just want to hear me say it?"

Even though my dick was fucking begging to be released, I still voiced, "I need to hear you say it."

"I want you, Beck."

I moved my lips to her throat, inhaling more of that erotic scent. "And what do you want me to do to you?"

"You're really trying to drag me out of my shell, aren't you?"

"By the end of the three nights, if you want my tongue on your pussy, I expect you to climb up my body and sit on my face. That's the level of comfort I'm talking about. But in order to get there, we have to start here." I waited, and when she didn't reply, I added, "Tell me, Jolie, what do you want?"

"I want you to get me naked," she whispered.

Words, I could tell, weren't easy for her to say.

Since my mouth was just above the zipper of her sweatshirt, I kissed around her jaw while I lowered the metal slider all the way to the bottom. Once it was unlatched, I peeled the material off her arms and dropped it on the floor. Beneath, she had on a tight shirt that was tucked into her jeans, and I lifted the top over her head, leaving her in just her bra. I kept that on while I got to work on her pants, pulling those down her legs while taking off her sneakers at the same time.

What was left was a black pair of panties, made of what appeared to be satin, and a matching bra that pushed her tits high on her chest.

I ran my hand over the top of my head as I stared at her, taking in every fucking inch. "You have no idea what I'm looking at right now or what I'm thinking ... do you?"

"You mean, my body?"

I nodded.

"I would guess it looks like most others that you do this same thing with."

I let out enough air that made it sound like a laugh. "No."

"No?"

"Not even close." I slid my hands up to the highest part of

her thighs, stopping at the edge of her panties. "I want these off."

"Okay."

I yanked them off her hips and down the legs that I'd just touched, and once they were out of my hand, I gripped the back of her bra. "This too."

When she held her arms out straight, I unhooked the two parts and dragged the straps past her biceps, her tits falling from the cups before her bra joined the rest of her clothing on the floor.

"Jolie ... fucking Jolie." My head shook as I took her all in. The soft creaminess of her pale skin. The curves of her waist, the roundness of her ass. The dips of each tit—not large, but just big enough—with her light-pink nipples. And hanging past her shoulders, stretching almost to the flatness of her stomach, were those wild red locks. "You're perfect."

"You're funny."

"I'm not joking." I made no attempt to hide which part of her I was staring at. "Shit, I've never seen a woman more perfect in my life." My eyes squinted, my teeth gnawing away at my lip until I swore I tasted blood. "This is going to be so much fucking fun."

Her head pointed down, breaking eye contact.

"Look at me," I ordered.

A bashful expression covered her face as she glanced up.

I was about a foot away, giving myself enough room to really look at her. But I came in closer, holding her cheeks, speaking near her mouth. "When I say to you that you're the most gorgeous woman I've ever seen naked—or ever seen, period—tell me you believe me."

After a few seconds of pause, she said, "I believe you." She rubbed her lips together. "Whether I believe it myself, that's a whole different story."

Damn, those bullies had done a number on her. It was always the jealous ones who caused the most destruction—and everything I'd heard tonight was their fault. This was the result of their antagonizing mockery.

Which fucking killed me.

She wrapped her arms around her stomach, positioning them in a way that covered her tits. "I have an idea."

"All right."

She smiled. "Why don't you show me how perfect you are?"

"You're saying you want me naked?" I chuckled.

"Quickly." That grin grew. "Very quickly."

She clearly hated the spotlight.

Which was fine because I fucking thrived when it was shining on me.

I undid a few buttons at the top of my shirt and lifted it over my head, adding it to the pile of her clothes. As I slipped out of my shoes and let my jeans and boxer briefs drop, I heard, "Oh my God."

Her eyes were round and large as she gawked at me while I stood naked in front of her.

"You good?" I asked.

"Good? I'm in awe." She waved me closer since I'd backed up to strip. "I need to touch you."

I laughed. She was already getting more comfortable—and I liked it.

She went to my chest first, rubbing each of my pecs before moving to my shoulders and biceps. A solo finger then crawled down the center of my abs, stopping just below them.

"When it comes to guys, I've always been most attracted to their arms—I don't know why, they're just my thing. But, Beck ... you've converted me."

"To what?"

"An everything girlie."

She traced the black tattoos that covered the top part of my chest—a piece I'd had done a few years ago—and down my arm, where the designs continued all the way to my wrist.

"Family. Hockey. College. Before you ask, that's what it means—some in obvious forms of art, some symbolic."

"It's all so beautiful."

I touched the inside of her wrist, where a small *L* was tattooed. "Is this your only one?"

"Yes."

I would have asked more questions, but I'd delayed things enough, and I didn't think I could wait much longer to have her. "We're going to talk about your tattoo. We're just not going to talk about it right now."

"Deal."

"I'm going to grab a condom from my suitcase in the closet." I pointed my finger at her. "Do not move."

"I won't."

I went into the walk-in, where my suitcase was open on the floor, unzipping the inside pocket, pulling out one of the metal foil packets from the box that I kept in there. As I returned, tearing off the corner with my teeth, she was looking at me from the dresser. Perched upright and fucking stunning. The bedroom light caught the lighter parts of her hair, the color so much like fall, and the lightness of those round, hard nipples.

"Jesus," I sighed.

"What?"

Instead of taking out the rubber, I left it inside the metal and set it on the dresser. As I halted in front of her, I held her hips. "I can't believe I get to fuck you."

She was blushing. "Stop."

"And even though that's what I planned to do right away, I've changed my mind."

"What do you mean?"

I aligned my nose with hers. "My dick needs you, Jolie. It needs to be inside you. It needs to be fucking you so hard that we're both shaking."

"But?"

"I need to do something else first ..."

"Which is?"

I moved my hands to the lip of the dresser, spreading my arms out wide, and I let my shoulders and head drop. This new spot put my face in front of her legs. I wedged in between them, and with my mouth only inches from her cunt, I whispered, "I need to taste you."

FOUR

Jolie

"What"—I gasped so hard that my chest felt like it was about to cave in as I glanced down, between my legs, where Beck's face was resting—"are you doing to me?"

It wasn't a real question.

It was a reaction.

Along with a shocking realization of what was actually happening from a night I never could have predicted. But I was here, lost in his movements, overwhelmed by how he was making me feel.

And how amazing he was at everything.

Beck had his arms stretched across the front of the dresser, his face holding my legs apart, his mouth buried in me. His tongue was giving my clit fast, hard sweeps. Each time it landed or massaged that spot, some kind of noise came out of me.

Like now. A mix of breathing and moaning and crying, "Oh! Yes!"

I couldn't stay still.

My hips were rocking forward, my legs shaking. I was gripping the edge of the dresser, and when that didn't feel like enough, I stretched up my arms and pushed them against the wall behind me. And when that didn't feel like enough either, I grabbed Beck's hair.

Beck.

A name I couldn't believe I was repeating in my head.

Or saying out loud.

Because no matter what was happening—like every time I looked down and saw the top of his head or his eyes met mine—I had the hardest time comprehending that he was here. That I was with him. That his mouth was on me.

This time, with our stares completely glued on one another, his tongue moving faster than it had, his finger now deep inside me, I begged, "Don't stop."

There was absolutely no way he could halt, he could slow, he could do anything but what he was doing.

Not when I was this close.

And that was something else I couldn't believe—that Beck had the ability to actually get me here without knowing my body. My last boyfriend had done this—not nearly as talented as Beck, but he'd done the act—and although it was all right, I never got off. But aside from the location of where they put their mouths, there was nothing similar between what the two men had done to me.

Not the speed.

Not the way they moved their tongues.

Not even in the way they touched me.

Beck's finger expertly arched up, hitting a place that was new to me. Undiscovered. One that was so extremely sensitive. And he kept it lodged inside, turning just the tip of it in a circle.

I found myself panting.

Arching.

Shouting, "*Ahhh*," as my body began to work its way toward the most paralyzing, mind-boggling peak. I tightened—my fingers in his hair, my muscles as the tingles spread, my body—and everything started to happen at once. "Beck! Holy! Fuck!"

Two things stood out the most.

The first were my sounds. Noises I was positive I'd never made before.

The second was this feeling. It was more than pleasure. It was a total takeover, owning my insides, causing my outside to shudder.

"Gah!" I screeched.

Earlier in the night, I'd described to Beck the real moments of vulnerability, but this was on an entirely different level. Because Beck was bringing me here. He was keeping me here. And he was watching me come down from here.

My eyes closed as the initial shock began to vibrate through me, my head pushing against the wall, my body experiencing every quake of energy. The blackness behind my eyelids prevented me from being in the heat of his stare—something I could still feel even though I was no longer looking at him. But I knew he was watching me, catching my breathlessness, seeing the movement come over me, hearing the way my sounds were filling the silence.

"Yes!" I drew in a giant gulp of air, things still swirling and bursting, building in momentum. "*Yesss!*"

Just the way he knew when my orgasm was building, he also seemed to know when it was on its way down. He slowed his speed, sensing exactly when I needed total stillness.

My eyes flicked open, my teeth gnawing my bottom lip as

his finger gently slid out, his tongue lifting from me, sinking back between his lips.

But his mouth stayed, kissing what he'd just finished licking.

"I could spend the whole night right here, licking this perfect fucking spot, eating your pussy nonstop. That's how good you taste." He held my thighs as he stood straight, the wetness on his lips showing under the bedroom light. "You've got one hell of a cunt."

What? Is he saying?

To me?

All I knew was that I was dying—over and over and over again.

"I honestly don't know what you just did to me ... but I still can't breathe."

He moaned as his gaze dipped down my body and rose to my face. "I gave you my tongue. That's all it was." His stare grew, like he was attempting to see through me. "You've had a man do this before, yes?"

"Yes—I mean, sorta. It wasn't like *that*, and nothing like *that* has ever happened."

He cocked his head. "You're telling me another dude's mouth was on your pussy and he didn't get you off?"

I nodded. "Yep. That's what I'm telling you."

He wrapped his arms around my waist, his face even closer to mine. "Now that's a real fucking shame. Because a pussy like yours should be worshipped. Do me a favor—don't ever be with an amateur again. Only be with men who will treat your clit the way it deserves to be licked."

I smiled, and when that felt too simple, I laughed. "Says the guy who just set the highest bar ever and who has a tongue that could probably win awards."

He showed it to me by dragging it across his bottom lip.

"You'll find someone who will savor you the way I just did." He took the condom off the dresser and pulled it out of the foil.

I touched his arm. "You don't have to put that on yet."

"What are you talking about?"

"I'm saying, I think I owe you for what you just did to me."

He ignored me, rolling the condom over his shaft.

Since we'd met, Beck had called me perfect more than once, but that title really applied to him. In fact, I didn't think he could be more perfect—a theory that was confirmed as I took in his beautifully thick, powerfully long dick, his mushroom head bubbling with pre-cum.

"You can suck my dick later. Right now, all I can think about is putting it inside you."

He gave his cock several pumps and tugged me toward the very end of the dresser, tucking my legs around him and putting me in a position that aligned him with my entrance.

"Kiss me," he demanded.

My wetness was even on the strands of his mustache.

"But I'm all over you."

"And?"

He punched forward a little, giving me a sample of his size. It was just a hint, a tease of his crown, nothing more.

"I can't even imagine what it would be like to taste myself."

"I want you to find out." His lips hovered above mine, but they didn't touch me.

"But—"

"Tonight is going to be all about things you've never had or tried." He brushed his thumb over my clit. "Like what I just did to your pussy—that was one. Kissing me while your cum is all over me—that's two."

I wrapped my arms around his neck, and as I locked him in my grip and attempted to reply, "I—" he drove all the way into me, his lips slamming against mine at the same time, stopping me from responding.

But what he couldn't prevent was my moan.

The loudness of it. The way it vibrated against his mouth. The way it slashed through my chest and cut through the air.

Oh God, he felt incredible.

Especially when he twisted his hips, rotating within me, hitting walls that didn't know they needed friction, but they did.

He stayed just like that, giving me small pulses while he ravished my lips, keeping me from voicing words so all I could do was make sounds.

And I let out plenty.

Because the more he kissed me, the more I tasted the flavor of Beck Weston, the less I cared about what was on his beard or where his mouth had been, and I could only focus on him.

The pure pleasure he was giving me.

That only continued to get better.

He leaned back just enough to hiss, "Fuck yes," and he held on to the base of my neck, his fingers tightening as he thrust in and out of me. "You're so fucking tight, Jolie."

"And wet." I couldn't believe I'd spoken those words, but I also couldn't believe how wet I was. How wet he'd made me. How wet he was still making me.

"Damn, this feels good." His strokes turned harder.

His forehead pressed to mine, his breaths hitting my face, the smell of him as good as his taste.

My arms unraveled from around him and went to his pecs, cherishing each muscle and the outline of his abs, the grooves between each one swallowing my finger. "Beck!"

"Do you want me to slow down?"

"No. I want you to go faster."

"Yes ... that's my fucking girl."

After a few more plunges, his hand dropped from my neck and moved around my waist, and he lifted me into the air, carrying me off the dresser to the lounge chair by the window on the far side of the bedroom. But where I expected him to place me on the cushion and kneel in front of me, he was the one who sat and straddled me over him.

I assumed he wanted me to ride him, and that was why he put me in this position, so with my feet on the ground, his hands wandering my body, I lifted to his tip and slowly lowered.

"Hell yeah," he moaned. "Do that one more time." I did, and then he said, "Now I want you to turn around."

I took in his hazel eyes. "Turn around?"

"Put your back to me and face the opposite direction."

Reverse cowgirl.

Something else I hadn't done before.

"You must somehow know I've never tried that?"

He chuckled as he pinched one of my nipples. "It was an easy guess." He slapped my ass. "Come on. Turn around."

I carefully drew him out of me and got off the lounge chair, facing away from his eyes, only to straddle him again. It didn't matter what angle of me he was looking at—they all made me nervous—but this one felt even more personal than the last.

With him seated and upright, as I sat, he wrapped his arm around my breasts and pulled my back against his front. Once our bodies were pressed together, he guided me toward his tip.

His mouth was at my ear, his breathing making my skin even warmer. "Wait until you feel how intense this is going to be."

I sank all the way down, every inch of his dick inside me.

My head fell back, my lips parting. "Oh God."

He was right.

This was intense.

Because he was hitting me from a totally different direction.

And even though the amount of fullness had been epic before, it didn't compare.

"This is"—I tried to take a breath—"fucking wild."

"I told you." His voice was gritty, deep. Dominant. "Now fuck me." His hands were all over me, on my tits, my neck, palming my navel, rubbing my clit. "Jesus, you feel so fucking good."

The mix of his strokes and clit play was an unexpected combination.

But a combination that was blowing my mind.

I used the sides of the lounger to hold on to, to bear my weight and grind over him, and I was getting hit with multiple sensations.

I could barely keep myself together.

"Oh!" I heard myself scream. "Shit!"

He was meeting me in the middle, arching his hips up, pounding from the bottom while I came down from the top. "Just like that, Jolie." He nibbled my earlobe. "Faster."

I didn't know what was happening.

But as he circled my clit, the sparks of an orgasm were returning to my body.

The desire burning, the sparks surging through me.

And it only grew when he tugged on my nipple, the pressure hard enough to make me scream, "Yes!"

He lengthened each plunge, letting me go as far back as his crown before hammering in, whispering, "I can feel you tightening. You're going to come."

I wasn't sure I could even form a sentence at this point—I was so far gone. But I knew I wanted that for him too. I wanted to not only feel that side of him, but I wanted to see it. To know what vulnerability looked like on Beck.

I turned my face, my cheek pressed against his lips. "Come with me. Please."

"You want that already?"

"We have all night and two more evenings together ... don't we?"

"We do." He lunged his hips up. "And I'm going to have endless amounts of this pussy."

"*Mmm.*"

"And I'm going to make this cunt"—he tapped my clit—"come so many fucking times."

I sucked in some air. "Beck!"

I was there.

At the top.

My toes threatening to slip over the edge while I waited for him to catch up.

And he did; because even though I was frozen and couldn't move or I'd lose it, he took over the control, and every sign told me he was close. His drives were deep, sharp, his breathing matching mine as he growled, "Jolie!"

That was when I knew he was as far gone as me.

"Beck!"

I immediately began to fall.

My body exploded with shudders; my stomach convulsed. My exhales were coming out in pants, my voice turned scratchy as I yelled, "Ah!"

"Take it! Fucking take it, Jolie!"

I wasn't the only one losing it; he was too. I could feel the tremors racking his body, the quakes that were blasting through him the same way they were igniting through me.

"Fuck yes! Fuck!"

Our orgasms reached the end at the same time, and even though our breaths were coming out heavy, our sounds were turning light. Beck's movements gradually slowed and softened until he turned still.

He leaned back into the lounger and brought me with him, my body rising and falling every time he inhaled and exhaled. I stared at the dark screen of the TV that hung on the wall across from us, my brain a busy intersection of what had just happened and what the future of the next couple of days would look like.

I didn't know how, but I already had a feeling our goodbye would hurt more than I was ready for.

"Take a shower with me," he said after what felt like minutes of silence.

A shower.

With Beck Weston.

Who was still inside me.

A sexy combination of muscle and warmth and thick chestnut-brown hair—all things I felt as he lay under me.

I couldn't wrap my head around any of this.

"I would love that."

Even though the thought of more vulnerability—standing naked with him under running water—was a lot to process.

His arm was across the front of me, but instead of lifting to get us up, he held on even stronger. "I'll carry you there in a second. Right now, I like this enough to not want to move."

I agreed.

It was all …

Perfect.

Still damp from our shower, Beck and I lay next to each other in bed. My arm was stretched across him, and he was holding my wrist above his face, massaging the inside of it. The glow from the TV lit up the space around us, but neither of us was watching it.

His thumb stalled on the small tattoo in the crook beneath my thumb—a spot that could be hidden by a watch, which was why I had chosen it.

"A best friend or an old boyfriend?" he asked.

He was questioning who *L* was.

"Luke. My ex." I sighed. "We talked about him earlier."

"We talked about him—*oh shit*. The dude whose mouth didn't get you off—I'm assuming that's who Luke is?"

"Yep."

He stroked the thin line of the cursive letter. "It's the only tattoo on your body. He must have meant a lot to you."

"We dated our senior year of high school and through our freshman year of college. He goes to Northeastern, not even a ten-minute walk from me."

"What happened?"

I adjusted the pillow, my head sinking back into the fluff. "He broke my heart."

"Asshole."

I laughed. I could now. But for a while, I couldn't even bear the thought of his name, let alone attempting an expression like the one I had on. "When the others were mean, he wasn't. But college changed him. Or maybe I changed—I don't know." I turned my wrist, catching a glimpse of the ink. "We got these a week after we graduated. He has a *J* in the same spot. What's ironic is, around the same time, my parents were griping about how one of their friends' sons got a whole bunch of tattoos for a girlfriend, and how they ended up breaking up, and how stupid it was of him. And then I went and did this."

"Do either of your parents' names start with *L*?"

"Sadly, no."

He released my wrist, his arm tucking behind me, his

fingers rubbing my bare back. "Tattoos are removable, if you ever want to go that route."

I leaned up on my elbow, gently touching his chiseled, tattoo-covered chest. "One day, I'll definitely get it removed. For now, I guess it's a good reminder of why I need to stay focused on school and work. Those two things, for the most part, monopolize my life. So, I really don't have time for assholes." I smiled.

"Men are a distraction." He laughed. "Hey, look, I pulled you away from whatever you and your friend had planned for after the bar, along with everything that you had scheduled for the next couple of days." He gently bit my chin. "You're my hostage."

I let out a soft moan. "But you're worth it. Men like Luke, not so much."

His hand stilled at the top of my butt. "How do you know I'm worth it, Jolie?" He paused. "Are you saying that because I'm Beck Weston? Or are you saying it for a different reason?"

"I've known you, for what, less than an hour? And within that short time, you put your mouth between my legs and actually cared enough to give me something no other guy had. Even the one who had said he loved me." I traced up to his neck. "And you've made me try things that no one has ever taken the time to encourage me to do—again, not even the one who said he wanted to spend forever with me." I flattened my hand, not realizing the placement was over his heart. "I might not know you on a personal level, but based on those things alone, I would say you're worth it."

He rolled toward me, my hand falling to his back. "Tell me something, Jolie. How did Luke break your heart?"

I rubbed my lips together. "My dad has always said, 'It's not what they tell you, it's what they show you.' That's when the true nature of a person's soul is revealed." I went quiet for a moment. "Luke showed me who he wasn't, and the disappointment broke my heart."

"Your dad sounds like a smart man."

I nodded. "The smartest I know, which means my future husband is going to have a lot to live up to." I squeezed both sides of his mouth. "Since he'll need to have a tongue like yours and a brain like my dad's."

FIVE

Beck

Even though we were in the middle of a run-down bar with plenty of wild shit to stare at, my eyes didn't leave Jolie. They couldn't; she looked too fucking gorgeous as she sat across from me at the small high-top table, face bare of makeup since she didn't have any to put on, hair untamed and beautiful as ever.

I finally forced myself to take a quick glance around. "Shit, it's been a long time since I went to a college bar."

"Have you missed it?" She propped up her elbows, and I could tell from the movement that she was swinging her legs. "I imagine the places you go to in LA make this place look even divier than it is."

I chuckled. "I've got nothing against a dive bar. In college, that's mostly what I went to."

I lifted the glass of a light draft I'd never heard of, and while I was bringing it up to my lips, she turned her head, giving me a chance to take in her profile. And that dress. *Fuck.* The style was a knee-length sweater that hugged her tits and narrowed in tighter as it reached her waist—a spot I couldn't see, as it was hidden by the table. My assistant had done a good job at picking it out, along with the knee-high boots. Both had been delivered to the hotel this morning, and they were sexy as hell on Jolie.

"When I do go out in LA, I mostly go to a club my family owns. It's just easier that way since I get all the privacy I want."

"Your family owns a club? Is it bad that I didn't know that?"

I put my hand on the visor of my baseball hat after I set down my beer. "Not at all. It's actually a relief that you don't know. Most people who do, they tend to ask all the questions. Ones I'm not always up for answering."

"If I'm ever in LA, I'll have to check it out." She tucked some of her locks behind her ear, but they didn't stay, springing right back to her cheek a few seconds later.

I wanted to touch them.

I wanted to fucking touch her.

"It's called Musik," I explained. "We have several of them, all in different locations, and we're building more. We own restaurants too." I waited until our server delivered our next round of drinks before I continued, "Have you ever heard of a restaurant called Charred?"

Her neck craned back, a sight so stunning that my dick ached inside my boxer briefs, dying to be released. "Everyone has heard of Charred. At least everyone in my world. It's one of the most popular restaurants here. It's where my parents took me for my birthday."

"That's ours."

Her eyes widened. "For real? Wow."

"I'm not that active in the business as far as the day-to-day stuff is concerned. My siblings mostly run the operations. I pop in when they need me. Time, the obvious issue."

"That's badass though. Having multiple hustles going on at the same time, especially the ones you have—hockey, food, the club scene—and all of them being super successful."

"We've had our ups and downs, but yes. Thank you." I smiled. "Tell me, what's going to be your hustle after you graduate? You said you work. What do you do? I don't even think I know what you're getting your degree in."

"Marketing—digital mostly. I'm not bad at the art aspect, although I much prefer managing accounts to designing creatives. I am getting a minor in digital art, so I can handle both sides if I need to." She rubbed her fingers together, the silver of her nails sparkling. "I work for my dad."

"What kind of company is it?"

"He's a venture capitalist and private equity investor. In an attempt to turn the companies around or build them—whatever the case is—he keeps the marketing in-house. That's where I come in. And of course, his slew of other employees."

"Did you just start working for him?"

"No." She shook her head. "I started working for him as soon as I was big enough to carry mail from the mailroom to the offices." She ran her finger around the top of her tumbler. "I've held almost every position at his company—phone answerer, photocopier, lunch grabber, errand runner, restroom cleaner"—she grimaced—"and now, all these years later, I have two of my own accounts. Once I graduate, assuming I continue to prove myself, I'll be able to take on much more."

"Assuming you prove yourself? You're saying your dad won't just hand you more responsibility once you get your degree?"

Her back straightened, a posture that looked all business. "You don't know my dad. When it comes to his company, I'm not his daughter. I'm his employee, and he treats me that way, which I suppose is how it should be. So, no, I get no special treatment, like getting handed something I haven't earned. I'm expected to deliver a service, the same way everyone else who works there is."

I liked this side of her. It wasn't a soft side; it was a confident side.

It was no wonder her father wanted her to work for him. You put someone breathtaking and brilliant, like Jolie, in front of a client, and that was the most powerful combination.

Hell, I wanted to hire her for The Weston Group.

"My dad was the same way," I told her. "He was a chef, and when it came to his first restaurant, he didn't fuck around. All of us kids were expected to work, and he took no shit from any of us."

"So, you get it."

I nodded.

"If I'm being honest, there are times I wish things were different because I swear the man is trying to emotionally break me. There isn't anyone in this world who can test me like him." She let out a long breath. "But I also know he's doing it to teach me, to make me better and stronger, and for that, I'm grateful." She licked her bare lips. "So, most of the time, I wouldn't want it any other way." She winked. "And some nights, I guzzle whiskey sours in my dorm room until I'm drunk enough to stop screaming."

From the moment I'd met her, Jolie had never come across like a twenty-year-old. Now I knew why. She was mature beyond her age, and a lot of that had to do with how long she'd been involved in her father's company—a sophistication gained from responsibility and pressure that only working kids could understand—along with the way her parents had raised her.

A childhood that sounded similar to mine.

Some kids were truly kids, and some spent weekends and

after-school hours at their family's business, filling in gaps that the employees couldn't.

"What's it like when you're home?" I asked. "Is he still in boss mode or dad mode?"

"He's my best friend. We go to hockey games together—I've told you that's our thing. During the season, that could be several times a week. And during offseason, I see my parents at least once a week for dinner and to do a little laundry exchange." She covered her face, like she was embarrassed they did her laundry—something I would take full advantage of if I were her. "We leave work at work." Her head tilted. "Because the thing about my dad is that even though he lets me get away with nothing, he allows me to share and express myself. So, I get out everything I need to, and by the time I see him again—whether that's at home, or at the office, or at a game—I don't want to strangle him." She laughed. "Or maybe I still do, but not as badly."

"He plays fair. I appreciate that." I flicked my bottom lip with my teeth. "Based on the location of his company, it sounds like Boston is where you're going to stay."

She took a drink of her whiskey sour, her smile then reaching as high as her light-blue eyes. Eyes I could stare at forever.

Goddamn it.

"I love it here. I think it'll forever be my home. Unless I end up not working for Dad, but I don't see that happening. Being a part of his company is all I've ever wanted to do." She nodded toward me. "The same way I'm sure hockey is for you."

An answer I could understand. An answer that made perfect sense.

But an answer that hit my stomach, and that was what made no fucking sense.

"I'll play until my body gives out." I shook my head,

attempting to get my thoughts straight—thoughts that weren't on hockey at all. "I hope to make the choice before it happens. And hopefully, it won't happen anytime soon."

"You're twenty-seven, right?" She smiled even larger. "I might have googled you while you were at practice this morning."

I returned the gesture. "I am."

"You've got plenty of years ahead of you." As she was lifting her drink, she added, "Do you think you'll stay in LA after you retire?"

"Probably." I rubbed my hand over the sticky table. "I'll become more involved with the family business at that point, I'm sure. But at least I'll have a lot more flexibility with my schedule. Now, hockey runs my life."

"As it should."

I drained the rest of my beer and picked up the one the server had recently delivered. "Let's talk about tomorrow. I know you're not taking me to Quincy Market since we did that today for lunch. Or to the path by the Charles River since we knocked that out too. And since we've also checked off your dive bar, tell me what else you've got planned."

She pushed her drink to the side, making room on the table. "Everyone who comes to Boston *has* to see the North End, where you're going to have the best cannoli you've ever tasted." She hummed out an exhale. "Then maybe a quick walk through the Public Garden." She was now hiding her smile. "And then I've pulled a few strings to get something arranged for later in the day, but I won't know if it's going to happen until tomorrow morning." She pulled out her phone and looked at the screen, her smile no longer masked. "Scratch that. It's going to happen." She put her phone away. "There's just one problem."

Jesus Christ, why can't I get enough of this one?

Why do I want to shove the table away and fuck her right here in the middle of this bar?

I swallowed. "And that is?"

"You're going to have to let me go back to my dorm, or your assistant is going to have to order clothes that are much warmer than this." She pulled at the top of her dress. "I'm talking stuff that's *extra*, extra layered."

I slipped my phone out of my pocket and shot off a text to my assistant, letting her know that the both of us needed some heavy clothes delivered to the hotel by morning. "Done."

She shook her head. "You make everything seem so easy." When she crossed her arms, finally filling the space in front of her, her hair fell over them, and her tits pushed up higher. "I know you've been to Boston a bunch before, but by the way you were reacting today during each of our little outings, I could tell you hadn't seen much of the city. What we're going to do tomorrow night is going to show you a lot more of it, but it's going to show it to you my way."

"Your way, huh?"

"Even though you're a California boy who isn't used to the New England cold, hopefully, you'll still enjoy it." She winked.

And that fucking wink was so hot.

"I went to college in Michigan. I know cold."

She nipped her lip. "You say that now"—she laughed—"but just wait."

SIX

Jolie

Champagne wasn't what I had in mind for breakfast, but that was what room service had just rolled in now that Beck was back from practice. Once the delivery dude was gone, after leaving the cart in the center of the living room, Beck took the bottle out of the ice and poured some into two glasses. I wrapped my fingers around one of the flutes and took a seat on the couch, watching the little bubbles shoot from the bottom of the liquid to the top while I waited for him to join me.

The breeze of air that swished past me as he sat beside me made my eyes close.

Over the last couple of days, I'd learned that Beck had his own unique scent. It didn't matter what products he used in the shower or the cologne he sprayed on after he was dressed. His body would absorb each of those aromas and create something entirely different.

And it was pure spice.

A smell that clung to his skin, hair, even his beard.

I'd never forget it.

"All I thought about during practice was how badly I wanted to get back here." His eyes weren't just staring at me. They were eating me. "To you."

I smiled, my breath quivering in my lungs, and I held my glass in front of his. I tried to think of a toast, and since the only thing that came to me was how badly I didn't want him to leave tomorrow, I said, "To getting drunk."

He chuckled. "Breakfast is coming in about twenty minutes. I ordered every kind of meat they had on the menu. For you, avocado toast with a poached egg." He pointed at his glass after he finger-brushed the sides of his mustache. "The cocktail is to celebrate. The food is to make sure we don't get too drunk and ruin everything you have planned." His finger left the air and landed on my thigh.

Tingles instantly exploded in my chest. "What are we celebrating?"

"Our last day together."

Once the truth hit my heart, those tingles began to die down. Given that it was a subject I didn't want to dwell on, I said softly, "You know, that's my favorite breakfast order."

"I've seen you eat, what, three meals and a couple of snacks? You've ordered clean every time, so I figured it would be something you'd enjoy."

"It's like ... you know me." I grinned.

"To another day—the final day—of holding you hostage." He smiled and clinked his glass against mine.

That smile.

My God.

I swore, there was nothing in this world more beautiful. There couldn't possibly be. Certainly nothing sexier, from the way his lips spread around his straight white teeth—a detail we'd joked about after we left the bar last night since hockey players were notorious for getting their teeth knocked out—to the tiny grooves next to his hazel eyes, and to the hairs that teased his lips when he pulled them wide.

Hairs that had teased my lips too.

A sensation I would desperately miss.

"Cheers," I whispered. I wouldn't allow any emotion to come through my voice, but the reality was, this goodbye was going to suck.

I could feel it in every part of me.

Like a spring shower, when the sky turned completely dark and a breeze rushed through the city—you could see it coming; you could feel it in the air. That was now. And tomorrow, my heart was going to ache when he left to go to Washington, DC.

I didn't care that Beck had only come into my life the evening before last.

Whatever these feelings were, they were real.

And these feelings were going to hurt when they watched him walk out the door.

"Did the clothes arrive?" He took a drink. "The ones my assistant was supposed to send?"

"They're all hung up in the closet. We won't need them until later this afternoon. What I have planned for the first part of today won't be as chilly, even though it's cold outside."

His brows lifted, his forehead one of the few places on his face that wasn't covered in hair. "And you're still not going to tell me what those plans are?"

"Nope." I laughed. "There's something so satisfying about surprising you."

He cupped the bottom of my neck—a spot that he touched more often than any other place on my body. "You know, you've already made this stay more memorable than I ever imagined." His thumb stroked back and forth. "Thank you for giving me these couple of days." He paused. "I won't forget them."

Stay.

Please.

Even though I know there's no possible way that you can.

"I won't forget them either."

Our eyes were locked, and the silence was too much. His stare was too. So, I looked away and downed my entire glass of champagne, setting the empty on the table in front of us.

The flavor of the drink mixed with the mint on my tongue—an odd combination, but I needed the booze, so it didn't matter. Because it was the drink that gave me the courage to ask, "What time is your flight tomorrow?"

That was a Band-Aid that needed to be ripped off. My brain was desperate to fill in that missing piece, the unknown more than I could handle right now.

Since he'd mentioned their itinerary was going to be discussed at today's practice, I knew he had the answer.

"Nine." He turned toward me on the couch, his hair still wet, the smell of shower faint, but the spice strong. "The team will be leaving the hotel a little before eight."

"It's a private flight, right?"

He nodded. "And we have to be film-ready. Our social media crew wants footage of us walking on and off the plane and will be shooting during the flight." He sighed. "Any bit of hype they can stir during our winning streak, they take full advantage of."

Even though we were talking about something different, that didn't mean I felt better about his departure. That I wasn't mentally dwelling on it. "I can't blame them. You guys have won your last five games. Momentum like that drives up ticket sales."

He moved his hand behind my head, his fingers lost within

my locks. "It does, but we fucking hate it. We want to be in a zone when we get on the plane and stay focused during the flight. The same is true for when we exit and go to the hotel. Having a camera in your face, especially while in the air, fucks everything up."

"I'd hate it."

He nodded. "Some moments, you just don't want to be *on*."

"Well ..." I inched a tiny bit closer. "I'm going to do everything in my power to try to make you forget about being on. At least while you're still here."

His LA Whales sweatshirt was zipped up to the top, and I lowered the zipper a little, sticking my fingers inside. He was wearing a soft cotton T-shirt beneath, and the heat from his skin was coming through the fabric.

No one had ever felt as warm as Beck.

Tomorrow, I would crave this moment. I would think back to it. I suspected I would do absolutely anything to rewind time.

He lifted my legs and stretched them across his lap, holding my shins, rubbing them. "You already are, Jolie."

"I want to tell you something." Beck's hands were hanging over the rail at the front of the fifty-five-foot yacht we were on, the freezing wind blowing his hair back as we cruised through the harbor. "No one has ever done anything like this for me before."

My parents had hosted countless parties on this boat. We'd entertained clients on it for various reasons, and this was where Dad's company celebrated their yearly Christmas party. But tonight was the first time I had ever reserved it for personal reasons. Aside from the captain and his assistant, Beck and I were the only ones on board.

"No one has ever taken you on a boat ride?"

Earlier in the evening, I'd pointed out the highlights of Boston, testing my knowledge and history of the city. This part of the cruise was solely for enjoyment.

He continued to stare straight ahead as we passed one of my favorite skylines. "A woman hasn't, no." He finally looked at me, the hazel of his eyes a dark green tonight. "Just you."

I smiled. "I'm glad I could pull it off."

"How many strings did it take?"

I laughed. "Just one. The owner is a client. I promised I'd work some overtime on his account and I wouldn't bill him for the hours." I nudged his arm. "Seeing your face when I walked you up to this boat makes up for every extra minute I'll have to put in next week."

He chuckled. "I was shocked that this was what you had planned. I still am, I think."

"Because it's too freezing to boat in this weather?" When he didn't respond, I rubbed my arms over the sleeves of my coat and said, "I was worried it would be so cold that we wouldn't be able to come outside and we'd have to stay in the cabin—a view that isn't nearly as good as it is out here. But I figure it's worth bearing these icy temps to have this kind of scenery since there's truly nothing better."

"No, that's not why I was shocked." He turned toward me, his hands going to my face. "It's because you're showing me, you're not telling me, Jolie."

"Oh. I ..." I let my voice drift off. I didn't know what to say, but I knew I couldn't say what I was really feeling.

His hands dropped, and he pulled our bodies together. "You're shivering."

"I'm fine."

THE WILDEST ONE

"You're fucking shaking."

"It's the wind. It's a lot on my neck, but I promise, I'm okay."

I didn't want to go in the cabin. Although it was nice, that was where the captain drove the boat, so we wouldn't be alone.

He hugged his arms around me. I was in a Beck bubble, and suddenly, I couldn't feel even the slightest breeze despite my hair flying all around us.

He was silent as he gazed down at me, but his eyes were saying so much. This wasn't the first time he'd looked at me like this today. It had happened several times. Each occasion lasting a little longer. Like now, how it felt like a few minutes of quietness had already passed.

"I wish I could bring you to LA with me."

His voice was unexpected, but what was even more surprising was what he'd said.

"In a perfect world, I would," he added.

My heart was pounding.

It wasn't one-sided.

He felt it—whatever this was—too.

"But we don't live in a perfect world, Jolie. You're here, living a life you can't walk away from. I'm there, in a life that takes me on the road non-fucking-stop. We couldn't be further apart." His arms unraveled, his hands moving to my face again. "I liked this. I want you to know that."

"Me too."

His thumbs stroked my cheeks, and every time they left, even if it was just for a second to move back to the original spot, I missed them.

"That night at the bar, like I told you, I just wanted to go to my hotel and ride out these next few days, catching up on sleep and resting my body." His stare became even more intense. "And to think, if I'd done that, I would have missed out on you."

I smiled. "I'm so happy you didn't." The emotion was in my chest. It was in my throat. I was doing everything I could to keep it from entering my voice. "This has been amazing."

He brought his lips to mine, hovering just above them. Each of his breaths turned the air white.

It was like he had more to say, but he wouldn't. Or he couldn't. And he was letting his hands and his eyes and his close presence say the rest.

Until I heard, "Thank you."

I found myself moving back so I could get a better look at him, which put several inches between our lips. "For what?"

He fanned his fingers across my cheeks in a way that tilted my head up. "For being everything I didn't know I wanted."

Tomorrow morning was when he'd leave, but this was his goodbye.

I could feel it.

I could see it.

I knew there were far too many states between us and we were in different stages of life.

But I also knew this wouldn't be Beck's last visit here.

"You don't play in Boston again this season. We fly to LA instead. But maybe we'll make the playoffs, and I'll get to see you."

He laughed, shaking his head. "Boston isn't making the fucking playoffs."

"Hey"—I pointed at his chest—"that's my team you're talking shit about."

"I happen to know a lot about your team, and I know they don't have what it takes to clinch a playoff spot this season." He ran his thumb over my bottom lip. "I'm just being honest."

"Then how about next season?" When he didn't say anything, I continued, "If you have time while you're here, we can grab a drink ... or something. You know, after the game."

He moved back to the position he had been in before, our lips almost touching, the smell of the air filled with the spiciness of his scent. "Next season is an eternity from now."

My eyes briefly closed. "I know."

"Fuck, Jolie." He rubbed his nose over mine, and when he stopped, pulling it away to align our mouths, he whispered, "Kiss me."

And I did.

With a level of passion that showed just how much I was going to miss him.

SEVEN

Beck

A raging hard-on was what caused my eyes to flick open, my heart immediately pounding as I recalled the dream I'd just had. The one that was all about Jolie's lips. The way they parted for my dick, how deep her mouth bobbed down my shaft. How I came on the back of her tongue and she swallowed me.

Basically, a fucking recap of what had happened after we left the boat and got back to the hotel last night. She was so good at giving head that my brain didn't want to let it go.

The room was still dark. I had no idea what time it was. I checked my phone, and I still had a couple of hours before my alarm would go off and I'd need to go to the airport.

In the meantime, there was no way, with my dick this stiff, I'd be able to go back to sleep.

And there was no way my dick was going to soften anytime soon.

Not when I was looking at the outline of Jolie's naked body, fucking stroking my cock as I stared at her.

Her hair covered every inch of her pillow, and there was a faint hint of vanilla amber in the air.

Jesus, I was going to miss her taste.

Her smell.

And the feel of her skin, a kind of softness I'd never touched before.

I moved in closer, my tip brushing against the bareness of her ass, my hands reaching around her waist to hold her navel. As my crown teased her cheeks, my mouth went to her shoulder, kissing across the back of it and up to her ear.

That was when she started to stir. "*Mmm.*" She reached behind her head, her fingers diving into my hair. "What time is it?"

"A little past three."

"I was dreaming about you."

I lifted her hair and kissed behind her neck. "Tell me about it."

"You want to hear about my dream?"

I arched my hips forward, sending my cock toward her pussy. I didn't have a condom on—I would get one, but I needed this first. Just a little piece, enough to show me what I was missing by wearing one. When my tip met her wetness, I moaned, "Fuck yes." I lifted my hand to her tit, pinching the edge of her nipple.

She was pushing into me, her nails stabbing into my skull. "We were on the couch in the living room of this suite, and you put me on the back of it. You know, the hard wall part behind the pillows."

I dropped her hair and began to kiss down the center of her back. "Keep going."

"And you ... spread my legs over it."

My dick was so close to sliding into her; my pre-cum mixing with her wetness was like an invitation to thrust in. "What did I do to you on that couch, Jolie?"

"You got on your knees."

My eyes closed as my hips gave one final push, and just the very end of me slipped in. Once it did, my forehead pressed against her back, and I hissed air out of my nose. The tightness was already there, her pussy sucking the end of me, causing my shaft to pulse. It was taking every fucking ounce of willpower I had not to drive in the rest of my dick.

I pulled back and growled, "Tell me what I did while I was on my knees."

"You know."

She was getting more comfortable at voicing things compared to when we'd first met; however, she still took a little coaxing.

"I want to hear the words, Jolie." As I kissed down the rest of her back, my body lowered. So did my hand, cupping the front of her pussy, my lips finally reaching her ass.

"You were licking me."

I was gentle when I nibbled, but I still made sure she could feel the bite of my teeth across each of her cheeks. "Did I make you come?"

"Yes. It was amazing. I swear, there's nothing like your mouth."

I rolled her onto her back, separating her legs, and I knelt between them. "Is that what you want right now? For my mouth to make you come?"

Her knees stayed apart and bent. "Yes."

"Ask for it."

I got into position, wrapping my arms around the inside of her thighs, overexaggerating each exhale so they hit her clit.

Even though the room was too dark to see her eyes, I could sense them on me, her fingers gripping the hell out of my locks.

"Tell me, Jolie."

"I want you to lick me."

"Where?"

She used her other hand to point. But it wasn't a single finger. She used three, holding them at the top of her cunt, giving it a little rub. "Right here. On my pussy."

"Fuck yes, that's what I want to hear." I used my face to push her fingers away, clearing enough room for my mouth. But I didn't give it to her right away. I knew this was the last time I would do this, so I needed to make sure neither of us ever forgot it. My nose went to her clit and sucked in as much of her aroma as I could breathe in, memorizing the scent. "God, you smell so fucking good." I dragged my nose down the rest of her pussy, coating it in her slickness, and when I reached the bottom, I stretched my body across the end of the bed and pulled her toward me.

Her legs tightened around my face, and I assumed she wanted to feel the roughness of my whiskers—something she'd certainly experienced a lot of over the last few days—but she said, "Can I keep you right here? Forever? Because I want to."

Forever.

Fuck.

There would be another motherfucker who would one day lick her pussy. Whether I liked that thought or not, it didn't matter.

I wasn't in a place where I could make this work.

This wasn't the right time.

Our scenario was ... impossible.

And I wouldn't even try to consider making it possible when I knew it would just hurt her in the end.

That was one thing I wouldn't do—hurt her.

"You've owned this tongue since I first gave it to you. Trust me, it wants to stay right here."

I rimmed her entrance, and the second my tongue left that spot on her pussy, my finger went inside, arching upward. She rocked against the bed with each plunge. But she needed more—and more was something I had a feeling she hadn't ever gotten. So, while I positioned my mouth over her clit, I took some of her wetness and spread it to her ass, massaging it around that hole.

"Have you ever been fingered here?"

"No."

I smiled even though she couldn't see me. "You're about to."

Before she could ask any questions or worry out loud if it was going to hurt, I gave her my tongue, knowing that was one hell of a distraction. Fuck, the woman dreamed about it.

"*Ohhh,*" she moaned. "Yes!"

And while I flicked the tip across her clit, I slowly and carefully worked my finger into her ass.

"Whoa."

"Give it a second, it'll feel a lot better."

She was even narrower in here than in her pussy. My dick wanted it; it wanted to be buried between those fucking cheeks. More pre-cum leaked out as I thought of how it would feel. But fucking a virgin ass—that was for someone who was going to tell her he loved her, not someone who was going to leave her in the morning.

When my finger was finally all the way in, I stayed there, holding steady, making sure she could handle this before I pumped both holes at the same time.

Because once I did that and mixed in the humming of my tongue, she wouldn't last. She'd come almost immediately.

I didn't want that yet. I wanted to stay in a little longer, so the soreness would be with her all day tomorrow, giving her a constant reminder of this moment.

Of me.

Of the way I fucking savored her cunt.

"You're right. It does get better." She twisted my hair and cried, "Don't stop."

My speed had decreased so much that she was getting only delicate swipes.

But the desperation in her voice made me say, "I'm not stopping, baby. I'm letting you get used to this first."

Baby?

A response that surprised the shit out of me, but it felt so right as it rolled out of my mouth.

"Make me come, Beck."

A demand she hadn't ever given to me before.

Her confidence was building. So, how the fuck could I delay this and drag it out when she had the courage to ask for what she wanted?

I couldn't.

I upped my pace again, my fingers gaining momentum, too, and I added pressure to the tip of her clit by sucking it into my mouth. I kept it in there with my teeth, a sweet bite that I knew wouldn't cause her any pain, and once I had it secured in place, I licked the end of it.

As hard as I could.

And as fast.

"Oh my God!"

Her legs spread, giving me more access, and my teeth released her, my tongue then flattening against her whole clit, sweeping upward in a quick pattern while my fingers ground inside. Each lap made her hips buck, made her clench my skin, made her clit turn even harder.

Wetter.

"Beck!"

The sound I wanted to fucking hear.

But because I knew this was just the beginning of her climb, I gave her what she needed, and that was more pressure.

More friction.

More power.

"Fuck," she gasped. "Fuck!"

I watched the shadow of her body move over the bed, her shudders blasting against my face as I tasted the thickness that came from her.

"Ah!" Her legs didn't stay apart; they caved in toward my face. When my beard hit her thighs, she screamed, "Oh, yes!"

My mouth didn't slow, nor did my hand. I kept up the same speed, the one that had sent her over the edge, until I knew she was well past the peak and on her way down.

"Gah," she cried.

That was when my movements turned tender, the intensity long gone, and I waited until I knew it was time to slow.

And become completely still.

"Beck ... I can't even think. Or talk. Or tell you what that just felt like ..."

"You don't have to. You showed me instead."

While I kissed her clit, I eased my fingers out, my mouth staying there to press against each spot I'd touched tonight. And eventually, my lips moved to her stomach and chest, each of her nipples, before I made my way to her face.

"That was one," I told her.

She was breathless. "One what?"

"One orgasm. You're about to have three more."

Even in the blackness of the room, I could see her eyes widen.

"From your mouth?"

I chuckled. "If that's what you want." I rubbed my tip

against her clit, taking in that feeling once again, fucking torturing myself. "But I'm hoping at least one is from my dick."

"I want that." Her hands took hold of my shaft and began to pump. "Go get a condom. Right now."

Traces of faint morning light were coming in through the blinds, showing hints of Jolie's face and body as she lay, covered by the thin white sheet. Where she had fallen asleep after her fourth orgasm, I'd stayed up. Watching her. Listening to her breathe. And when it was time, I climbed out of bed and put the last of my things into my suitcase, rolling it to the door.

I didn't like goodbyes, and since I didn't know what ours would look like, I took a few minutes to write her a quick note. While I stood in the doorway of the bedroom, staring at that unforgettable body, I reread the words I'd jotted down on one of the hotel's notepads.

> *You looked far too beautiful and peaceful to wake up. When you read this, don't rush out. The room is reserved until tomorrow morning—I extended it for you. Order breakfast, lunch, dinner—whatever you want, it's on me.*
>
> *I'm leaving my number. Use it. Or don't. Just know, I'll never forget these three nights.*
>
> *—Beck*
>
> *P.S. Since I fucked the Boston off you, I thought it was only fair to replace it with LA.*

I glanced toward the bed again. The red of her hair was such a contrast to the white bedding. The shape of her ass, the arch of her back, the softness of her neck, even hidden—it was making me want to get back in and have one more taste.

But I forced myself to walk into the living room, setting the note on the table next to my LA Whales sweatshirt. I paused for a second—only a second—and wheeled my suitcase to the door. I left my key inside the suite and quietly shut the door behind me.

UNKNOWN
Hey, it's Jolie.

ME
Good morning, gorgeous.

JOLIE
You're gone. SOB.

ME
I just got to the plane.

JOLIE
I can't believe you left me your sweatshirt.

ME
I think you should wear it to the next Boston home game.

JOLIE
You're funny. 😊

ME
I wasn't joking.

JOLIE

Listen, I want to thank you. I'll never forget those three nights either—even if I'm going to have to get an extension on my paper that I was supposed to write and spend allll the hours at the office to get caught up, you were worth it. If you ever find your way here again, you have my number. Use it. Or don't. Just know, I want you to.

ME

LOL. I hear you ...

JOLIE

Have a safe flight, Beck, and good luck at your game tonight.

"Who the fuck are you talking to?" Landon asked as he took the seat beside me, attempting to bypass the security screen on my phone and see what I was typing.

I shoved my cell into my pocket and reclined my seat, securing the headphones over my ears even though a song wasn't playing. I'd muted it once Jolie's text came through. But because there were multiple cameras on this plane—probably one pointed at me now—I wasn't going to get into it with Landon.

This was a conversation for when we were alone.

"The redhead from the bar," I whispered, blocking my lips with the back of my hand so they couldn't be seen or read. "The one who stayed in my room."

"You've got it bad for her, don't you?" He kept his voice down—he knew what was at stake.

"Bad? No. But I had a hell of a time with her."

He pulled at the knot of his tie, loosening it a little. "So, you're telling me it was worth going up to her and talking to her? Which means you're happy you listened to me and I saved you from making one of the biggest mistakes of your life." He waited. "Come on. Tell me I'm a genius."

I punched his arm. "Asshole."

"Let me fucking gloat for a second. You know I'm right."

I shook my head while I looked at my friend. "All right, motherfucker. I'll let you gloat, but only for a couple of seconds, and then I'm turning up my music and focusing on our upcoming game."

He banged his head to a silent rhythm. "She was that good, wasn't she?"

I held the back of my neck, my fingers meeting the stiffness of my starched shirt, my brain concentrating on only one thing —and that thing had nothing to do with our upcoming game. "Yeah, man, she was."

EIGHT

Jolie

"Get up and get dressed. I'm taking your ass out."

Ginger stood in the middle of our room, extending her hand in my direction, her attempt at pulling me out of bed. Except I didn't have any fingers to give her—all of mine were holding Beck's sweatshirt, my nose buried in the fabric, inhaling his spicy smell that had soaked in.

"Jolie, come on. Please get up."

I had known this was coming, so my response, "Go without me," was already prepared.

"Ha!" She flopped down beside me. "Listen to me, girl. We're going to the hockey house. Whether I have to put makeup on you myself and dry-shampoo your hair into a ponytail, you're coming. I'm not going without you."

I groaned, "I'm most definitely not going to the hockey house."

"Please?" She rubbed my knees, almost shaking them. "You've been moping in this room since you got back from

Beck's hotel this morning. You didn't eat lunch. You didn't eat dinner. I get that you're all up in your feels, but you're going to snap out of it and have some drinks and get him off your mind."

"I'm not moping." But I was moping. I couldn't help it. Waking up to a Beck-less room and a note and his sweatshirt and the slapping realization that he wasn't coming back had been a real kick in the gut. "I'm watching the game."

LA at Washington wasn't a game I'd normally care about. I had no interest in any team other than Boston. But Beck had changed that, and seeing him on the ice tonight weirdly made me feel closer to him. It made the sting of his absence and the hollowness in my chest feel less intense.

But the game was just a temporary fix. Beck wasn't coming back—not in the way I'd just experienced over the last three nights.

"Babe, the game is almost over. There's, what"—she turned toward the screen—"two minutes left?"

I hugged his sweatshirt closer to my chest. "So?"

"And you don't even like LA."

I closed my eyes and sighed.

I'd watched every second of this game, even the intermissions. Although it wasn't really the game I was focused on; it was Beck. He was in the first line, and my stare didn't leave him whenever he was on the ice. And if he wasn't, I tried to catch a glimpse of him on the bench.

The way he looked in his uniform—*God*. I could see hints of his beard through his navy-and-silver mask and those hazel eyes every time the camera zoomed in on him.

"Jolie? Are you even listening to me?"

I was staring at the screen. The clock was running out. Beck was no longer playing because LA had such a big lead, and the third and fourth lines were in.

I gradually glanced over at her. "No."

"I'm begging you—let's go."

I shook my head. "The press conference will be coming on in a couple of minutes. I have to see it. He was the top-scoring player in the game, I know they're going to interview him."

She grabbed something on my bed and stood, backing up several paces toward her side of the room. "I'll make a deal with you." She waved the TV remote in her hand. "I won't shut the TV off and throw the remote out of the window if you promise to get dressed the second the press conference is over and come out with me."

The scowl was heavy on my face. "You wouldn't."

She went over to the window. "We both know there isn't anything I wouldn't do for you—and letting you mope in this room is not going to happen on my watch. So, yes, I would toss this sucker out the window." She cranked the semi-broken old latch, and I felt an immediate breeze as the window pane opened a crack. "Remember, I'm doing this for you." When I didn't answer, she said, "I don't want you hurting—and I know you are."

"But I shouldn't be hurting." My voice was getting quieter with each word. "It was three nights. That's nothing. That's like a long weekend at best. So, why do I feel like this?"

She closed the window, leaving the remote on her desk, and she rushed over, putting her arm around my shoulders. "People have fallen in love in much shorter time frames. Trust me, it's possible."

I lowered the sweatshirt from my face and set it on my lap.

Every breath of his spiciness made me miss him more, causing my brain to spiral.

One day, probably soon, his scent would fade, and the only thing I'd have left was watching his games. Yet he'd have many more overnighters in cities across the country, where he'd probably spend those evenings with someone else.

I heard the rumors. I knew how things worked when it came to single professional athletes.

I wasn't stupid enough to think this was the first time Beck had done this or that it would be his last.

It didn't matter if we'd had the most amazing time.

I was replaceable.

And that made me ache harder. It made my stomach turn. It made the knot in my chest move into the back of my throat.

"Jolie, you're in your head. I can see those wheels spinning. Don't do it, don't dwell on it, don't try to make sense out of it. It will keep you in your feelings, and that's not where you need to be right now."

I left the screen to look at her and say, "We just had so much fun together."

She gently nodded. "I know."

"And I knew I'd feel like shit after he left—I'd tried to prep myself for it. Maybe that should have stopped me from carrying on through the whole three nights, but ..." Flashes of our time together were filling my vision. The way he had held my hand when we walked to the boat. The way he had hugged me whenever I was cold. The way he'd looked at me—each time, not one single time. "I just didn't want it to end."

She rubbed the middle of my back. "Based on the note he left, I'm positive he felt the same way."

I wasn't going to cry.

I couldn't.

Getting emotional over this wasn't going to help the situation. It wouldn't make me feel better. And it wouldn't bring Beck back.

I had known what I was signing up for when I told him I'd leave the bar with him.

We were both beyond single. We'd made that clear.

He made no promises.

But that was then.

In the time we spent together, I saw hints of the man behind the hockey mask. I saw flashes of his heart, a rawness that was usually covered by his uniform.

Sure, Beck Weston was a hockey star, and that was what had initially attracted me to him. But he was so much more.

My hands went over my face. "It doesn't matter, Ginger. He's gone."

"Yes, it does matter." She clenched my arm, forcing my fingers to fall and land on top of the sweatshirt. "He said he wished he could bring you to LA with him. He said in a perfect world, he would. And he told you he liked this—meaning what was going on between you guys."

I could hear his voice saying those words.

They had been replaying nonstop since I'd gotten home.

"He even gave you his number. He didn't have to do that." Her hand stilled. "But by doing that ... babe, he was showing you."

My eyes left the screen again. "Showing me. I—"

My voice was cut off by the commentators announcing the press conference, and I quickly glanced back at the TV. The screen changed, showing a long table, wrapped in the NHL's logo, with two players from LA sitting in front of mics.

One was Beck.

I found Ginger's hand, squeezed it in mine, and slid to the end of my bed.

He hadn't showered. He'd come straight from either the ice or the locker room. His hair was wet, his face sweaty. He didn't even bother wiping it off with the towel that hung around his neck.

Something I was strangely grateful for. The way sweat looked on that man should be illegal.

"I'm about to die," I confessed.

"I don't blame you. I kinda am too."

A group of reporters, not in the angle of the camera, were calling out questions for Beck and his teammate. I saw Beck's mouth moving in response, I heard his voice, but I wasn't processing anything he was saying.

I was too fixated on his face. On his eyes and how riveting they looked. On his lips. Ones that I'd kissed not that long ago. On his beard that was untamed and devilishly sexy.

"What the heck is on his mustache?" she asked.

I couldn't glance at Ginger. Nothing in this world could pry my eyes off my TV. "What are you talking about?"

"Right above his lip and below his nose, like halfway, stuck to the hair ... is that ... a ... piece of a protein bar? Or something like that?"

"A what?" My heart was pounding so fast. I released her hand, got on my feet, and walked to the TV to get a closer view. "Oh my God."

Ginger was right. There was something woven into the hairs above his lip. It wasn't large, and if you weren't looking as intently as we were, you would probably miss it. But it was definitely a ... *questionable crumb*.

"I don't know what it is," I admitted. "It's brownish, almost tannish."

"But it's something," she pressed.

I sucked in some air and nodded. "Yeah. It's ... something."

"Definitely food, right?"

I took another step, knowing that wouldn't give me the answer, but it was still worth a try. "A piece of a cookie? Or a protein bar, like you said?" I touched the screen. "Or maybe pizza crust?" I laughed. "At least crust that isn't burned, like the kind I make."

Several seconds passed before she said, "The internet is having a blast, trying to figure out what it is."

I backed up, but I didn't take my eyes off him. "What do you mean?"

"The memes have already started."

I continued to step backward until I reached the bed and held out my hand for her phone. Once it hit my palm, I placed it in front of me, scanning from the TV to her cell, back and forth, so I wouldn't miss any of Beck. "My God, they're ruthless. It's like everyone has to be so perfect. No one is allowed to have a real moment—"

I cut myself off when I realized what I'd just said.

A real moment.

"And you think I'm a man who only seeks perfection? Shit, I'm far from that, Jolie. Listen to me. We all have real moments. Athletes especially. We're under a microscope, and some of our most vulnerable experiences are caught on camera and blasted all over the internet."

As I stared at Beck's mouth while he was replying to one of the reporters, I recalled our conversation as though it had happened moments ago.

That crumb on his face—whatever it was—had to be a coincidence. He'd taken a quick bite of something to eat before he came out for the press conference and forgot to wipe his mouth.

Like I'd done before rushing into first period that day in ninth grade.

Right?

I blinked several times as Beck got up from his chair, as he and his teammate walked out of the press conference and the commentators filled the feed.

That was when I slowly turned toward Ginger.

Since I was still holding hers, she now had my phone in her hand, scrolling. "Girl, you should see the comments coming in. Some say it's a piece from his helmet. Some say it's food. Some say he put his face in the DC goalie's ass and—"

87

"Can I run something by you?"

She put my phone down. "Of course."

I tossed her phone on the bed to free up my hands and wrapped them around me. "Now, I could be wrong—and I'm sure I am—but I told Beck the story about the barbeque sauce that was on my face in ninth grade and how I was teased endlessly for it. That conversation led to a talk about real moments and vulnerability. He tried to make me feel better by telling me that things like that happened to athletes all the time and how they were caught on camera and would go viral."

She crossed her arms and smiled. "What are you saying, Jolie? That Beck put a crumb on his face on purpose?"

"I'm wondering if he did, yes. It doesn't make sense why he would do that, but—"

"Oh, it makes perfect sense to me."

Why wouldn't my heart stop pounding?

Why was it beating so fast that when I voiced, "Why would you say that?" I sounded breathless?

Her smile grew. "It's just a hunch I have."

"Explain your hunch."

"*Hmm*, where do I start ..." She tucked her legs in front of her and rested her hands between them. "Beck's still hockey rough with his unruly beard and messy hair, which looks messy on purpose, but it's still messy."

I slowly filled my lungs and moaned, "Yep."

"But at the same time, he's pretty. He's put together, and for the most part, he's groomed. He cares how he looks. The suit he had on before tonight's game was so sharp. Even when he was dripping in sweat after the game, his hair wasn't standing up in every direction—it was tamed—and his beard was finger-combed. Trust me, that guy wasn't walking into a room of reporters with something on his face unless he wanted it there."

I grabbed a bunch of my hair and lifted it off my neck, the room suddenly so hot. "You're saying he left the ice, stopped somewhere to put that crumb, piece of helmet—whatever—on his face, and went to the press conference? But why?"

She shook her head back and forth, letting out a long breath. "One day, you'll know your worth. I swear it's my mission. But we're so far from being there, it's not even funny."

I rolled my eyes at her. "Ginger—"

"The reason Beck would show a real moment is because he agrees with me and everyone else in thinking you're the hottest woman alive. And he knows, if things were different, you would be his, and that man would never let you leave his side."

"Ginger—"

"He also knows damn well you're watching him on TV tonight and that you're going to see the memes. He wants you to know you're not the only one who has real moments, and he wants nothing more than to make you smile about it."

"No." I looked at my bare feet. "That whole theory is bananas. I don't believe it."

"Jolie ..." She waited until I glanced up. "That boy is thinking about you, babe. The same way you're thinking about him. And he's showing you."

ME

> I have to know ... was it a real moment or a staged one?

BECK

> You should be asleep. It's almost four in the morning.

ME

> I've had all the drinks. Like, alllll the drinks.

BECK

Dive-bar night?

ME

Aww, I love that you know that.

But no. The hockey house.

BECK

LOL.

ME

Ginger's idea, NOT mine.

She stayed there. I'm back in our dorm. But before I fall asleep, I have to know …

BECK

You think I'd put something on my mustache to cause the internet to explode? And draw even more attention to me? Shit, you know how I feel about social media.

ME

I don't think you care what anyone says about you, which means you'd do something like that to prove a point.

BECK

I've got nothing to prove.

ME

Fair.

But maybe there's something you wanted to show.

BECK

Did it show you something?

ME

Yes.

BECK

Sweet dreams, Jolie.

NINE

Beck

"Look who the fucking cat dragged in," my oldest brother, Walker, said as I came into the conference room of my family's corporate office.

It had been a while since I'd been here. My main contributions came in the form of financial support when they needed liquid cash to put down on a piece of land or to vote on the location of a new restaurant after my siblings did the tedious task of researching why the different spots would benefit our brand.

But since I was in town for a decent stint, I figured making the weekly strategy meeting would be a good place to see everyone at once.

I clenched Hart's shoulder as I passed him, his black suit jacket and red tie making him look sharp as hell this morning. Only two years older with the same height and build as me, he should have been a professional athlete, but Hart, like Walker, had had his sights set on building this business from the ground up.

"Welcome back, brother," Hart said as my fingers left him.

I gave Eden, the youngest, a kiss on the cheek before I sat between her and Colson, pounding fists with my second-to-oldest sibling.

"Are you doing all right?" Colson asked.

I wasn't surprised the only parent in the room had inquired about how I was doing. Although any of them would eventually, Colson always asked.

"Hanging in there." I lowered the hood of my sweatshirt and ran my hand over my head, my strands still damp from the cold plunge I'd done before coming here. "But I'll be honest—*dragging* couldn't be a more accurate description." I leaned back in my chair and rested my hands on top of the table. "It's been a long couple of weeks on the road."

"Is the body hurting?" Walker asked, wearing his chef's whites, the brightness of it glowing under the overhead light, showing there wasn't a single stain on the fabric. Within a few hours, I was sure that would all change.

"Something fierce," I answered.

"Well, you look half dead." Eden turned in her chair to face me, her blue eyes locked right on me. My sister's assessment and opinion were forever honest and so fucking dead-on. "When was the last time you slept?"

I whistled out a mouthful of air. "I got about six hours last night."

"It wasn't enough. Your body needs more," Colson said. The dude was so laid-back, unlike Hart and Eden. He was wearing a polo instead of a button-down. "That was a long stretch on the road. You're home for a week or so, yeah?"

I nodded. "Thank fuck."

"You'd better be taking care of yourself while you're here,"

Hart added. "You've got the usual treatments scheduled?" He had a pile of folders in front of him that he leaned his arms on.

A pile that told me today's meeting was intended to be all business.

"Massage, hydrotherapy, hyperbaric chamber treatments, chiropractic work—all of it." I held the back of my head, my arms bent, elbows pointed out. "I'll be good."

"I'll stop by and prep some meals for you," Walker said.

Walker had been born with the same talent as our father. He could turn simple ingredients into a masterpiece. But the pressure that came with that skill was immense, especially given the business we'd built. He was in charge of the menu and new recipes at Charred, our steak houses, and Toro, our seafood and raw bars, constantly having to keep our restaurants fresh and competitive.

And even though I loved the guy, his attitude reflected what he was feeling at all times, and that was fucking stressed and usually pissed off.

"You don't have time for that," I told him. "You're running the kitchen of LA Charred and controlling operations at hundreds of our restaurants." I looked at Hart and winked. "I'll have Hart cook for me."

Hart laughed. "Don't hold your breath, asshole. Things behind the scenes are as busy as our kitchens. I don't remember the last time I even cooked for myself."

"Which is why all of you have a personal chef." Eden rolled her eyes. "Let's stop wasting time talking about things that aren't ever going to happen—like Hart cooking for you—and let's discuss the elephant in the room." Eden reached across the space between us and held my cheeks as though she was inspecting my face. "What was under your nose at the press conference?"

I chuckled. "I can't believe it took you this long to ask me. You're slacking. That's not like you."

"We had more important things to discuss through text message"—she pointed at the pile of folders in front of Hart—"like some of that."

"Speaking of that"—I nodded toward Hart's pile—"how many more locations of Charred are we opening—"

"Nope," Eden said, cutting me off. "First, we're discussing the face crumb. Then, we can talk about work."

"This one is relentless." I smiled. "I had a bite of a chocolate chip cookie before I went out to the press conference. What's the big fucking deal?"

"The internet thinks it's a big deal. They're having a blast, coming up with theories of what the crumb was. Listen to this: Vegas is even allowing people to take bets on whether it was a protein bar or a piece of your helmet." Her hand slapped the table—her attempt to really drive in her point.

That was why my agent had called the next day and asked what it was—Vegas probably needed him to confirm the answer.

The expression I gave her backed up this point. "You know I give no shits about what the internet thinks."

"But you do give a shit about what you look like." She crossed her arms. "Which has me wondering ..." Her eyes narrowed as she stared at me.

"I'm with Eden." Walker pushed up his white sleeves. "You're the prettiest one out of all of us."

"And the king of being camera-ready," Hart contributed.

I waved both of them off, even though they weren't wrong, and said, "Wondering about what?" to my sister.

"A few weeks before, there was the ice-humping scandal"—she covered her eyes with her black-painted nails—"something

I don't even want to talk about—I'm scarred for life because of it." Her hand dropped. "Now we have the face incident. So, yes, both of these things have me wondering: Are you trying to stay in the limelight for reasons other than hockey? Are you raising your middle finger to someone? Or ..." Her brows furrowed.

I replied, "You're reading too much into it."

She shook her head. "I don't think I am."

Of course, the fucking detective of the group had called me out. I wasn't surprised. I just wasn't going to admit why that piece of cookie had been on my lip. The person who had needed to see it did. That was what mattered.

I looked at Walker, Hart, and Colson, knowing the three of them were probably stirring and that this wasn't the first time they had heard our sister bring this up. "Do any of you have anything to say? Or can we talk about what's in those files?" I nodded again toward Hart.

Hart smiled at me, the kind of grin that said he was up to something. "Let's talk about Boston." He licked his lips, leaning even further onto the table. "How was it?"

"Out of all the places I played at during this stretch of away games, you want to talk about Boston?" I was rocking in my chair, but stopped. "It was fine. Why do you ask?"

Hart's brows rose. "It was just *fine?*"

"I walked into a fucking lion's den this morning." I let out a loud laugh. "Do you have something to ask me, Hart?"

"Do you have something to say?" he countered.

There was no question in my mind who could have told my brother this information. Not that I gave a shit. I didn't hold back anything from my siblings—minus the reason for the face crumb—but I was going to dig into my goalie for this one.

I laughed. "Nah. I'm good."

Hart rubbed his hands together. "I bet you're real good after those three nights."

"Oh my God," I groaned with a grin. "Here we go. Lay it on me. Give me everything you've got."

"Hold on a second. Is there tea?" Eden asked. "That only Hart knows about?" She glared at Hart. "How dare you not tell me!"

Hart pointed at his chest. "It's not my story to tell."

"Fuck, there is no story," I said to my sister, and when I glanced around the table, I could tell that not a single face I looked at appeared convinced. "Things happen when you're on the road. It's the same shit on a different day."

But that wasn't true. At least not the latter part.

Jolie wasn't like anyone I'd ever met.

I never spent three consecutive nights with a woman or even three accumulative nights. The way I lived my life, I considered that a fucking commitment.

And it was a commitment I'd been thinking about nonstop since I'd walked out of that hotel.

Eden turned her chair even more, her body fully facing me, and she crossed her legs. "We all know that things happen on the road. We've heard your stories. You're not one to hold back when it comes to us. Which is why this suddenly feels strange ... because you're not sharing what happened during those three nights. And that, Beck, is not like you at all."

My hands dropped from behind my head, and as I placed them on the table, I glanced down. I had shelves full of LA Whales sweatshirts, like the one I was wearing, but my favorite was the one I'd given to Jolie. At this moment—and so many fucking moments before this one—I wanted nothing more than to fuck the LA off her.

"Here's what I'll say ..." I looked up, immediately connecting eyes with my sister. "I met someone in Boston and spent those three nights with her. But neither of us is in a place where we can make anything of it. What happened there, it's going to stay there."

Eden's expression softened—something that wasn't common. "That's too bad."

I waited a second before I asked, "Why do you say that?"

"Because what I'm hearing and what I'm seeing are showing me how much you like her."

"There isn't an inch of my fucking body that isn't screaming right now." Landon winced as he unlatched the straps of his shoulder pads and chest protector and lifted the heavy gear over his head. Every new piece of equipment he took off, he set it in front of his locker. "Today felt more like a game than a practice."

The gray T-shirt he wore beneath his pads was soaked with sweat, and while he still had it on, I punched his shoulder. "Pussy."

"Fuck that." He shook the sweat out of his hair. "Even you were fucking hard on me."

"I was the hardest on you—get it straight." I pulled my grays over my head and tossed the wet T-shirt into the laundry bin. "That's what you get for ratting my ass out."

He froze as he looked at me and then started laughing. "Oh shit, Hart said something to you about Jolie?"

"I'm surprised as hell that he waited until this morning to bring it up, but yeah." I took a seat in front of my locker to untie my skates. "How did he get it out of you?"

Landon stood next to me, holding on to the side of his locker. "He reached out after the Boston game, asking where we'd gone to celebrate. He wanted to buy the team a couple of bottles. He said he called you and you didn't answer, so he tried me. That's when I dropped the news that you were no longer at the bar."

I rubbed my chest, the muscles in there and my biceps and shoulders all sore from today's stick work and shooting. "Dirty bastard."

His head hung. "I knew he'd give you shit for it, especially when he texted me during our flight to DC to follow up and ask how things were going between you two. Hopefully, he didn't lay it on too hard."

"It's all good, my man."

Landon was friends with my family, and since he didn't have any here, he'd spent a few holidays with mine. I wasn't at all shocked that he'd told Hart—he'd probably assumed I would tell him anyway—nor was I bothered by anything he was admitting.

"Have you talked to her since you guys were texting on the flight to DC?" He sat beside me to unlace his skates.

"No."

He paused to look at me. "Do you think you will?"

Each locker was built out of wood and framed like a cubby. I leaned into one of the separating walls, pushing my back into the edge, letting the hardness work into my muscles.

"I've thought about it. But it's a situation that won't get any easier."

Not with her being a sophomore. If it were her senior year, we could possibly wait it out since maybe there'd be a chance her dad would let her work from home and that home could be LA. But as a fucking sophomore, at a school on the other side of the country, she was years away from having any freedom. And with a schedule as inflexible as mine, that really made things impractical.

"If we talk, it'll make me want her more, and she can't give me more."

More? *Fuck.* Who would have ever thought I'd want that?

"And if you don't talk to her?" he asked.

There was this feeling in my chest that I didn't like. To try to tame it, I bent forward and rested my arms on my hockey pants. "I'm going to miss her like hell."

TEN

Jolie

ME

How has it been a month since I saw you? You're kicking all the ass in the meantime— I've been keeping track. Who would have ever thought I'd be cheering for a team aside from Boston? Not me, certainly, LOL. Anyway, I'm going to be in LA next weekend. I know you're going to be in Dallas for a game, and then you're off to Canada. It just feels weird to go there and not reach out to you.

BECK

Jolie ...

You're flying in on Friday and heading back on Sunday?

ME

Yep.

BECK

Extend your trip.

ME

I can't. I have a test first thing on Monday morning.

BECK

I get back to LA on Monday afternoon.

ME

Sigh.

BECK

What if you flew to Dallas on Thursday and then flew to LA on Friday? That would give us one night together.

ME

I'd love nothing more, but I can't make it happen. I'm meeting with a new client on Thursday, and we're taking them on the yacht.

BECK

Busy girl.

ME

Me? Ha! More like you're the busy one.

But, hey, at least I tried. I hope I get to see you soon.

BECK

You will.

BECK

Hey, you.

ME

Hey, YOU.

BECK

Your sophomore year is coming to a close. You must be excited. Things going good for you?

ME

I still have a couple of months to go and finals—shudder, LOL. But, yeah, things are awesome.

Your season is almost over. It has to feel amazing, knowing that a break is coming soon.

BECK

Regular season, yes, but now we have to survive playoffs.

ME

I imagine that's a whole thing.

BECK

Yes, a whole fucking thing. 😉

Listen, I've got a bye week coming up. I can't travel since I have practice every day, but I was thinking, why don't you come out and stay with me? If you can't swing the whole week, come for a couple of days or as long as you can.

ME

Ooh. Sounds fun. What are the dates?

BECK

March 12–18.

ME

Beck, nooo! Tell me you're kidding. Tell me those aren't the dates?!

THE WILDEST ONE

BECK
You've got plans?

ME
I'm in South Beach that whole week with my friends for spring break.

BECK
You'll have a blast.

ME
I thought that too ... until I got your invite.

ME
I swear I didn't breathe that entire game! AH! I'm screaming for you right now and sending ALL THE CONGRATS! What an amazing victory, Beck. Stanley Cup winner—I couldn't be happier for you.

BECK
Jolie ...

I appreciate that. Thank you.

ME
I hope you're celebrating.

BECK
We're doing a shitload of that, yes.

ME
I wish I were there with you. Enjoy every second. 🩶

BECK

Hey, beautiful. How's summer treating you?

ME

Hi, stranger. It's summer? I wouldn't know. The only time I'm outside is when I'm walking to and from work. I've been dreaming about sand, surf, and a tiny bikini. Sigh. How are you? Are you eating up every second of your break?

BECK

Fuck yes. I've been in the Maldives, and I'm heading to Europe soon, where I'll be spending the next month or so until I have to report to practice.

ME

Another season already? Whoa!

BECK

Another school year. Junior year, baby.

ME

Shhh. We don't bring up school. I'm soaking up every second of this homework-less and test-less life, LOL. 😌

BECK

You know what I think you should do to celebrate that no-school life?

ME

Tell me.

BECK

You should meet me in Paris. I'll be there next week. And since you'd be gone over the 4th of July, I even promise fireworks.

ME

Do you know how dreamy that sounds? Except next week, I'm in Cape Cod. A bunch of us rented a house to celebrate the holiday.

> You know what I think you should do to celebrate that no-practice-and-no-game life? You should come to the Cape with me.

BECK

That's a tough one.

ME

> Cape Cod vs. Paris—there's a clear winner there. 😊
>
> Plus, it's been, what, 7-ish months since I kissed you? That's just mean.

BECK

Just because I'm not coming to the Cape doesn't mean I don't want to kiss you …

ME

> Happy start of your new season. How is it possible that summer is over and another season is beginning? Sigh.

BECK

No shit. It feels like the season just ended and Europe never happened.

ME

> Was it amazing? I wish your assistant had posted pics from your trip on your Instagram account and not just hockey and brand deals. I was dying to see your adventures, and she shared nothing about it.
>
> I get why you're so private. I just selfishly wanted to see more.

A photo came through of Beck in front of the Eiffel Tower. It was nighttime, and the tower was lit with beautiful white lights. His body wasn't pointed toward the camera; it was more of a side angle, and he was looking over his shoulder with a slight grin. But that face? *My God.* It was shaved down to a heavy stubble, his hair short, his hazel eyes filled with a fiery gaze even though it was dark outside.

This was the groomed version of Beck when I'd been with the wild, untamed one.

I had no preference. The man was so hot either way. But now that I had this photo on my phone, what it did, what it showed me, was that I would do anything to rewind time so I could go to Paris instead of the Cape.

What was I even thinking when I made that decision?

BECK
What you missed ...

Words that rubbed salt straight into the regret wound.

ME
I hate myself. In case you're wondering.

But ironically, I'm reaching out because I'm trying to see you. I know it's a long shot, especially after checking your schedule, but I'm going to be in LA for one night—October 21. Any chance you'll be flying back after your game in Chicago? It looks like you've got a three-day window between that game and your game in Vegas.

BECK
We leave Chicago and fly straight to Vegas.

ME
I was afraid that was going to be your answer.

I swear, the universe is doing everything in its power to keep us apart.

THE WILDEST ONE

BECK

Jolie ... I'm sure you know we're coming there in a few weeks to play Boston.

ME

Yep, I know. I can't even believe I'm about to type these words.

BECK

You're going to be out of town, aren't you?

ME

I'm heading to Lake Como with my fam for Christmas. I was going to text you soon and tell you. It's just, at this point, I kinda can't believe we're missing each other AGAIN.

Do you know what next week is?

BECK

No.

ME

The one-year anniversary of us meeting.

BECK

One year? No shit.

ME

It's a crime that I haven't seen you since. Those three nights, Beck—I think about them. A lot.

BECK

Me too.

ME

> That was such a tough loss. You guys were SO close to winning the conference finals. I can't believe it came down to a sudden-death match during overtime. I hope you know that even though you didn't get the win, you guys had the most incredible season. Be proud of yourself, Beck. I'm certainly proud of you.

BECK

I appreciate you.

Congrats on finishing your junior year. I'm assuming you're about done with finals?

ME

> Almost, yes, and then it's another summer packed full of work with a few trips to the Cape thrown in, LOL.

BECK

It's your last one before your life becomes all work. Enjoy it.

ME

> Enjoy Europe—I'm guessing that's where you're headed during your time off?

BECK

Europe, Africa, and Asia.

ME

> Ah! Amazing! I've always dreamed of going on a safari.

> Can you imagine listening to the sounds of all those animals and looking up at the dark sky, gazing at the stars with me? Put me in your suitcase, pleeeease.

I stared at my screen, the bubble beneath his name showing that he was typing. I slowly filled my lungs with air, the anxiety kicking in as I wondered what his response would be. Would he invite me to join him, like he had asked me to come to Paris? Would he offer to go to the Cape?

Even though we hadn't seen each other in a long time, that hadn't stopped us from trying to get together.

The want was there.

He showed me that consistently.

Luck just hadn't been on our side.

I set my phone down on my bed, the bubble still moving beneath his name. I went into the kitchen of the apartment I shared with Ginger and another friend, and I grabbed a can of sparkling water from the fridge. Both girls were already sleeping. I was the only one who had stayed up for the game, so I quietly tiptoed back to my room, making sure I didn't wake them.

I sank into the row of pillows on my bed and picked up my cell. I waited a few seconds, but the bubble was gone, and it didn't return.

And there was no message from Beck on the screen.

He didn't want me to go.

A devastating blow that dug straight into my heart as each hour passed.

My chest was a gaping hole the next morning when there was still no text from him.

And when a whole week went by and all I got from him was silence, my heart completely shattered.

"Why don't you look as excited as I thought you'd be?" my father asked as I sat on the other side of his desk. The news he'd just shared was pulsing inside my chest, hitting walls that held in my heart and ricocheting. "I thought you'd be grinning ear to ear."

But his news had come out of nowhere.

And it was information I was having the hardest time processing.

"I am excited, Dad." I rubbed my hands over my black skirt. They weren't just sweaty; it felt like each finger weighed hundreds of pounds. "I think I'm a little overwhelmed by it all." When they were as dry as they could get, one dived into my hair, twirling the strands as my brain spiraled.

A spiral that took me from one dead end to another, causing me to mentally turn and run in a different direction.

"Understandable." He picked up his cell as it rang on top of his desk and silenced the call. "We have a lot to discuss. I want to get into details, but I don't have time to do that now."

My chest was thumping far too hard and fast for me to say much more besides, "No, I get it." I checked my watch, knowing I was cutting it close to the meeting I had with my client. This pop-in with Dad had been unscheduled; he'd just asked me to come to his office a few minutes ago. "I have to run too. How about I come over for dinner tonight and you can break everything down?"

He picked up the silver classic pen from his desk—a gift I'd given to him when I was in the first grade, *Best Dad* engraved toward the top—and he tapped it against his blotter. "Salmon piccata or lasagna?"

"Dad," I groaned, "you can't ask me that. You know they're both my favorites that Mom makes."

He smiled. "See you tonight."

I nodded and got up from my chair, walking out of his office and closing the door behind me. As I reached my cubby, I found it harder and harder to breathe, especially since one of the first things my eyes landed on was Boston's schedule. It was pinned to the wall right next to my computer, where I'd circled the home games in pink highlighter.

Three weeks from now, we were playing the LA Whales. At home.

Beck hadn't reached out to ask if I would be in town. We hadn't even spoken since LA had lost the conference finals at the end of last season.

I didn't want the silence.

I also didn't want to bother him or bombard him with messages.

When he hadn't replied, something had told me that was the end of us. Not that there had been an us, but the effort on both sides had been exhausted, and we were accepting that whatever happened, happened, and it wouldn't be happening again.

But he was coming here to play, and he knew my dad had season tickets. I was sure he knew that if I was in town, I would be there.

I rested my elbows on my desk, my hands going over my face.

But after the news I just heard ... *will I be there?*

ELEVEN

Beck

The sound of the siren signaled the end of the game, but not a single one of my teammates left the ice. The only movement was Landon, who skated away from his goalpost to join the five of us near the center line, where Boston's third string and goalie were waiting on the other side.

Both teams were staring each other down.

I could feel the fight brewing, my skin tingling at the thought of hitting someone.

I could see it in the eyes of my teammates, the tension building with each one of their breaths. The anger, on both sides, hitting a peak.

Boston had made us look like a bunch of amateurs tonight. We couldn't do a goddamn thing right.

We hadn't fallen apart. That would have meant we'd started off strong and dissolved over time, and that certainly wasn't the case. From the moment this game had begun three periods ago, we weren't able to find a rhythm, and there was no sync between any of the lines; we'd looked like a group of novice figure skaters, cleaning the ice with our fucking asses.

"Break it up, boys." The ref, who should be leaving the rink, came over and positioned himself between the teams, his arms outstretched. "Back off. Now!"

He was quickly joined by a second ref and a third, but their presence was barely noticed, as there was so much shit talking going down between each team.

For us, it was because LA didn't lose.

If it happened due to the other team being better than us, that was one thing. But Boston wasn't better, even though tonight had been a shutout, and we weren't taking the defeat well at all.

"Take your asses to the locker room," one of the refs threatened. He skated to my side. "Weston, bring your guys in right now." His hand was on my arm, shaking me, attempting to get me to react to him. "The league will fine you. I'm warning you."

His words hit and bounced off. I was too busy telling Boston's left wing what I was going to do to his fucking face.

"Locker room! Now!" another linesman shouted toward each team.

"I'm going to break your goddamn nose and cover the ice with your blood!" one of my guys yelled at a defenseman.

"Come do it, asshole," the defenseman replied.

The ref moved in front of me and grabbed my face mask. "Do you know how many thousands of dollars that punch is going to cost you?"

"Do you know how many thousands we make each game?" one of my guys shot back.

None of us gave a fuck if we got fined. I would guarantee Boston felt the same way.

The satisfaction of hitting one of those cocky, loud-mouthed, *wished they were as good as us* motherfuckers would be worth every dollar we had to shell out.

And we were going to be paying because the guys were closing in, the heat coming off their bodies telling me we were inches away from brawling.

There was only one person who could stop this fight.

One person my boys would listen to.

That was me.

But I wanted nothing more than to get this anger out of my body. I wanted to hurt something. I wanted to shake the guilt that was fucking consuming me by connecting my fingers to flesh.

My hands tightened inside my gloves, and I took a quick glance toward the stands.

A place I'd looked at hundreds of times tonight.

Each time searching for her.

And each time, the last text I'd sent, replayed in my fucking head.

Come to Africa. I'll pay for everything. I want to look at those stars with you.

I turned, refocusing on the ref. The second I took these gloves off, fists would go flying. Blood would be shed. Pictures of me would appear across every news channel and online. I could see the headlines now, calling me a sore loser.

I didn't want more attention. I already knew this evening's warm-up would be made into a meme and get blasted across social media. Eden kept me updated on shit like that even though I had told her not to.

This fight, since it would happen after the game, would be even worse.

And it would give Boston what they expected from us at this point. What would be even better was if we beat them in a shutout when they came to LA and played us in a couple of weeks.

Goddamn it, there were times I hated myself when I made decisions with my head.

"We're out of here," I told the boys. "Come on." As I skated past the line, I pointed at Boston's captain and roared, "You're fucking lucky."

He laughed at me. "I can't wait to embarrass you in front of all your fans."

I ground my teeth together. "Never going to happen, you cocksucker. You know we're going to destroy you. And you know you'll never be as good as me, and it fucking kills you."

"Weston, you think tonight showed me that you're any good? You're a fucking joke. LA is wasting their money on you. If they haven't already realized how bad you are, they will by the end of the season, and they'll trade your ass." The captain smirked. "Boston knows you don't have any skills, so you won't be coming here."

It took everything in me to keep heading toward the exit. To swallow my anger. To not turn around, change my mind, and punch that disrespectful chump in the back of his head as he took a victory lap around the ice.

"Don't worry, we'll get even," my right wing said as we got closer to the exit. "When they're in LA, they won't know what hit them."

"Fuck them," I replied. "I can't fucking stand that team."

The door to the rink opened, and I stepped onto the concrete, making my way into the tunnel that led toward the locker room.

"What the hell happened to you?" a man voiced from above.

Several fans were hanging over the railing that looked into the tunnel. The man had to be one of them.

"Over fifty shots on goal, and not a single one landed," the same man continued. "What happened to my team? You're fighters. This isn't like you, and gosh darn it, I'm so disappointed."

I glanced up and connected eyes with the gentleman as he spoke. He had on a vintage Whales hat—the same one my father wore to games, a design that was no longer sold. He'd either paid a fortune for the merchandise or he'd been a longtime fan.

Something told me it was the latter.

And we'd let him down.

No. That wasn't true.

I had let him down.

And he had every right to be disappointed in me.

Fuck me.

I turned my gaze to the end of the hallway and pulled off my helmet, the sweat releasing from the top of my head and pouring down my face. I used my padded arm to wipe it away, and when I reached the locker room, I took a seat on the bench.

I took my gloves off and threw them across the room. "Fuck!"

Towels were thrown in response. Sticks were broken across players' knees. Equipment was shredded off and dropped with enough force to make one hell of a noise.

It was only a matter of time before Coach came in and chewed us apart for the way we had played, and I'd have to hear about the disappointment all over again.

Landon took a seat beside me. "What happened out there?" He was removing his skates.

"We fell apart."

"Bullshit."

I slowly glanced at my goalie. His question was sitting in the center of my chest, gnawing a hole around my heart.

He saw the game from a completely different angle, not even the same one that Coach did.

"We both know you were off tonight. Why?" he questioned.

"I don't know."

"Yes, you do, Beck. Tell me what's going on with you." When I didn't say anything, he added, "You set the tempo for every game. You're the nucleus that holds us together. When the nucleus is off, nothing works right."

"There are three other lines, Landon. The guys on the second, third, and fourth—what about them? Why didn't they have it together? Why didn't they score? Why didn't they stop the puck—"

"Beck, come on, my man. You can bullshit the media when they ask—and they will ask—but you can't bullshit me."

My elbows went to my knees, and I held the top of my skull, the steam coming off my skin like I was in a sauna.

"Where's your head right now?" he asked.

Where?

That was a good question.

I was tired. We'd been on the road for over a week. I craved the routine I had at home, one that helped my body feel its best. I needed a break from hotel rooms and to sleep in my own bed.

I needed some of Walker's cooking.

But I was used to this lifestyle and being on the road for a majority of the year, and I accepted that traveling this way was part of the gig.

But that wasn't the reason I felt lost tonight.

It was something else.

It was a feeling in my chest. A fucking emptiness. A sensation so foreign that I didn't know what it was at first. And then, hours ago, once the game started, I realized what it was.

And that was when I first found myself looking up at the stands, scanning the faces of the audience.

Something I never did. Even when I was near the glass, I was too focused to notice who was sitting on the other side of it.

Nothing affected my concentration during a game—not the music, the clapping, or the cheering.

But from the beginning of this one, something had pulled me toward the seats; it had forced me to study the hair of each woman, looking for those wild red locks, wondering why, after everything she had said in her messages, she hadn't wanted to go to Africa with me.

"My head is at ..." My voice trailed off while I squeezed the sides of my temples. "I don't know."

"Can I ask you something? And you promise not to chew into me?"

The air was vibrating off the roof of my mouth every time I exhaled. "What?"

"Is it her? Is that what you're thinking about? Is that why you were off your game tonight?"

My hands dropped, and I glanced toward him. "Who?" My brows furrowed. "Jolie?"

Of course he was talking about her.

We were in Boston. There was no one else he could be speaking about.

"Yes," he replied.

I sat up straight, gazing at the faces of my teammates with expressions that were as miserable as mine.

I owed them an apology.

The coaching staff too.

Fuck.

FUCK.

A loss as devastating as this one, all because I couldn't get my goddamn thoughts together.

And no matter how hard I tried, I couldn't stop thinking about her.

"While we were on the plane, you told me you weren't seeing her tonight, but you didn't have time to elaborate with all the cameras that were in our faces. Is it because she's out of town? I know she was the last time we were here."

Two years had passed since I'd seen Jolie and over six months since we'd last texted.

The time between our texting had been growing, going from monthly to every few and even longer. That didn't mean I wasn't thinking about her. Wanting her. Dreaming about tasting her again. The opportunities that presented themselves had just never worked in our favor.

"I don't know if she's out of town or if she came to the game," I said to him. "We don't talk anymore."

"You never told me that."

I took off my jersey and got to work on releasing the clasps on my shoulder pads. "There was nothing to say. I invited her on my trip to Africa. She blew me off. We didn't speak again." I handed the shoulder pads to the team's equipment manager. "She could have declined my offer, and when she didn't even do that, when she said absolutely nothing, I took that as a sign that she was done."

"Check your phone. See if she reached out. Whether she's here or not, being how big of a fan she is, by now, she knows Boston won. She would probably text you for that reason alone."

I shook my head, the sweat drips falling to my bare shoulders. "Nah, man."

"Just do me a favor and look."

There was no reason to even waste the effort of pulling out my phone. Plus, I was sure there were texts in our family group chat, attempting to make me feel better about the loss, and I didn't want to read them. It was too early, the loss still too fresh.

But to appease Landon, since I knew he wouldn't stop nagging me, I reached into the bag behind me and got my phone, watching the screen light up with more notifications than I wanted to deal with.

I went straight to the texts, and aside from the ones from my parents and siblings, there was nothing from Jolie.

"Nope. I was right." I shut the screen off, too angry to look at it.

With his skates removed, he turned toward me. "I'm not going to lie ... I'm finding this strange as hell."

"Why?"

"From everything you've told me, she was into you, Beck. Really fucking into you. And the kicker is that she's graduating this year, isn't she?"

I huffed out some air. "Yeah, in May."

"Which means, in a handful of months, her life will be completely changing, and she won't have school holding her back."

"School didn't hold her back during the summers when I asked her to come to Paris or Africa."

Even after he rubbed it, his blond hair was too wet to spike the way it normally did when it was dry. "True, but going full-time with her dad, she's got vacation, I'm sure, and a bit more flexibility since she'll be giving him so many hours."

Now I was questioning why I'd told him so much.

Jesus.

"What are you? A fucking closet relationship expert?"

"I'm piecing it all together and coming up with a conclusion."

"Do you have one?"

He hung his head. "Unfortunately."

"Which is?"

He squeezed my shoulder. "She's dating someone."

Those words shouldn't hit.

There was absolutely no fucking reason for them to hit.

Two years had passed since I'd touched her, over six months since we'd texted.

At this point, she should have been a faded memory.

But she wasn't.

That was the impact Jolie had made on me.

The same shoulder he was gripping, he now shook. "I wish you knew that answer instead of a bunch of unknowns. That's why you should have texted her today."

"No."

"What do you mean, no? You want to see her—it's obvious. It's been eating at you since you stepped out onto the ice—that's why tonight's game got fucked. I don't care what you say, she's the reason we lost. And had you texted her, you wouldn't be sitting here, guessing."

"I'm not fucking guessing, Landon."

But I was guessing.

He nodded toward my lap. "Text her now."

"Now—"

"Get showered and get dressed," our coach said as he walked into the locker room, cutting me off. He stood in the center of the team. "Our plane leaves in less than an hour." His hands went to his hips. "If you're wondering if we're going to talk about the way Boston crucified us this evening, the answer to that is yes. We'll be doing that on the plane, and we have a lot to discuss."

I turned to Landon. "Why bother? We're leaving in less than an hour. Even if she came, I wouldn't be able to see her."

He released my shoulder and gave me a smile. "For the second time in your fucking life, just listen to me. You've got to admit, I have a solid track record when it comes to this shit, considering the first time you listened to me was when I encouraged you to go talk to Jolie in that bar."

I glanced down at my phone, my fingers moving on their own—pulling up Jolie's name in my Contacts and hitting the button for Messages, our texts loading on the screen.

"What the hell do I even say at this point? *Want to meet for ten minutes before we leave for our flight?*"

He stuck his hand out. "Give me your phone."

I chuckled. "Hell no."

"Give it to me, Beck. I'll show you the message before I send it."

Reluctantly, I handed him my phone.

And within a second, he was groaning. "Dude, you're a fucking idiot."

"Why do you say that?"

He tilted the screen toward me. "Do you see the last message you sent her? How it's in green?"

"Yeah."

"That means it might not have been delivered. Do you notice how the other texts you sent to her have *Delivered* beneath them? That means they went through. But this last one, not so much."

My stomach was churning.

"What are you saying, Landon?"

His expression softened—his attempt at being sensitive. "I don't think Jolie got your invitation to Africa—that's what I'm fucking saying." But then he stared at me like he didn't recognize me. "You really didn't know that a green message was always questionable?"

I shook my head. "I'm into hockey, not technology. I don't even go on social media." I pulled at the strands of my hair. "Do you know how many fucking times I looked at that text and wondered why the hell she hadn't written me back?"

"Now you have your answer." He tapped my shoulder and handed me my phone back. He walked to the showers, leaving me alone on our section of the bench.

This whole fucking time, Jolie had no idea that I wanted her to go away with me. She didn't know that trip, in my head, was the start of something more. And this whole fucking time, I had thought she had blown me off.

But she hadn't.

It was nothing more than an oversight, like not wiping your face well enough to get off all the barbeque sauce from breakfast.

A goddamn real moment.

And it was ... all my fault.

TWELVE

Jolie

"I could get real used to this," Ginger said as she stood along the balcony of the second floor of the club, looking down at all the people grinding below. While she danced in place with the club's signature pink drink in her hand, the straw bounced, and the booze sloshed against the sides of the glass.

"Get used to what?" I took a sip of the same cocktail, the mixture sweeter than I normally liked, but all the women in here were drinking one, and I'd wanted to see what the hype was about.

"This." She twirled her finger in a large circle, and I could tell she was including the ceiling, which was as decked out as the rest of the interior, the VIP room we were in, and the dancers shaking their asses below. "Everything about this place is beautiful. Even the people—I don't think I've seen a single one who isn't gorgeous. It's just"—she shrugged—"my vibe—what can I say?"

She was definitely right about the club. The entire inside

was done in only black and white—a design as eye-catching and attractive as the people she had just described, especially the ones who were dancing in cages that hung from above. There were mirrors everywhere, so I couldn't tell if I was looking at a reflection or if there were really that many people in here.

She rubbed her shoulder against mine. "And I kinda love that we're out, together, on a Friday night, having all the cocktails. It's been a while since we did this. Things have been a bit ... stressful."

I sighed. "You can say that again."

Now that I really thought about it, this was probably the first time we'd gone out, just the two of us, in about a month. Up until a few days ago, I'd been working nights and weekends to prep for all the change that was coming.

She wrapped her arm around my upper back and hugged me against her side. "But we're over that stressful hump."

The sound that came out of me was a laugh, but Ginger knew I didn't find this funny. "Are we really? Because I feel like we're still climbing toward the peak and we're nowhere even close to being over it."

"Listen, I'm drinking out of a glass that has boobs." She held it in front of me so I could see, even though mine was identical. "Let's spend tonight focusing on the good rather than the upcoming anxiety we're about to face."

I smiled, lowering my head to look at my hand. One of the first things I'd noticed when the bartender gave me my order was the shape of the glass—how it dipped and curved and jutted out, resembling a woman's body.

When I glanced back up, I raised my brows and said, "We both have anxiety?"

She tucked a piece of hair behind my ear, knowing my locks never stayed. "Part of a bestie's role is taking on the other person's anxiety. So, yes, by default, I'm taking on yours, which means we both have it."

Anxiety.

I hadn't anticipated having it this bad—or at all.

Because I had a plan.

I was going to graduate from college. Ginger and I would stay in the same apartment we had rented our junior year and keep it until we could afford something larger, however long that took. I was going to work full-time for my dad in his Boston office, and instead of him comanaging my accounts, they would become mine, and I would take on several others.

The graduation part had happened.

But nothing else went according to plan.

And it all started that day my dad called me into his office, dropping a bit of news that completely came out of nowhere.

News that had rocked my entire world.

My hand went to my chest. "Is yours right here? Your anxiety, I mean." I pushed harder against it. "Because this is where I feel it. It's burrowed a hole, and it won't stop digging."

She circled her fingers around mine. "That means you haven't had enough to drink. You need to down these"—she tapped my glass—"until that feeling is gone."

My head fell back, and I tried to breathe. When I couldn't, I said, "And tomorrow, when I wake up and it's still there, what do I do then?"

She smiled. "We do it all over again."

I made a face as I thought about what that hangover would feel like. "Horrible plan."

"I know. But it's all I've got."

I slid my hand over the top of my hair and bunched some into my palm. "What the hell am I going to do about Monday—"

"Oh my God."

Ginger hadn't cut me off because she was tired of hearing me groan. What told me that were the way her eyes were going wide and how her mouth was hanging open. An expression then grew across her face, like she'd just witnessed an alien land behind me.

"Ginger?"

She quickly downed every last drop of her drink, which she set on a nearby table as fast as she had shot back the liquor, and she put her hands on my shoulders. "I need you to listen to me."

"Ginger, you're freaking me out. What's wrong?"

"Do not move. Do you hear me?"

"Why?"

"Because I said so."

"But why?"

"Jolie, you're not listening—you're talking—and I really need you to listen." She took a deep breath, her behavior getting stranger by the second. "You're going to put your drink on the table beside us, and then you're going to give me your hand, and we're going to walk across the front of this balcony until we reach the stairs, and at the bottom, we'll sneak out the back—if there's a back. If not, we'll slip out the front."

"Huh?" I searched her eyes.

She nodded toward my hand. "Come on. Drink up."

"Why are we leaving? I thought you loved it here?"

"I do."

"And I thought you were going to have me keep downing these"—I raised my glass—"until my anxiety was gone?"

"Plans have changed. We're going elsewhere to make that happen."

"Why?"

As her chest deflated, she briefly closed her eyes. "Just trust the process, okay?"

"Seriously, what has gotten into you?"

Every time I shifted or looked over my shoulder, she would mimic me and try to block me or shake me to keep my attention on her.

"Is there something behind me you don't want me to see?"

I attempted to turn, but she did everything in her power to stop me.

"I don't understand what's happening—" I didn't let her control my movements this time, and I peeked in the direction she was trying to have me avoid.

Oh God.

Now it made sense—why she had been acting that way.

My entire body froze.

Except for my heart.

That was beating to the point where I could feel it in my throat.

A wave of redness was covering my skin, not just my cheeks —I was positive I was flushed all the way down to my toes.

And the air—it was gone from my lungs.

Beck Weston.

Here.

And only feet away from me.

My eyes were already locked on him, but they dipped, taking him in, remembering, but also getting an immediate refresher.

His trimmed, well-groomed beard—since preseason was just starting next week, he had months and months of growth ahead of him. Those talented lips. His riveting hazel eyes. His thick neck, a gold chain dangling just below it, and his muscular chest, covered in tattoos, which were hidden by a black button-down. His shirt was fitted enough that it showed the outline of muscles in his arms and the flatness of his stomach.

But it was his face I couldn't stop staring at. A face I'd seen in my dreams. That I'd looked at on social media. That I'd watched on TV.

That I'd stared at from the stands when LA last came to Boston and played in our arena.

"Ginger ..." I whispered.

"Babe, I know."

I didn't know where she was standing—I was far too focused on Beck—but I heard her directly in my ear.

"Turn around before he sees you and it's too late—" Her voice cut off when he glanced in my direction and zoomed right in on me. "Fuck. He's spotted you."

I tried to swallow the anxiety—a layer much thicker than I had been feeling minutes ago—but I couldn't. It was there. Building. And getting worse by the second.

"What do I do?"

I couldn't think, never mind try to make a decision.

"There's nothing you can do. He's headed toward you right now."

THIRTEEN

Beck

I was lifting a glass of bourbon to my lips when I saw Jolie. She was near the balcony that overlooked the dance floor, her back facing me, but she had glanced over her shoulder, and we connected eyes.

Those beautiful light-blue eyes and that wild red hair.

She was as stunning as the first time I had seen her—even more so. But it was like seeing a fucking ghost.

One that continued to haunt me, even to this day.

Fuck.

Why was my dick instantly hard?

Fuck.

Why was my heart screaming, like I'd just finished over a hundred suicide drills, and I couldn't catch my breath?

Fuck.

Why did my body react so quickly to her?

Fuck.

My hand had frozen midair, halfway to my mouth, but I

felt it lower to my side, and my feet were moving toward her, only stopping when I reached her.

Whether this was the right moment to speak to her or whether I should wait a few minutes to get my thoughts straight —it didn't matter. My body had made that decision for me.

"Jolie ..." As the word left my lips, I smelled her.

Vanilla amber.

A unique twist on a traditional scent that I'd only ever smelled on her.

And an aroma that brought back the most vivid memories of the three hottest nights.

"Beck ..." Her hands were empty, and one went into her hair, holding a chunk of locks, her fingers lost within them. "Hi."

I leaned toward her, and at first, I was just going to give her a one-armed hug, a greeting that felt appropriate, given our past. But as I neared her face, I found not only my arm wrapped around her, but I was kissing her cheek too.

I hadn't been prepared for the softness that hit my lips.

Or the intensity of her scent now that I was this close.

Or the way her eyes closed as my mouth stayed on her skin, breathing her in.

How had I gone so long without speaking to her?

Touching her?

Tasting her?

Her hand landed on my biceps, holding it and then squeezing it. Fingers that stayed in that position until I pulled away.

"It's good to see you." I gave her a smile and shifted my focus to Ginger, extending my hand in her direction, recalling her being there the night I'd met Jolie at the bar in Boston and Jolie telling me stories that involved her. "We've never officially met, I don't believe. I'm Beck. And you're Ginger, I assume?"

She nodded with an intense amount of energy. "Oh my God, you know my name. Yes, hi! It's so, so amazing to meet you!"

I chuckled.

Ginger's gaze turned to Jolie at the same time I released her hand. "I'm going to give you guys a couple of minutes. I'll be over there." She pointed to the other side of the bar.

Jolie followed Ginger's finger before her stare returned to me.

I couldn't tell by her expression where her head was. I was sure she was shocked to see me—there was no way she could have known I'd be here. I'd just decided to come less than an hour ago, and I'd slipped in through the back, so if there were any paparazzi lingering around the front of the club, they wouldn't see me.

If there was excitement, I didn't see it on her face. If she was annoyed or feeling disgruntled, I didn't see that either.

All I saw was this nervous energy rising across her and coming out of her fidgety body.

"What brings you to LA?"

Her arms crossed over her stomach, the movement causing her tits to lift, the tops popping out of her black dress. "Work." Her throat moved as she swallowed.

"Ah, yes." I finally took a drink. "That must be your life now? You're graduated and employed by Dad?"

She nodded. "Things are quite different now compared to two years and nine months ago."

"Two years and nine months," I repeated, calculating how much time had passed and realizing she was correct. "I can't believe that's how long it's been since I saw you."

She rubbed underneath her lips. "I know."

"Shit, that seems like forever."

"Because it was." Her hand left, and she smiled. "I didn't even have to use a fake ID to get in here."

I laughed. "Finally of legal age." I took another sip, keeping my finger there to wipe off the wetness the bourbon had left behind. "That's a good thing, too, since my guys can detect a fake regardless of how good it is. Although, for you, they might have made an exception just because of how gorgeous you are."

Her face turned as it became redder, but her eyes stayed on me. "What do you mean, your guys?"

"The bouncers outside work for my family and me. Everyone in here does. We own this place." I crossed an arm and held the tumbler near my chest. "I think I must have told you that?"

"Musik." Her hand went over her mouth. "You're not going to even believe me, but I didn't realize we were here—at Musik, I mean. Ginger arranged all the VIP stuff ahead of time, and I was on an important call with my dad when we arrived, completely distracted. I could have been landing on the moon for all I knew. She told me she was bringing me to one of the most popular clubs in LA, and I didn't ask any questions."

"If I had known you were coming, I would have had your entrance fees waived."

"I didn't even know I was coming." Her eyes narrowed. "But if you had known …"

"Yeah, as in if you'd texted me."

She let out a sound that was somewhat like a laugh. "We haven't texted in a long time, Beck, and this isn't the only trip I've made to LA that you didn't know about."

I hissed out some air. "Scandalous."

"What are you even talking about? You're the one who stopped messaging me. Not the other way around."

I wanted to touch her. I wanted to put my fucking hands all over her.

I wanted to pull her toward me and kiss her.

"I want to talk about the texting ..."

"Oh God," she groaned. "If you're about to give me an excuse, it's okay, you don't need to. You're one of the most popular players in the league. Women throw themselves at you. You didn't need to keep in touch with a twenty-year-old—or however old I was at that point—who was living on the opposite side of the country as you and who you were likely never going to see again."

"That's what you think?" My brows shot up. "That your age and location are the reasons I stopped reaching out?"

"Both of those combined, along with the fact that you probably have an identical situation"—she swept the air between us with her finger, the movement signifying the three nights we'd spent together—"whenever you have a break on the road."

My head shook back and forth as I laughed. "That's what you believe?"

"A million percent."

"I told you, there's never been anyone like you."

She shrugged.

"And you didn't believe me." I waited. "You still don't."

"Why does it matter what I believe, Beck?"

I stared at her silently for a moment, debating whether I wanted to do this or not, and then I pulled out my phone, hitting my Contacts, where I filled in her name and pulled up our last group of texts. I turned the screen toward her. "Do you see the last message in green? The one I sent, inviting you to go to Africa?" I stalled while she read the words. "The look on your face right now and the fact that you never responded—that tells me the message definitely never went through."

She grabbed the phone out of my hands and held it in front of her face.

"You need to know that I thought it had gone through, Jolie.

And I thought you'd ignored the invite and blown me off. I didn't realize there was a difference between green and blue messages, and the green meant it wasn't guaranteed to be delivered until I was in Boston last season. I was in the locker room after the game, pissed off that we'd lost so badly and—if I'm being real fucking honest—pissed off that you hadn't reached out. My buddy told me to message you, and when he saw my screen, he told me the text probably hadn't gone through."

She slowly looked up from my phone and gave it back to me. "You meant to invite me to Africa ..."

I shoved my cell into my pocket. "I wanted you there. I wanted to look at those stars with you. I wanted it to be the start of something more." My dick fucking ached as I stared at her. "The same way I'd wanted you to come to Paris."

"And the text never went through."

It was as though she was processing the truth by speaking it out loud.

"I know I should have reached out once my buddy told me you probably hadn't gotten my text. Shit, I should have. I don't know why I didn't. That's on me, and I take full responsibility for it. I guess I felt like a fucking idiot, and some time had passed, and ... I don't know." I was starting to repeat myself, but the regret was coming on hard, making me feel even worse. "I also could have told you I was coming to Boston to play. But at the same time, there was no doubt in my mind that you knew I was going to be there. I guess—and it was probably wrong to guess—that with the way things stood, with you uninterested and not responding to my invite, I figured you didn't want to see me." I shoved a hand in my pocket to stop it from reaching for her. "Or you were dating someone."

"And that's what I assumed too." Her voice was so soft. "Just flipped the other way around."

I took a drink, hoping the liquor would put out this fire in my body. But I knew—fuck, I knew—it would only ignite it more. Especially as I said, "Jolie, things between us never had to stop. Just because I hadn't seen you, I still thought about you. And I wanted to see you. I would have kept trying even if Africa hadn't worked out." The honesty was lifting from my chest, and I didn't try to tame it. I had nothing to lose by telling her the truth. I was beyond single—a phrase that made me smile inwardly—and not a single woman I'd come across after all this time even came close to measuring up to her. "You're still on my mind. Even now."

The deer-in-headlights look was sexy as fuck on her, which told me the reality of this situation was shocking the hell out of her.

"You're telling me"—her hand went to her chest—"that you haven't forgotten about me."

"Forgotten? Hell no. It would be impossible to forget a woman like you."

"But at the same time, you didn't care enough to reach out after learning the text hadn't gone through. If you had cared, things would have played out much differently."

"Don't portray me that way. I fucked up, Jolie. I didn't handle things perfectly. I own that. But never once did I stop caring."

Her head dropped. "Beck ..."

"The second my eyes landed on you, what did I do? I came straight over here to talk to you." I took a step toward her, my hand going to her waist, her head instantly lifting, my eyes studying another expression that I couldn't define. But the feel of her, goddamn it, it was good. No. It was the fucking best. "Wanting you hasn't gone away either." I leaned my lips toward her ear. "That want has only grown."

"It's ... grown." Her voice was now a whisper.

I downed the rest of my bourbon and reached toward a

table, placing the glass on top of it so my other hand could grip her, and I guided her a few inches closer. "Are you dating anyone?"

She hesitated to respond but finally said, "No."

"Which means you've thought about me ... haven't you?" My fingers stretched up her back.

"Of course I've thought about you." Her voice still hadn't gotten any louder, but those light-blue eyes were fucking shouting at me. "I cared about you too, Beck. But I didn't want to bombard you with messages. Given your job and where I lived, I knew the chances of anything more happening between us were slim. I still wanted something to happen though, and I really wanted nothing more than to bombard you with texts." She put her hands on top of mine. "After the Africa thing, I just sorta ... gave up."

"You shouldn't have."

She scanned my eyes. "Why?"

"Think about what that would have shown me."

She turned silent, and her hands lifted off mine.

"Did you ever think about what it would feel like if you saw me again?"

She nodded.

"What did that look like in your head?"

She attempted to take a step back, and when I gripped her tighter, she stayed put. "It doesn't matter."

"It matters."

"Why?"

My hands lifted to her neck, and I held both sides. "Because you're here. I'm here. And there's a reason the fucking universe finally put us in the same place at the same time." I paused, my thumbs stroking the bottom of her cheeks. "I'm not going to let you go."

Her lips parted, her gaze turning even more intense. "What are you saying, Beck?"

"I want you to come home with me tonight."

She let out the same noise as earlier, the one that sounded like a laugh, but wasn't. "No."

"Why? What's stopping you?"

"*Everything* is stopping me."

"Give me one reason. I want to hear it."

She glanced away and focused on something other than me until her eyes closed and her head fell slightly back.

"Do you know how many times I've asked myself what it would feel like to kiss you again?" I rubbed my nose over hers. "How fucking good it would feel to taste you." I placed my mouth on her cheek. "Give me tonight, Jolie. Let me have your body. Let me do to it what I've been dreaming about. Let me show you how much I've missed you."

When her eyes opened, they were finally giving me an emotion I understood.

So, I said, "Don't question this. Don't even think about it. Just give in to what your body needs—what you know I can give you."

"I've always wanted you—that's the problem." She chewed the inside of her lip. "I'll never be able to get you out of my head, and that's also a problem."

I didn't see how either of those was an issue.

"Are you here for the night?" Based on how late it was and how she didn't seem rushed to leave, I assumed she wasn't taking a red-eye back to Boston, but anything was possible.

"Yes."

"Are you leaving early tomorrow?"

Her chest rose high, and she didn't let the air out when she replied, "No."

"Then I don't think there's any problem here."

She stared at my right eye before shifting to my left, going back and forth until she said, "You're just asking for one night?"

I smiled. "We'll start with one. But if you're here for longer, I'll take as much as you'll give me."

"Beck ..." She put her hand on my chest. She just rested it there; she didn't push against it. "This is a horrible idea."

"Was it a horrible idea when we did it in Boston?"

"Boston was Boston." Her fingers curled. "This is ..."

"Another chance."

She shook her head. "Don't say that." Her head didn't still when she added, "There's no reason why I should do this."

"And there's no reason why you shouldn't."

"But there are. There are actually so many reasons." Her hand dropped down and landed on my abs, her thumb running down each of the grooves. "Fuck."

I moved my mouth toward hers, allowing only inches between us. "Tell me you want me to take my hands off you and back away, and I will." I tilted her face up. "But if you don't tell me that, Jolie, I'm going to walk you to my car right now. I'm going to take you home with me. I'm going to lick every inch of your body, and I'm going to make you come all fucking night long."

FOURTEEN

Jolie

"Babe, what's going on? Are you okay?" Ginger whispered as I pulled her into the restroom, taking her into the corner so it didn't appear as if we were in line for a stall.

"I ... don't know." I placed my back against the wall and positioned her in front of me, my hands immediately diving to my forehead, holding it as though my brain were about to fall out.

"I've been watching you guys—" She put her hand up, like she had to defend herself. "I swear I wasn't trying to. I just can't help myself. You went from talking, to touching, to practically getting it on, to bolting over to me, and then you dragged me in here."

I used the wall to hold me up and grabbed the drink from her hand, downing it in one gulp, and I set the empty on the floor next to our feet. I wiped my lips, letting the burn of the alcohol die a little before I said, "He wants me to go home with him."

"That's obvious."

"And the whole Africa thing? He wanted me to go with him, he even invited me through text." I paused. "He showed me on his phone how he'd thought the text went through, but it never got delivered. Therefore, I never got it."

Her eyes became big again, like when she'd spotted him here tonight. "So, this whole time you thought ..."

"Yep."

"Whoa. Doesn't that change things?" Before I could reply, she added, "Are you going to go home with him?"

I shrugged. "I told him I needed a second. I'm ... freaking out."

She pushed my hair off my face. "Don't freak out."

"Of course you would say that."

"How do you feel about everything?"

I banged the back of my head on the wall, and when that didn't feel like enough, I did it again. "That man mesmerizes me. It's like he puts me in this trance, and I can't focus on anything other than him. And maybe when I first met him, it was because of who he was, but now that has nothing to do with it." My eyes closed as I admitted, "It's the way he makes me feel. It's what he does to me. It's the person I know he is."

"That makes him the most dangerous man alive."

My eyelids flicked open. "You know what's going to happen, don't you? If I do go home with him, I'm going to get everything I want. And that means I'm going to get a taste of that peanut butter, and then the mouse trap is going to come right down on me and crush me."

"Are you seriously calling yourself a rodent? And Beck is one of those scary rat traps found all over Boston that snaps when you touch it?"

I winced. "You get the drift."

She put her hands on my shoulders. "I know why you're

feeling this way. It's justified. I also know how you've never forgotten that man, and at any point, you would have dreamed of a scenario like this."

I laughed. Like really laughed. "A scenario? Like this? No." I glanced up at the ceiling. "This is a scenario from hell."

"Just because your circumstances have changed—"

"Ginger, you know I can't do this. You know I shouldn't do this. I don't know if those two things mean the same—I can't even think straight at the moment—but the answer is, I need to run. And I need to run fast."

"But what if you do go with him—just for the night? It's not going to hurt anyone per se."

"Are you—"

She shook me. "Jolie, you haven't slept with anyone in two years and nine months. If you don't have sex with that man, things are going to close up down there"—she nodded toward my legs—"and I swear, they might never reopen again." She let out a long breath. "Babe, just do it and deal with the consequences later. That's the best and only advice I'll give you."

I was panting through my nose. "You're the worst."

"That's why you love me."

I thought about everything she'd said, the decision not any clearer in my mind. "If I do leave, what are you going to do? You'll catch an Uber, yeah?"

"Please don't worry about me. I'll be fine." She smiled. "Besides, you have my location on your phone."

I studied her face, making sure what she said matched up to what I was seeing in her eyes, and then I took her by the hand and led her out of the restroom.

As soon as we got through the short hallway, I instantly saw Beck. He was standing at the bar, leaning into it with his hands crossed, looking at me mostly from across his shoulder so I had more of a profile view of him.

Oh God.
That man.
There was no one hotter in this world.
No one more talented.
And certainly no one more perfect.
"Jesus fucking Christ, he's everything," Ginger whispered from my side. "Just look at him."
As I did, unable to take my eyes off him, his words began to repeat in my head.
"I'm going to walk you to my car right now. I'm going to take you home with me. I'm going to lick every inch of your body, and I'm going to make you come all fucking night long."
I sighed in response.
"You don't have to tell me what you decided. I already know." She hugged my shoulders. "See you tomorrow, babe. Have *alll* the fun."

FIFTEEN

Beck

As Jolie stood at my kitchen counter, watching me walk toward her with two glasses—a whiskey sour for her, a bourbon for me—I couldn't take my eyes off her. She looked so tiny in front of my massive island, under ceilings that were well over twenty feet high. At six feet, three inches tall, I towered over her, giving me the perfect view to take her in.

A black dress that hugged every one of her curves.
Curves that I knew intimately.
Curves that had only gotten sexier since I'd met her.
And a dress I wanted to fucking rip off her.
Even though her body got lost in a space that was so massive, her presence screamed across my house. I could feel her when I went into my living room to pour us drinks at the bar. I could smell her as I returned to the kitchen.
She was electric. Consuming. She had a sensuality that came effortlessly to her, seducing me with a mere blink of her gorgeous light-blue eyes.

"For you." I set the whiskey in front of her, and she immediately reached for it, gazing at me through her eyelashes. "More whiskey, less sour."

"You remembered."

I chuckled. "I remember everything about you."

She took a drink. "I think Ginger was a little taken aback that you knew her name."

"She's going to be even more taken aback when the manager of Musik lets her know I've sent a car for her so I know she gets home safely."

Jolie's brows lifted, and her mouth dropped open. "You did that?"

"Of course I did. She's your best friend. And I recalled her name because you'd spoken about her often." I held the bourbon near my mouth, but I didn't take a sip.

"But that was so long ago."

"Not long enough to forget." I set the glass down, tired of holding it, and I stretched my arm across the space between us, my fingers landing on the side of her neck, two of them split just wide enough to hug her ear. "Graduated and free. A period of your life I've thought about many times."

"Why?"

"Why ..." I let my head drop. When it came to her, the honesty was always present. It flowed right out of my mouth. She wasn't the exception to every rule. Because when it came to women, I didn't hold on to them long enough to set rules. "I wondered if freedom would change things between us."

"You mean, would it bring us closer?"

I nodded. "I assumed, when you got to that point, there would be instances when you could work from home. My house could become that home."

She huffed, "Beck ..."

"Don't tell me you didn't think about it at some point."

"Oh, I did." She moved the glass between her hands and flattened both palms on the quartz. "I definitely thought about it. I wished for it to come true. It just ... didn't. We went silent instead."

My hand slid back a little, moving beneath her chin. "When do you leave to go back to Boston?"

"I ..."

Both of her hands surrounded the glass this time, and as she brought it up to her lips, I moved behind her, the urge to hold her becoming too strong to fight. While she was swallowing the drink, I positioned her just the way I wanted her. And as she set down the empty glass, I folded my arms over her chest.

"Jolie ..."

Her eyes closed when my lips went to her cheek. Her mouth parted when I pressed our bodies together. She let out a small moan when I ground my hard-on against her ass.

My lips were now on the shell of her ear. "I'm going to fucking lick your entire body, and once I've covered every inch of your skin, I'm going to give you what you love."

She was pushing her ass against me, her back so tightly aligned with my chest that there wasn't even air between us. "Do you remember what that was?"

"Your tongue ..."

I took her earlobe into my mouth and nibbled the end, my hand moving under her dress until my finger could slide through the slickness between her legs. A wetness so thick that I would have thought my mouth had just left her.

"Yes. It's going right on your cunt. And I'm going to lick you until I get so many orgasms out of you that you feel like you can't come anymore."

She leaned her head back against me, and I clasped the bottom of her neck.

"But first ..." I hiked up her dress, past her thighs and over

THE WILDEST ONE

her ass, releasing it to cling to her waist. I then lowered her thong, pushing until it was around her heels. "I need to be inside you."

"And I need that—right now."

She turned around, stepping out of her thong, and began to unbutton my shirt, peeling it down my arms. Once that fell to the floor, she was unclasping my belt, unhooking the button of my jeans, and lowering the zipper, pumping my dick the second it sprang free from my boxer briefs.

"You've missed my dick, haven't you?"

She looked feral as she glanced at my hard-on, her tongue jutting out a little before she said, "I haven't been with anyone since you."

Her words hit.

And then they slashed across me again.

"Jolie, it's been two years and nine months." A number that had been reconfirmed when she said it at the club.

"I know."

I touched the front of her cunt, and she gasped. It was just a quick swipe of my thumb across her clit, and she reacted as if I had sucked it into my mouth and was flicking it relentlessly.

Oh, she fucking needed this.

And she needed it badly.

"Why did you wait?"

She shook her head. "Anyone I met ... they weren't you. And I just got this feeling that if I let them in, they wouldn't treat me the way you had, so I didn't let them in. I didn't even let anyone get close."

All this time—and her pussy was still mine.

Neglected.

Untouched.

Waiting for me.

I was petting her, stroking just the outside of her sweetness and dipping to where I was about to stick my cock in. "You were saving this for me."

"But I didn't know this was ever going to happen."

I backed her up until she was against the waterfall side of the island and spread my arms out, my hands landing on the edge of the quartz on either side of her. "What do you want, Jolie? Tell me. I'll give you anything right now."

"You mean ... sexually?"

As much as I wanted to fuck her, if she needed my mouth, I would give her that first.

"Yes."

Her hand went to my lips, crawling across them with her fingertips. "This—I want after." With her palm, she rubbed around my tip, spreading my pre-cum over her skin. "This"—she stroked me even harder—"I want now."

I didn't bother to take off my shoes or my pants. I just put my hands on her cheeks and pulled her face toward me, capturing her lips, parting them enough to fit in my tongue.

That flavor.

I could almost taste how much she desired me.

I could certainly hear it since each of her breaths ended in a moan.

"I need you." Those were the words I growled across her mouth when I separated us. With my hands on her hips, I turned her around to face the counter, making sure she was holding on so my thrusts wouldn't send her across the stone. "I just want to feel how fucking wet you are. I'll put on a condom in a second."

My tip wedged between the cheeks of her ass and lowered until I hit that spot.

The one that was dripping.

The one that was goading me to slide inside.

THE WILDEST ONE

She wrapped her arm around my neck, pulling the front of me down, my cheek now next to hers. "I have an IUD, Beck."

Birth control.

We'd be double protected.

But still, I had to ask, "What are you saying to me ..."

"You don't need that condom. Unless you insist on wearing one or there's a reason you feel you should."

She was giving her pussy to me.

Bare.

And even though she hadn't said this specifically, she was giving me permission to come inside her.

"Don't fucking tease me." I took a bite of her neck, arching my hips upward so just my crown was pushing through.

"I'm not."

My teeth released her. "You're telling me I can have it all?"

She pushed into me, and what that did was sink every inch of my dick inside her. "Yes."

"Shit," I hissed as the feeling took hold of me. "You dirty, dirty fucking girl."

"Ah!" Her nails were stabbing my skull, her body bouncing over my shaft—not all the way, just small pumps that gave her several inches of friction. "Please. I need it. I need to come—" The way I reared back cut off her voice, and the way I drove in caused her to fucking scream, "Beck!"

"You're even tighter than I remember."

Her pussy was like a goddamn vacuum, and with each thrust, it was begging for my cum. That feeling alone would get me off quicker than I wanted, but when combined with her wetness and heat, it was too fucking much.

Jolie wasn't just the perfect woman.

She was the perfect woman with the most incredible cunt.

"Do you know what that tightness is doing to me?" My mouth moved to the side of her neck, her nest of wild red hair covering most of my face. "Do you know how badly I want to fill you with my cum?"

"Please!" Her hands lifted off the counter and slapped back down. "I want that." She drew in some air. "I so want that."

Through her dress and bra, I tugged on her nipple, earning a moan that was the loudest one so far, and I continued down her body until my hand was on her pussy. With two fingers, I rubbed her clit, feeling it dampen and harden.

And with each rotation, she started with an, "*Ahhh*," and exhaled with an, "*Ohhh*."

My movements were turning sharper because she was narrowing in around me. Because she was moving with me. Because her body was giving me every sign that she wanted me to come.

And I was doing everything I could to hold it off.

"Baby, you need to slow down," I warned.

"No. I want this."

"But I'm going to fucking fill you."

"You'd better."

My forehead rested on her cheek, my mouth on her shoulder, and I arched upward, aiming for her G-spot. "Was that a demand I just heard?"

"Yes!"

I knew when I hit that special spot because she jumped—not out of pain, but out of pleasure. And instead of increasing my speed, I upped my power, pounding her pussy with an intensity she hadn't yet experienced tonight.

"Shit!" She held her arms outstretched and steady, using the counter to help her move with me. "Fuck!"

I knew she was seconds away. I could feel it. I could hear it. So, I stroked her clit like it was the screen of my phone, my thumb endlessly swiping, and she immediately fell apart.

I did too.

From the sound of her.

From the sensation of her tightening around me, the rush of wetness that followed—both sent me straight over the fucking edge.

The moment the burst hit my sac, building through my shaft to explode out my tip, I shouted, "Jolie! Fuck! Yes!"

And she followed—in sounds, in words, in movements—bouncing over me before I bucked back and shoved my way in.

"Do you feel that?" I moaned during a break from her yelling. "The way I'm emptying inside you, filling you with every drip of my cum."

I didn't know if she could process what I was saying, or if she was too lost, or if there was a heavy mix of both going on. But when she said, "Oh my God, I can feel it," I knew she understood. "Give me more, Beck." She plowed her ass back and rocked forward, adding, "Give me more!"

That was when I assumed she was hitting her peak, and because I knew her body so well, when she started moaning my name, I knew she was on her way down.

So was I.

My movements slowed, my thumb softly caressed her clit, and I held us together, locked and completely still.

"*Mmm*." I kissed around her shoulder and up her neck, stopping behind her ear. "Round one of a fucking hundred tonight."

She laughed. "A hundred? I won't be able to walk tomorrow."

"I don't have to report to the rink until Monday. That means, tomorrow and Sunday, the only thing I want to have on my schedule is tasting you ..." I moved my mouth back to her cheek. "If you'll still be here."

"Sounds like a repeat of Boston."

"Are you opposed?"

She was still laughing when she said, "Not at all."

"Good. Then, I'm going to carry you into the shower, so I can wash me off you and I can eat that fucking pussy the way I want to."

"*Fuuuck!*" Jolie screamed, her stomach shuddering, her fingers stretched against the glass wall of my shower, where I was kneeling on the floor with her pussy on my mouth.

Two orgasms. Both from my tongue.

"Oh my God," she gasped.

With the ripples still making their way across her navel, telling me she was at her climax, I kept up the same pace with my licks, and my finger, which was deep inside her, did the same.

Jolie liked the combination.

And, fuck, there was nothing better than getting to taste her and feel her at the same time.

"Beck!"

Even the sound of her drove me wild.

So did the view.

I glanced up her body, meeting the flatness of her stomach and the curve of each tit, her unruly hair clinging to them. My gaze went higher to the delicateness of her neck, her full and parted lips, and her beautiful light-blue eyes.

Years later, and she still had no idea how gorgeous she was.

And that softness, that humbleness—it was something I would endlessly crave from her.

When her body began to still, her sounds turning from shouts to dull murmurs, I lowered the momentum. My tongue went from flicking to slow, agonizing laps, and my finger eventually slid out. I kissed up and down her pussy, back and forth, swallowing the thickness before I rose to my feet.

She didn't pull her hands off the glass. She didn't even move. She just looked at me with the most animalistic expression and said, "What are you doing to me?" She took a breath between each word.

"I told you I was going to eat your pussy until you couldn't come anymore."

"We're already there." A hand went against her chest. "I'm a million percent positive that, after that, I can't come anymore."

I laughed. "We're not even close to there." I pulled her hand off her chest and held it in mine. "You need to be taken care of. We have two years and nine months to make up for."

"But you already took care of me in the kitchen. What happened in here, that was just ..." She shook her head as though she couldn't describe it.

"In here, that was for me."

She smiled. "You're a true unicorn."

"Why? Because I love to eat pussy?" When she nodded, I added, "Jolie, it's not all pussy. It's just your pussy." I held the back of her head and kissed her, the stream of water pouring between us. "The amount of satisfaction it gives me? I can't explain it. But I can tell you, I fucking crave it."

While I held her hand, I went to kiss the inside of her wrist, and I halted midway, staring at the blank skin, rubbing my thumb across it. For comparison, I lifted her other hand to check that wrist, noticing it wasn't there either. The thin, faint cursive *L* that had been there before was gone.

"What happened to your tattoo?"

"I had it lasered." She tilted her head back for a moment, wetting her forehead. "It was a graduation present to myself."

"It's completely vanished. They did a hell of a job."

"Which is a major relief. I swear, if I had to stare at that *L* for one more second, I was going to be a very unhappy girl."

"You could have covered it with a *B*." I winked at her.

She laughed. "No more initials on my body. One and done, mistake-wise."

I kissed the spot where the *L* used to be. "We'll see about that."

SIXTEEN

Jolie

Guilt was what caused my eyes to flick open before the sun rose. It was what made my heart race. It was what had me carefully lifting Beck's arm off my stomach, sliding out of his bed, and setting his arm on the mattress, hoping the movement didn't cause him to stir. It was what had me tiptoeing around his room to grab my dress and shoes and purse, quickly layering them on my body. And it was what had me standing in the doorway of his bedroom, staring at him while he lay on his stomach beneath the sheet and comforter.

Two years and nine months ago, while I had slept in his hotel room, he had taken off to fly to Washington, DC, and I was doing almost the same thing to him now.

In fact, I still had the note and sweatshirt he'd left me. The note lived in my nightstand. The sweatshirt folded on a rack in my closet. I hadn't worn it in a while. But for a long time, that sweatshirt had come to bed with me every night. I'd sniffed the thick fabric until I couldn't even smell the slightest hint of him.

Here, I wasn't leaving anything besides memories.

Ones that I'd have to hold on to for the rest of my life.

Oh God.

A realization that caused my eyes to fill. I pushed my hand against my chest as it hammered away, which did absolutely nothing. The tears still streamed. My heart still ached.

I shouldn't have come here.

I wished I hadn't gone to Musik last night. I didn't know he was going to be there. I didn't even realize it was his club I was at. But meeting him there, learning the truth about Africa, seeing how quickly we rekindled, and spending time with him—it only made this harder.

Because no matter what he had said to me last night or what had happened between us, there was no future between Beck and me.

What had gone down in this house would never go down again.

That meant I would never feel his arms around me. I would never get to kiss him. I would never get to experience the things his body could do to me.

And I would never get to tell him how much I cared about him.

This moment, right here, was the end.

The end of whatever could begin.

As I licked the wetness off my lips, my mouth filled with the salty aftermath of my tears.

They hadn't been shed out of guilt. They had been shed because I was in mourning.

And I knew this feeling would only get worse as I lamented over what we could have been.

I backed away from the bedroom, and using the light from my phone, I found my way to the front door, silently shutting it behind me. I figured there were multiple cameras pointed at me, so I rushed toward the gate, waiting for it to open before I went on my Uber app and ordered a car. To put some distance between his house and me, I walked toward his neighbor's entrance, and that was where I called Ginger.

"Are you okay?" Her voice was rich with panic as she answered my call. "It's not even six in the morning."

A squirrel ran past me, and I jumped. The darkness of his street and lack of lamps made things feel a little eerie at this hour.

"I'm fine. I just ordered an Uber. I'll be headed your way in a couple of minutes."

"An Uber? Why isn't Beck taking you home?"

"I didn't wake him. I ... didn't want to. I sorta just snuck out."

"Why, babe? Did things not go well last night?"

At the end of the block, knowing I'd probably walked too far for the Uber to find me, I approached the pole of the Stop sign. My arm weaved around it before my fingers clung to the cold metal. "No, things between us were perfect. Like, so perfect, Ginger." My voice was softening with each word. "That's the problem." I rested my cheek against the base of the sign too. "If I had been there when he woke up, I know he'd have asked more questions, and things would have probably been even better than last night—and I couldn't handle that. Not when I can't give him honest answers."

She cleared her throat, and I expected an immediate reply, but it didn't come for several seconds. "Eventually, you're going to have to tell him the truth. And the sooner you do that, the better, Jolie."

"Ugh." I released the pole and backed up to the brick wall that aligned with the sidewalk, a wall that acted as a fence to the mansion that sat behind it. "The thought of that makes me feel sick."

"But wouldn't you rather have him hear it from you?"

I pushed my head against it, the sharp pieces pulling at my hair. "Yes." My eyes closed, the guilt returning—or coming on stronger, as I was sure it hadn't left. "I just don't want to."

"I know." She sighed. "This is so messy."

My eyelids flicked open as a car drove by, but I knew it wasn't my ride since it never slowed. "This is why last night shouldn't have happened. What was I even thinking?"

"Well, I didn't help much. I was pushing you to do it. I feel terrible now."

"But I didn't have to listen to you."

"Babe, I told you things were going to close up, you know, down there. And to just do it and deal with the consequences later. This is later. And I'm a giant asshole."

"One, stop blaming yourself. I'm a big girl, and we both know I was going to do it regardless of what you said. None of this is your fault, and you're most definitely not an asshole."

"What's two?"

"Two ... I'm so fucked."

BECK

And here I thought you would stay long enough that I could give you breakfast in bed. You ran out early. Are things okay?

ME

Yeah, yeah. I'm so sorry about that. I just had to get going.

BECK

Baby, come back.

ME

I wish I could.

BECK
Are you still in LA?

ME
Yep. But work stuff, remember?

BECK
What about tonight? Will you still be here? Do you have plans?

ME
I can't.

BECK
No problem. When can you?

ME
Not sure—but let me see what I can do.

I stared at the words I'd just sent Beck, and my fingers shot into my hair, gripping the long strands while I rocked back and forth over the bed.

Not sure—but let me see what I can do.

What had I even been thinking when I typed that?

Why had I sent that response?

Why had I offered hope ... when there was none?

SEVENTEEN

Beck

I wiped the sweat off my forehead and tossed the small towel onto the incline bench, stretching out my chest and triceps before I did another set of chest presses and weighted dips. Music was blasting so loudly through my home gym—Eminem when I was maxing out, Jelly Roll when I was starting a new exercise, and Post Malone when I was walking out the pain—that there was no way I'd hear my phone ring or any texts come through.

Normally, while I was working out, I gave no fucks about anyone getting in touch with me, nor did I even bring my phone in here.

But since Jolie had left this morning, I'd been waiting for her to get back to me about when we could get together. And considering it was one of my final days off, it should have been flying by. Freedom always moved quickly.

Not today.

Her silence had caused the hours to fucking drag.

A silence I found odd, along with the way she'd left this morning—before the sun even rose—considering we'd had such a good time last night.

At least, I thought we had.

It had been her idea not to use a condom and my idea to give her a total of six orgasms that spanned across the whole evening.

I wanted to do it again tonight.

But, goddamn it, she hadn't said a word to me since I'd texted her when I woke up, realizing she was gone.

She was in LA. We'd reconnected after all these years. I just wanted to see her, and she was giving me nothing.

I checked the time on my phone. It was a little past four.

I mentally calculated how long the rest of this workout would take, along with a soak in the cold plunge, followed by a warm-up in the sauna, and began to type her a message.

ME
I'm going to head to Charred around six for a drink. You should meet me there, or I can pick you up at your hotel—whatever works best.

JOLIE
Can I let you know?

ME
Of course.

JOLIE
If I get out at a decent time, I'll swing by.

ME
And if you don't?

JOLIE
☹

A sad face? Meaning I wouldn't get to see her at all?

What the fuck?

I picked up the towel off the bench, and before I could even bring it to my face, I balled it up and threw it across the room.

I held my glass of bourbon between both hands, turning the tumbler in a circle over the top of the bar, bouncing the large block of ice with my finger. "Talk to me about Horned," I said to my sister as she sat next to me.

The whole side of the bar was blocked off for my family, so none of our diners were within earshot. That had been a surprising find when I walked into Charred, expecting to be the only Weston here, aside from Walker, who was working in the kitchen.

"Are the reservations still exploding?"

Horned was a restaurant we'd recently acquired, the Laguna Beach steak house now part of our collection, which we were currently expanding to three new locations—Portsmouth, New Hampshire, Charleston, South Carolina, and, as of a week ago, San Antonio, Texas. Land had been purchased. Build-outs were in motion.

"And the same with Toro?" I asked. "The social media hype for both spots hasn't died down, has it?"

Eden sent reservation numbers every Friday, but I hadn't looked at them at any point last night or today.

Time wasn't the issue.

It was that my head just wasn't in it.

My sister, already facing me, put her hand on my forehead as though she were checking my temperature. "It's Saturday night, Beck. We're a bourbon deep. And you want to talk about work? Now?" She pulled her hand away, but her stare didn't lighten at all.

"He doesn't want to talk about work," Walker said from behind the bar as he stood in front of us. "He's fucked up over something and trying to get his mind off it." He nodded toward me. "Look at him."

I didn't know if Walker was out of the kitchen for the rest of the night or if he was just taking a break, but his sleeves were rolled up, his chef's whites were unbuttoned at the top, and there was a drink in his hand that he was sipping from.

"Let the dude breathe for a second." Hart's arm briefly brushed mine while he lifted his old-fashioned. "He starts a whole new season of hockey in a couple of days. He's inside his head, and that's where he should be. That's why he's being quiet."

I stared at each of my siblings. "I'm not a fly on the wall, you know. I'm sitting right here."

"And you're acting weird as hell," Eden offered.

Where was all this coming from?

"First of all," I started, "I've been here for five minutes. I don't think I've been quiet at all—"

"You've been quiet," Eden countered.

I glanced from her to Walker and said, "And what's wrong with the way I look?" I glanced down the front of me, rather pleased with my outfit. The shirt had been sent over, along with about fifty others, from a brand deal my agent had recently signed me up for. The jeans had been supplied by my assistant, who had probably worked with a stylist.

"Did you just finish working out?" my oldest brother asked, crossing his arms over his chest. "We know you like late workouts when you're in offseason."

I pulled the bottom of my button-down to straighten out my shirt. "Yeah." I then moved to the collar, making sure it was sitting right. "I'm not even going to ask why that's a detail you remember."

"After your workouts, especially when you're getting ready for the season, you usually wear a pair of sweats and a hoodie." Hart had his elbow on the bar, his body turned so he was looking at the front of me. "Tonight, you're dressed up."

I smiled wide without showing any teeth, my brows furrowed. "I'm in jeans."

"But you're in clothes—and not some variation of workout clothes," Hart said.

I shook my head. "I'm at our restaurant. I should look nice."

"That's never stopped you from looking like hell before," Eden voiced, running her finger around the rim of her glass. "In fact, last time you were here, you were in a hoodie and sweats, and the hood was actually over your head and—"

"Jesus," I groaned. "You all need to fucking relax. I don't know why you're all over me, but stop." I shot back the second drink and set the empty on the bar top. "Fill it up," I said to Walker, pushing the glass toward him.

"Do you want to talk about it?" Eden asked softly.

Soft was reserved for special occasions; she normally stayed in hard mode.

I focused my attention on her, studying her face. She was doing the same thing to me, but her stare was far more intense, like I was some fucking assignment and she was about to write a hundred-page paper on me.

"Are you giving me any other choice?"

"No," Walker replied. "I think you know the three of us are going to dig like hell until you cave."

I tapped my hand on the wooden top, restless since there was no drink to hold.

I knew the second I opened up about this, they would hit me with endless questions, and I had no answers. To save myself the aggravation, I hadn't planned on saying anything unless Jolie showed up.

Then I would be forced to explain who she was.

But my silence had lasted all of, what, seven minutes before I found myself here?

"Last night ..." I let out a loud breath. "Guess who I ran into."

"I'm going to assume it was a woman." Eden waited to see if I reacted, which I didn't, and then added, "I don't have enough fingers to list all the ladies I think it could be." She smiled.

I rolled my eyes until they closed, my head slightly shaking. "I ran into Jolie."

Walker clasped his hand on mine. "The chick from Boston?"

I nodded.

"She's in LA?" Eden asked.

"She was at Musik last night," I told them.

"Did you know she was going to be there?" Hart asked.

Just like I thought—a verbal firing squad.

I stretched my arms up, my palms cupping the back of my head. "I ran into her randomly and couldn't fucking believe my eyes. Never had I thought she'd be there, and I'm sure she thought the same about me."

Eden held her drink close to her lips. "Did you tell her about Africa?"

"I did."

"Did she give you shit for not reaching out to her once you realized the text hadn't gone through?" Hart asked.

Although the stool didn't have any give, I rocked over the seat, the amount of questions nearing an overwhelming stage. "She gave me a little shit, but I deserved a lot more. I should have reached out to her after the Boston game. I don't know why the hell I didn't."

"So, that led to her going home with you ... I assume?" Eden took a long drink and set the glass down.

I laughed. "Solid assumption."

"Ugh. I wish you guys led with your brains and not that thing between your legs."

Still chuckling, I said, "What does that mean?"

"You haven't seen her in two-plus years. You fucked up. So, why not make it right and ask her out on a date? Why not spend time together that doesn't involve getting naked?" She waved the air. "Anyway, keep going."

Did Eden have a point?

Was that what Jolie was looking for?

But it had hardly taken any convincing for her to come to my place.

My arms dropped, and I gripped the edge of the bar. "She took off at around five this morning. She didn't even wake me up, she just left. I don't know how long she's going to be here for. And when I asked her to come here tonight, she told me she'd let me know."

"Holy fuck," Hart groaned. "I wish Colson were here instead of at some little kid's birthday party with Ellie. He's missing out on some good shit."

"I know one of you will be texting him to fill him in before the night is over." I looked at Eden, not because she was the drama spreader, but because she wouldn't want Colson to feel left out. "Am I right?" I winked at her.

"We need to back up for a second." Her hand was now on my arm. "You're telling me she took off before it was even light out? And you don't know if you'll see her before she flies back to Boston?"

"That's what I'm telling you."

Her eyes narrowed. "Did you piss her off?"

This time, when I exhaled, it came through my nose. "Not that I know of—"

There was a vibration in my pocket, and I took out my phone to read the screen.

> **JOLIE**
> I wish I had better news. I won't be able to make it tonight. Sorry!

I shoved the phone back in my pocket, balled up my fingers, and banged them on the bar. "Walker, I need you to hurry up with that refill."

As he lifted a bottle from behind the bar and tipped it toward my glass, I heard Eden ask, "Was that Jolie who just texted you?"

"Yes." My jaw was clenched. "She's not coming."

Eden's fingers hugged me harder. "I'm confused."

"That makes two of us," I admitted.

Once Walker finished pouring, I lifted the drink to my lips.

"Because something isn't adding up," she continued. "If things went well last night—and I'm figuring that if you asked her to come here, you believed things had gone really well—then why is she turning you down?"

"I don't know."

But I knew the anger I had about this situation and how badly I wanted to see her again, and I could only fucking imagine what she had felt when she didn't get a reply from me about Africa.

"And darting out in the morning without even a goodbye—also fishy," Eden said. "What if she's heading back to Boston in the morning and tonight was your only shot at seeing her again?"

"Women are so fucking confusing," Walker moaned.

Hart laughed. "I'm the only non-single one among us, and I'm still lost when it comes to how their brains work. I've got zero advice for you, Beck. I'm leaving this one up to Eden."

"I've got this, none of you need to worry," my sister said. "Except for you—you *do* need to worry." She was aiming her statement at me. "Even if she has something going on tonight—whatever that something is—and say she has another something planned for early tomorrow morning, she could see you during the in-between hours. That's what we do when it comes to something we care about—we run on no sleep, and we make it happen. Being tired isn't even a concern."

I placed my elbows on the bar and hung my head over my glass. "But maybe—whatever it is—it's too important to miss out on sleep."

"If you had a game bright and early the next morning, would that stop you?" Walker asked.

I stared straight into his green eyes. "No."

"Case closed," Eden replied.

I tilted my neck to gaze at my sister, and before my lips parted, I heard Jolie's voice in my head, speaking the line that had stuck with me for all these years. *"It's not what they tell you, it's what they show you."*

And what she was showing me? Fuck ...

EIGHTEEN

Jolie

> **BECK**
> It's too bad last night didn't work out. Let me know if you can meet up tonight. I'd love to bring you to Toro, our new sushi restaurant.

While I stared at Beck's text, my stomach did this weird thing, where it tingled from what he'd typed and the thought of seeing him. And at the same time, it churned because I knew I shouldn't see him again.

I couldn't.

Oh God, I hated this.

This whole situation.

The reasoning behind it.

The reality that I was facing.

A reality that came shooting down from the top of my screen in the form of a notification—the subject of the email raising enough anxiety within me that I abandoned Beck's message, clicking on the email. Once it was loaded, my eyes scrolled the words so fast; I went back to the beginning to read it again in case I'd missed something.

But it turned out, I hadn't missed anything.

It was all spelled out.

And each syllable made it even harder for me to breathe.

"Fuck. Fuck, fuck, *fuuuck.*"

"What's wrong?" Ginger rushed in from the hallway, coming over to the bed, where I was sitting. A towel was wrapped around her body, and another was over her hair like a beehive. Her skin was streaked with white lotion that hadn't been rubbed in all the way. "You look like you're about to throw up."

"I am." I handed her my phone so she could read the email. "When Dad called while we were walking into Musik, I thought this was going to be delayed ... and now he's telling me it's not."

Her eyes grew wider with each line of text. "Oh, hell no."

I could taste the acid in the back of my throat. "I know."

She set the phone on the bed and took a seat in front of me. "What are you going to do?"

I shook my head, and when that didn't feel like enough, I shrugged.

"Babe, you kinda need to know. Or have a plan." Her hands went to my cheeks. "Or at least have an inkling of an idea because ..." Her head tilted, like a dog's when you were speaking to them. "God, I do not envy you one bit."

"You're not helping."

"I'm being real. That's why you love me."

"At this moment, that love is being challenged." I clutched the base of my throat.

I didn't know what was going to take me out first—the heart attack that was on the verge of happening or the nausea since my stomach was threatening to empty the lunch we'd had delivered.

"I—" My voice cut off when my phone began to ring. I held my breath as I looked at the screen. "Shit."

"Who is it?"

"My dad." I could barely swallow; my heart was racing so fast. "This day couldn't possibly get any worse."

"Oh, but it can. You've yet to hear what he has to say."

"For the record, I don't love you anymore."

She smiled as she rolled her eyes. "Right." She lifted my phone and gave it to me. "Answer it."

I swiped the screen and brought the cell up to my ear. "Hi, Dad."

"I'm assuming you saw the email?"

I drew in as much air as I could hold, which wasn't enough. "Yes."

"Jolene ... we need to talk ..."

ME

I wish I weren't just getting back to you at 2:00 a.m. Anyway, I really hope your phone is on silent and you're sleeping. If you're free tomorrow night, let's grab dinner or something.

BECK

Dinner works.

ME

If you tell me I woke you, I'll die.

BECK

You didn't.

ME

Your first day of practice is tomorrow, Beck. You need to be sleeping and getting all the rest you possibly can.

BECK

I need to ask you something ...

Did I upset you?

ME

No! Why would you even think that?

BECK

It feels like I somehow fucked things up again. If you're mad that I didn't text you once I realized my Africa invite hadn't gone through, I'm sorry. I know I handled everything wrong. Since I saw you at Musik, it's been eating at me.

ME

Oh my God, please don't think that. I'm not mad. I'm not upset. I promise, it's not you, Beck. I swear on everything.

BECK

So, you're saying it's on you ...

ME

I'll explain everything tomorrow night. Try to get some sleep.

NINETEEN

Beck

I grabbed a whole bucket of pucks with at least fifty inside and dumped them on the ice, scattering them throughout the offensive and neutral zones. While I skated from one to the next, not going in any order, moving back and forth between sides, I didn't take my time while I shot toward the goal. I didn't focus on form. I didn't aim the way I would if this were a game.

Because this session wasn't about seeing how many goals I could make.

This session was to work out the gnawing feeling in my body.

But there was someone who was making that difficult, someone who was challenging me, and that was Landon. He was what stood between me and the goal, attempting to deflect every puck I shot his way.

The truth was, I barely even saw him. Not his stance, leg pads, stick work—it was all a blur.

All I saw was the puck.

While I used every goddamn ounce of power I had to sweep that puck toward the goal, all I heard was my text conversation with Jolie continuously repeating in my head.

Did I upset you?

No! Why would you even think that?

Because she had been blowing me off since she had left my house that morning. Because her responses were few and far between. Because I couldn't believe she wasn't making more of an effort to see me.

Jolie had given me a taste.

I needed more.

I wanted more.

Didn't she feel the same way?

It feels like I somehow fucked things up again.

Oh my God, please don't think that. I'm not mad. I'm not upset. I promise, it's not you, Beck. I swear on everything.

Then what the hell was it?

She was dating someone?

Was she uninterested in seeing if this could work between us?

Did she not have any feelings for me?

Was my tongue the only thing she wanted from me?

"Fuck!" I shouted. "What the *fuuuck*?!"

My body should have been battered from the hours of practice the team had just endured. I should have been breathless from the way I had been skating and shooting. My shoulder should have been screaming every time I lifted my dominant arm, my hips aching from the insistent twisting.

I felt nothing.

But I wasn't done.

I needed more.

I needed to get this out—this feeling that was consuming me.

And nothing, not a whistle or someone yelling, could stop me from slamming that piece of vulcanized rubber toward the opposite end of the ice.

So, you're saying it's on you ...

I'll explain everything tomorrow night. Try to get some sleep.

Sleep? How the hell could that have been possible when my mind was racing between theories?

When I was filled with endless questions.

When my sister was planting regret bombs in my head and they were detonating every second.

"Dude, are you trying to fucking kill me?"

It took a moment before I realized I wasn't the one who had spoken those words. It was Landon, skating toward me, covering his face even though he was wearing a mask because my stick was pelting pucks right at him.

"Beck! Chill, you motherfucker!"

My arm halted midair, my jaw clenched, my breathing coming out in deep grunts. "I'm sorry. I ..."

"What the hell crawled up your ass today?" He moved around me in a circle. "You were a beast during practice, and now you're shooting at me like you're at a fucking gun range."

I slipped my hand out of my glove and pulled off my helmet. I hadn't even felt hot, but the sweat poured straight down the front of me, and as it started to drip into my eyes and sting, I wiped them. "It was a long night."

And a long couple of days, but the last thing I wanted was to talk about it. Besides, Landon didn't even know that I'd run into Jolie, which meant I'd have to start from the beginning, and that was a tale I wasn't getting into now.

"You all right, my man?"

While we skated toward the opening in the rink, I handed

my stick to one of the team's helpers and replied, "Yeah, I'm good."

"You sure?"

I shook some of the sweat out of my hair. "Positive."

Even though he eyed me down, I stayed silent. My siblings had been giving me a fucking earful since we'd met up at Charred on Saturday night. Even Colson had voiced his thoughts after Eden filled him in on our family group chat. The last thing I needed was another opinion swirling around in my head.

Landon took off his helmet and stepped off the ice after me, groaning as soon as his skates hit the concrete. "Fuck day one of practice." His hand went to my shoulder, giving me a surprising amount of weight as we walked to the locker room. "I'm not going to be able to move in a couple of hours."

"You need a cold plunge, followed by at least twenty minutes in the hyperbaric chamber." Adrenaline was what was keeping me moving, but as soon as that wore off, I was going to be in pain. Fortunately, I had both of those at my house, so I didn't have to use the team's. "Do it, trust me. You won't make it to tomorrow's practice if you don't."

"Ugh," he moaned.

I laughed at him. "You sound like a little bitch."

He tossed his glove and flipped me off. "I hope you're sore as fuck tomorrow. Asshole."

I continued to chuckle. He took a seat at his locker, which was right next to mine, and I stayed standing to strip off my practice jersey. I then unhooked my shoulder pads and the rest of my gear, handing each piece to our equipment manager, leaving me in just my compression shorts.

"What are you up to tonight?" Landon leaned forward to take off his skates. "Do you want to go out and grab some drinks?"

"Can't."

"You have plans?" He slipped one skate off and went to work on the other. "I'll wager a grand right now that you're even too sore to get hard. So, how about you cancel those plans and come out with me?"

I laughed. "Dude, nothing stops me from getting hard. And I don't care how sore I am, I'm never too sore for sex." One of the helpers threw me a towel, and I rubbed it over my soaked head. "I'm going to hit the shower—"

"Listen up," our coach said as he walked to the center of the locker room, glancing around where the team was either sitting or standing—all of us in different stages of getting undressed. "Before you leave or go take a shower, I need you sitting down for a few minutes so we can go over something."

The room turned completely silent.

I sat next to Landon, wondering if Coach was going to discuss how we'd played today. As a whole, we didn't look great. Most of the guys, including myself, hadn't been on skates in weeks. Their diets weren't in check. They hadn't lifted consistently. Their stamina was shit.

They liked to fuck off during the offseason, and I didn't blame them. We only had a short window of downtime.

But one thing we knew how to do was pull it together. By the first preseason game within the next couple of weeks, we'd be back to the team Coach expected.

"We have a few changes that are about to take place, but instead of hearing those from me, I'm going to let you hear it from the man himself. Please cover up, gentlemen."

Since I was in shorts and had nothing to cover, I glanced at Landon and whispered, "What the fuck is happening?"

"No idea," he replied.

A man I'd never seen before walked into the center of the locker room, shaking Coach's hand. He waited for Coach to join us before he said, "Most of you, I assume, don't know who I am, so let me introduce myself. My name's Mark Jameson, and as of a few days ago, I'm the new owner of your team."

Whispers began to fill the silence, including mine as I glanced back at Landon and whispered, "What the hell? We were sold? And no one told us?"

"I'm sure many of you have questions. I promise you're going to get those answers and you're going to get them from me," Mark said, clasping his hands, his gold wedding band shining under the lights. "But I want to start off by saying, the previous owner did an excellent job at running your organization, and I don't plan on making that many changes. At least not ones you'll feel at your level." His eyes scanned the horseshoe of lockers, making sure to connect with each of us. "What I do plan on doing is making this team more profitable. Ramping up marketing efforts. Making sure the Whales are getting the press you superstars deserve."

There was a brief round of applause from our team.

"Over the next couple of weeks, you're going to be seeing a lot of me. I'll be attending some of your practices. I'll be coming in during your weight training sessions. I want to get to know you, I want to see how you operate, and I want to get a sense of how you work as a team." He cleared his throat. "I'm hoping, at some point over the next week, I can sit down with each of you personally to discuss the things you'd like to see implemented and talk about your concerns." He held his chin, his other hand holding the elbow of his raised hand. "As players, you're the foundation. You see a completely different side of this sport, a side that's most important, and I want to make sure your needs aren't only addressed, but they're met."

I stole a quick peek at Landon, and he gave me a half smile, signaling he was impressed with what he'd heard so far.

So was I.

I'd been with this team since I'd joined the league, and the previous owner never came around. He left everything in management's hands. He'd never once asked for our opinion on anything.

When Mark's hand dropped from his face, he crossed his arms, the movement causing his black suit jacket to pull across the tops of his shoulders. "One of the biggest changes you'll feel at your level is marketing. I'm going to be honest—and I'm not telling you anything you don't already know—but what you previously had wasn't up to par. I dare say ... it was shit. Much of it was outsourced, and aside from game-day promotions, you didn't have a team on-site, giving you the publicity you need and deserve." He nodded at someone and added, "That team has been fired." He held out his hand. "I'd like to introduce you to your new head of marketing."

Two noises took over the room. The first was the clicking of a very high pair of heels, and the second was a murmur from my teammates.

The head of marketing came from the entrance behind me, and as she made her way toward Mark, it wasn't her bare legs—which looked fit and gorgeous and fucking endless, half covered in a skirt—that held my attention.

As she patted Mark's shoulder and turned toward us, it wasn't her tits—well hidden under a blazer, but pushed out enough to hint at how perfect they were—that captured me.

What owned me, what I couldn't stop staring at, were her light-blue eyes.

Eyes that were now locked with mine.

And her hair.

Those wild red locks that I knew far too well.

Jesus fucking Christ.

Jolie ...

TWENTY

Jolie

When I first walked into the arena this morning and entered the elevator that took me to my new office, one that had a window overlooking the ice and the team practicing on it, I had to force myself not to dry-heave. Since the beginning of my father's endless phone calls and emails, letting me know that today was the day of the takeover, the only thing I'd been able to get down was coffee. It was currently burning the back of my throat, and I was doing everything in my power not to throw up.

My anxiety was rearing its wicked head.

It was causing my entire body to shake.

It was making the guilt peak to a point that was impossible to come down from.

Or maybe it was Beck who was doing that to me.

As I stood in the center of the locker room, he was sitting at just about ten o'clock, wearing only a pair of spandex shorts, a hand towel hanging across his shoulders. His face was a tiny bit hairier than when I had left him Saturday morning in bed, his hair messy from his helmet, his skin glistening with sweat.

Oh God.

He looked beyond handsome.

But ... what was running through his head?

How was he processing this?

Was he putting two and two together?

None of that mattered at the moment.

First, I needed to find my voice.

I needed to get myself under control and my thoughts together.

Everyone was staring at me, waiting for me to speak. I only had one shot to impress the team, and this was it.

"Thank you for the introduction." I demanded my lips to smile, doing everything I could to keep the quiver out of my voice. "I'm Jolene Jameson, your new head of marketing. My office is upstairs"—I pointed up even though my statement was more than enough and the gesture wasn't needed—"so if there's ever anything you need, don't hesitate to come see me. I won't be working alone. I'll have two assistants, both arriving within the next few days from Boston, and the three of us will be managing the entire department."

I refused to look in Beck's direction, because I knew I wouldn't be able to get through this, so I aimed my focus at his other half-naked teammates. "To give you just a little background, I'm also from Boston, and I've been an avid hockey fan for as long as I can remember. I might not be able to call plays"—I grinned at the head coach—"but I have a deep understanding of the sport, and it's only on a rare occasion that I miss a home game."

"Boston!" someone shouted. "You'd better not be rooting for them now!"

I laughed. "There's no need to worry. There's only one

team I'm rooting for, and that's the Whales. Admittedly"—I could feel my face reddening—"I've been following your team for the last couple of seasons, so I'm well aware of what you guys can do and the strength and power and talent this team possesses." I shifted positions, feeling the weight of Beck's stare on my body.

"Mark briefly mentioned that marketing will be different now that it's under my control. One reason for that is because I'll be traveling with you. I know in the past, there was a never-ending carousel of marketing reps, a slew of unfamiliar faces, nonstop cameras pointed at you during times that felt inappropriate—that won't ever be the case with me. I will be your contact. It's my face you'll see—on the plane, at games, at practices—everywhere and anywhere." I used my fingers to list each point and paused to let the news set in for them. But for me, I halted because the thought of spending that much time with Beck—in this arena, on the team's plane, during one-on-ones—was what had made these last few days torturous.

"My team and I are here to make sure you're comfortable, and the best way to do that is by getting to know you guys. I'd also like to sit down with each of you to discuss our strategies and plans and make sure they align with yours." I attempted to find my breath. "Do you have any questions?"

I still couldn't look at Beck's side of the locker room.

I didn't trust myself if our eyes became glued again.

There was absolutely no telling what type of expression would come over my face or how my body would react. If his gaze would make the acid lift straight from my stomach and make me want to bolt from this room or make me break out in tears.

"Jameson," someone said. "Is it a coincidence you both have the same last name? Are you ... *married*?"

"No," I replied, my head shaking.

"Jolene isn't my wife ..." my father said, his voice carrying across the room.

But as his voice trailed off, I found my eyes moving. My brain was telling my body to stand still, but something wasn't allowing it to. Slowly, I shifted past twelve o'clock, nearing eleven, and stopping at ten.

Those hazel eyes weren't inviting. They weren't devouring. They weren't comforting.

My chest rose.

My stomach churned.

There was a pain so deep inside me as I saw exactly what I feared.

"She's my daughter," my father continued.

Beck's eyelids closed. His head tilted back. And I swore I heard him groan out in anger.

TWENTY-ONE

Beck

"He's a venture capitalist and private equity investor. To turn the companies around or build them—whatever the case is—he keeps the marketing in-house. That's where I come in."

As I stared at Jolie in our locker room, I remembered the conversation we'd had about her father, a man whose name I didn't know until now. At that time, I'd been interested in what he did for a living and her role in his company, given that I personally backed many of The Weston Group projects and considered myself a bit of a private equity investor.

But never had I thought the Whales would sell or that Mark would become the new owner of the team.

Or that his daughter—a woman I'd become fucking obsessed with—would be our head of marketing.

Head, manager, controller—whatever her title was, it was just a word. The reality was that she was Mark's daughter, which automatically made her an owner as well.

And that meant ...

Jolie had just become my fucking boss.

A point continuously driven into my brain while I fixated on her.

As she spoke, she was charming the boys with her warm, lovable personality, promising things we didn't know we wanted or needed, mesmerizing them with her looks.

There wasn't a limp dick in this whole fucking room—I'd bet thousands on it.

I glanced around at the faces of each of my teammates, annoyed as hell that their eyes were on her.

That they were listening to her.

That they were watching her.

I knew this was irrational.

I also knew there was nothing I could do to change the way I felt.

"My office is upstairs."

"I'll be traveling with you."

"It's my face you'll see—on the plane, at games, at practices —everywhere and anywhere."

What the fuck was even happening right now?

Was this some kind of sick joke?

Jesus.

I couldn't listen to another word.

I needed a time-out.

A drink.

To be in a room that she wasn't filling in some way.

My eyes closed.

My chin lifted.

And I groaned out the loudest roar of anger as the rest of the team applauded Jolie.

I had questions.

Hundreds of them.

I didn't even know where to fucking begin with any of this shit.

But I knew, after her message at two this morning, that she wanted to talk.

Of course she did. She needed to clean up the pieces after dropping this goddamn bomb on me.

But why hadn't she called me this morning to tell me before practice? Why hadn't she given me some kind of heads-up or warning before she and her father walked in here and unloaded this beast of information?

And why hadn't she mentioned this before I brought her home, before I fucked her without a condom, and before she came all over my tongue?

My chin dropped, and as soon as my stare moved straight, it locked with hers.

Jolie, why do you have to be so gorgeous?

But etched across that beautiful face was a war of emotions. I could see it in her eyes. In the tightness of her lips. In the furrow between her brows.

She was getting a piece of what I'd been going through since she had left my place on Saturday morning. Up until now, I'd had no idea what was going on with her. And starting now, she had absolutely no idea what was running through my head.

How does it fucking feel?

Regardless, this was a goddamn disaster.

I had seen what I needed—and I'd seen enough.

My gaze moved to Mark as he said, "If there's anything you need from us, let us know." His auburn comb-over with even redder eyebrows told me he was who she'd gotten her hair color from. "Take care of yourselves. Rest up. We'll see you all at practice tomorrow."

He held out his arm, allowing Jolie to walk out first, and the two of them left the locker room.

"Dude"—Landon slapped my arm—"I might be so off here, but that chick looked just like Jolie. They even have similar names."

I slowly faced my goalie. Whose ass I'd accidentally tried to pummel with pucks from being so worked up over her. "That was Jolie."

Landon's eyes couldn't possibly get any bigger. "You mean to tell me that was the three-night stand from Boston—"

"Yes." Both hands dived into the sides of my hair. "I ran into her the other night at Musik."

"Holy fucking shit."

"But I didn't know any of this." I took the towel off my shoulders and wrapped it around my wrist. "She spent the night at my place and said nothing. I just found out about her new position when you did." I was keeping my voice down so none of my teammates could hear. "And I'm fucking—"

"Damn, that fucking redhead. I'm calling dibs right now," my right wing said, his voice cutting me off as he shouted his comment across the room.

It had taken less than a minute for the shit talking to start—no surprise there. My team was a bunch of horny bastards.

"Fuck that, she's going to be mine," someone else said. "I'll have her begging for my dick in no time."

I tried to search for the second voice, but many of the guys were huddled in the center, where Jolie and Mark had been standing.

"I give her a week before she's spreading her legs for me," a third voice said.

"Did you see those legs?" one of my defensemen said, standing to join the group. "I'd like to have them wrapped around my face."

I turned toward Landon. "I'm going to fucking lose it."

"On who?" he asked.

"On every goddamn person in this room." I unwrapped the towel from my wrist, and I aimed it toward the huddle and tossed it like a football. "Enough!" I shouted at them.

Several of them looked over.

"She's the owner's daughter. Your dicks aren't getting anywhere near her."

"So, you're saying your dick is?" my backup goalie asked with a smile.

I flipped him off. "Get in the fucking shower and stop gossiping." I turned toward my locker and reached into my bag. My cell was on top, and the second the screen lit up, there was a message from Jolie.

> JOLIE
> I'll be over at 7:00 p.m. unless you tell me otherwise.

The message had been sent about twenty minutes ago, when I was still in practice. She had known she was going to come in here, she had known I was going to lose my shit, and she had known I would see this as soon as I was calm enough to look at my phone.

I tossed the phone back in my bag and began getting dressed.

"You're not going to shower?" Landon asked.

"With those fools? So I can hear them talk about her more? Shit no. I'm getting the hell out of here before I murder one of them."

TWENTY-TWO

Jolie

"Before you say anything, I could really use a drink."

Out of all the things I could have voiced to Beck when he opened his front door, those were the words that came out.

Part of that had to do with anxiety, which, at this point, was on the verge of sending me straight into a panic attack.

And part of that was because I really did need a drink or I was going to have that panic attack.

"A drink?" He gripped the side of the heavy glass door, his presence taking up the entire entryway, his hazel gaze zooming right in on me. "How about the truth? Why don't you start there instead?"

"You're going to get that." I clutched the strap of my crossbody. "But I'm a bundle of nerves, and we don't have any alcohol in our apartment since we just moved in. I could have stopped at the store, but I left work late, and I didn't want to arrive here a minute after seven and ..." My voice trailed off as he turned around and left the doorway, walking past his foyer, deeper into his home, like he was completely done listening to me.

"Okay ..." I shut the door behind me and followed him into the living room.

He grabbed a glass and bottle from the bar and set them on the coffee table. "Now talk."

With shaky hands, I unscrewed the top of the whiskey and poured some into the glass. I didn't ask for sour mix. I wanted nothing to come between me and this alcohol. Halfway to my lips, I asked, "Aren't you going to have one?"

"No."

I took a drink and then another, waiting for the burn to fade before I swallowed a little more. "Why not?"

"Because every time there's liquor involved, I can't seem to keep my fucking hands off you."

He was sitting in one of the chairs that was across from the couch, so I tucked myself in the corner of the large sectional, gripping a pillow with one hand and my drink with the other.

He brushed a hand over his soft hair, locks that weren't gelled or styled. "You're up. Let's hear it." And when that hand fell, he leaned back, his bare foot bouncing on the floor.

There was a coldness coming from him.

Not from his outfit—those gray sweats and T-shirt created a scorching look—but from his tone and posture.

I understood. Things were ... beyond disastrous.

Even though, over the last few days, I'd played this out many times in my head, I couldn't find a place to start. Starting should have been easy—it wasn't.

I traced my thumb around the rim of the glass and took in a giant breath. "I found out my dad was interested in buying the Whales three weeks before you guys played in Boston last season. When he called me in for that meeting, he'd already spoken to his attorney, and the deal was in motion." I tucked my legs off to the side. "When he dropped that news on me, that's also when he told me that if the deal went through, I'd be the one heading up the team's marketing and that would require me to relocate to LA."

He leaned forward, his elbows resting on his knees. "You're telling me ... you've known about this for that long?"

"Yes."

"And you said nothing to me?"

"Said nothing to you? I've signed so many NDAs over the course of working for my father, the sheets of paper with my signature on it would equal a four-hundred-page book." I huffed. "Even if I wanted to tell you, I couldn't until the announcement was made or my father shared the news—whichever came first, but you weren't going to hear that news from me."

"Bullshit." He nodded at me. "You could have fucking told me."

I stared at him, almost dumbfounded. "Let's say I could ... why would I?"

"Because you owed me that."

I released the pillow, the anxiety finally leaving my body, and in its place was a whole new feeling. A feeling that sent me to the edge of my seat after I untucked my legs. "I owed you nothing. Do you remember the whole Africa thing? Where it appeared that you didn't invite me? That I went this whole time thinking you'd ghosted me after my last message to you?" I flicked my hair off my shoulder. "Because of that, I wasn't exactly super excited to reach out even though I knew you were coming to town." I paused. "And even though I *was* going to be at that game."

He folded his hands together, looking at me through his lashes. "You were at that game ..."

"I was." There was no reason to sugarcoat this. I wasn't going to say anything he didn't already know. "You played like shit that night ... no offense. You seemed distracted, like your head wasn't in it at all."

His fingers were wiggling, his forearms bouncing between his open legs. His movements halted. "I couldn't stop thinking about you."

Words that should have sounded dreamy.

But not when they came through a set of grinding teeth.

"Another reason I didn't reach out was that it was going to be very hard to look you in the eyes, knowing there was a good chance my father was going to own your team. Since I can't keep my hands off you, with or without alcohol"—I let out a small laugh—"with the impending sale, I was too fearful that it would happen that night and I didn't get in touch." I was suddenly reminded of the other part of this. "Besides, it's you who should have been contacting me. Once you realized your text hadn't gone through, my phone should have been blowing up."

His head shook. "I already told you, I fucked up."

I wiped my sweaty hand over my skirt. "I'm just making a point." I took another sip. "Regardless of how we spin this, Beck, or who tries to blame who, if being together was the ultimate goal, then we're both in the wrong."

A conversation we'd never had.

Dating and a relationship—words we'd never used.

But I felt it.

His eyes told me he did too.

"Next on the agenda is Musik."

I found it interesting how he was the one who had told me to talk, but when I had brought up one of the elephants in the room—one that should affect him the most—he had absolutely nothing to say.

I filled my lungs. Slowly. "Not a decision I'm most proud of."

"Jesus Christ." He got up, and when I thought he was going to pour himself a drink, he turned and paced back to his chair, but he didn't sit. He stood behind it and gripped the top with both hands. "Why did you come back here with me?"

"The truth? You do something to me, and I can't resist you. And I know that's awful. I know I fucked up and shouldn't have done it. I was trying to fight the temptation, but even Ginger was encouraging me and telling me to deal with the consequences later, reminding me how long it had been since I'd slept with anyone." My head dropped, the guilt gnawing at the base of my throat.

"That last guy ... just happened to be me."

I glanced up, quietly replying, "Yes."

He extended his arms out wide while still holding the chair. "You're telling me you agreed to come here because you needed to be fucked?"

No, it had gone far deeper than that.

But that wasn't a part I was willing to admit—not now, and because of the circumstances, not ever.

My heart hadn't been still, but it also hadn't been beating like this. "Yes and no."

"What the fuck does that mean?" His brows rose.

"I didn't need to be fucked, Beck." I paused. "I needed to be fucked by *you*."

"And you told me not to wear a condom." The chair lifted off the floor, and he gradually set it back down. "But it didn't end there. I was on my fucking hands and knees, licking your pussy in the shower. You sucked my dick when we finally got into bed. I fingered your ass before I came inside you again. And you didn't think, at any of those points, you should stop things from going further?"

I shook my head. "I ... couldn't."

"You make no sense."

I drained the rest of my glass and poured a tiny bit more. "Listen, when shit got real, when the guilt caused my eyes to open before the sun even rose, I left. I came back to reality and faced it head-on."

He chuckled. "You faced nothing. You avoided me like the goddamn plague. And then you walked into the locker room today and dropped a bomb on me. That was a cowardly fucking move."

"I—"

"I don't give a fuck if you signed a million NDAs. Today was wrong, Jolie, and deep down inside, you know it."

"Jolene."

His face reared back as if I'd slapped him. "Are you fucking kidding me?"

"I can't have the entire team knowing you call me by my nickname. All that will do is raise suspicion, and the last thing I need is for them to find out I've had sex with their captain. I can't even imagine what my dad would say about that." I held my temple, the headache of that drama causing my brain to pound. "Trust me, Dad would have a whole lot to say on that topic, and none of those words would be pretty." My hand dropped, and I tried to regroup. "I need the team to respect me, Beck. I need them to work with me. What I don't need is them thinking I'm some puck slut who spread my legs the second I met you at a bar in Boston—even though that's exactly what happened."

He looked down at the chair, and I could tell the eye contact was hard for him to break. I could also tell he had this burning desire to throw the chair through the glass wall next to us.

That was confirmed when he glanced up, his eyes fierce, his mouth like a rabid animal.

"What are you saying to me, Jolene? What does all this really mean?"

I finished the rest of my drink and was tempted to pour more, but I had to drive, and I knew it wouldn't be long before I would be getting in my car.

But this was the part that hurt the most.

The part where the game ended in a loss.

There was no overtime.

No shoot-out.

"What happened between us"—I attempted to take a breath and couldn't—"can never happen again."

"You're saying, even if you want it to …"

"What I want doesn't matter." My hands turned clammier; my stomach flipped in a way that made me nauseous. "My dad owns your team. I work for your team. You're their star player and captain. There is no space for anything other than professionalism."

"Did your dad make you sign a nonfraternization policy? The league doesn't have one, but some individual teams do."

"No. I signed nothing like that. But I did sign a code of conduct clause, and in there it specifies things like respect and integrity and conducting myself with professionalism at all times." I hesitated before I said, "What's happened between us isn't professional, Beck. It's downright naughty."

"But what you're saying is that, legally, we're safe."

I shook my head. "I never said that."

"We're grandfathered in, Jolie. We were a thing way before you signed that clause."

"Regardless—"

"What about what I want?"

Please don't say it, Beck. Oh God, please don't say it.

"You fucking live here now," he continued. "You're going to be around me every goddamn day—at the arena, at practice, on our plane."

"And I'm going to treat you like every other player." I was doing everything I could to shut off my emotions, folding them into a part of my heart that I wouldn't ever open. "And you're going to treat me like—"

"Like I've never seen you naked? Like I don't know what your pussy tastes like? Like I don't know all the different ways to make you come?" He slammed the chair down, its legs hitting the wood beneath, making a noise much louder than his voice. "I can't act as if I don't know any of those things."

I sighed. It was that or moan, and I certainly couldn't do that. "You're going to have to."

"Right." He nodded sarcastically. "And you want me to just listen to my teammates go on and fucking on about you?"

I stared at him, oblivious to what he was talking about. "On and on about what?"

"You still think you're that girl with barbeque sauce on her face, don't you? You have no idea how other people see you."

I silently agreed, the movement of my head coming on slowly. "But what does that have to do with anything? What are they going on and on about?"

"Nothing."

"Beck—"

"I need to hear you say that deep down in your heart, you honestly don't want anything to happen between us. That you're going to be able to work with me every single day of this season and not think of me in any way aside from professionally."

He walked closer, and when he got to the couch, he got down, kneeling directly in front of me.

My breathing completely stopped.

My thoughts weren't in a safe territory.

My body was consumed with tingles, jitters moving through me at the speed of light.

But those were still on the surface, and what I was feeling was underneath.

Beck's attention, presence, gaze—they shrouded me, like I'd pulled a heavy comforter over my head, letting the weight of the down feathers block the light to create this thick, increasing warmth.

That was him.

A build that never let up.

"I need to hear you say you're going to be able to keep your hands off me. That you'll be able to look at these fingers"—he hovered them over my knees, but never set them on me—"and my tongue and not think about what they can do to you. What you want them to do to you."

Every word was a weapon.

Slashing me, cutting me so deep—he knew I was on the verge of bleeding out.

But I had to be strong.

I had to say what was right, whether I believed it or not.

"I'm telling you, Beck"—my lungs screamed even though I was feeding them air—"there is no other choice."

"What I'm hearing is that you want me to give up?"

I held the back of my neck so my hands weren't within his reach. "You have to."

"You really think I'm that kind of guy? One who just walks away. One who doesn't fight."

I said nothing.

"Let me tell you something. When I hear things like this, I'm the kind of guy who fights even harder. You'll see—and, yes, Jolie, you will see because I'm about to show you. It's game on."

"Fuck my life," I groaned as Ginger picked up my call, gripping the steering wheel as though it were the bottle of whiskey I was going to guzzle at some point tonight.

"Are you in the car? Driving home?"

I sighed, "Yep."

"I stopped at the store and got us some drinks. I figured you could use one. Or a thousand."

"I love you."

When I had agreed to move to LA, one of the best parts, aside from having the job of my dreams, was that my best friend wanted to move with me. That we wouldn't have to live across the country from one another. We looked at apartments together, and she had immediately found a job in finance.

"How did it go? Tell me everything."

"It went ..." I stopped at a red light, my eyes briefly closing. I didn't know where the emotion was coming from, but it was burning. And that burning led to dripping, tears streaking each cheek. "Nothing he said surprised me. Well, I take that back. The last thing he said before I wiggled my way off the back side of his couch because he was kneeling in front of me—that surprised me."

"Hold up. You're saying Beck Weston got on his knees for you?"

Would I ever get that vision of him out of my head?

The way he had looked at me.

The way he had wanted to touch me.

The way the silence had hung between us and I wanted to break it by wrapping my arms around him and kissing him.

That man was dangerous.

I couldn't be alone with him.

Not until I could trust myself.

If I'd ever be able to trust myself ...

"I guess he did," I replied. "But it wasn't exactly like that ... I don't know ... maybe it was. *Fuck*."

"What did he say that surprised you?"

I used my arm to wipe the other side of my face, my thumb tapping the steering wheel. "He basically said I was telling him one thing and showing him something entirely different."

"Of course you were. You're in love with the man. You can't hide that in the way you look at him."

My head shook, sending a tear straight to my lips. "But I have to, Ginger. I can't have these feelings for him. If Dad found out, he'd fire me. And if the team found out, they'd never look at me the same. I can't gain him and lose everything else."

TWENTY-THREE

Beck

Jolie was fucking everywhere. She would walk along the upper deck of the stadium before she went into her office, the color of whatever she was wearing catching my attention when I was on the ice. I felt her stare from the mirrored window across from her desk that overlooked the rink. She came into the weight room during our workouts, and she sat on our bench during some of our practices. And the day after Mark Jameson's announcement in our locker room, I had learned she drove an all-black Jeep Wrangler Rubicon with black rims and chrome running boards, so whenever I pulled into the private lot at the arena or left for the day, I saw her Jeep.

Every glance she made in my direction was like another bob of her lips down my dick. Every time we passed each other, it was like she was sucking the end of my tip. And every time I smelled her vanilla-amber perfume in the air, it was like she was goading the cum to rise but leaving right before I got off.

Her teasing was only part of the torture.

The fucking noise from my teammates was the other.

From the moment I entered the arena to the minute I left, it never stopped.

"What do you think she's jotting down on that tablet?" one of my defensemen said as we were leaving the ice. "All the different positions she wants me to fuck her in?"

"Nah, she's sketching how I look naked," the backup goalie voiced. "It's an accurate portrayal, too, considering I hit that last night."

I stopped halfway in the tunnel, staring in the goalie's direction, waiting for him to continue. My fingers pulled back from my gloves so they could ball into fists, my teeth positioned in an underbite, my top lip curled.

I wasn't out of breath from all the skating and drills we'd just finished.

My body was letting out the air in preparation for destroying this motherfucker's face.

"You're full of shit," the defenseman said to the goalie. "You wish you'd hit that."

The goalie laughed. "No, she wishes I hit that. But, fellas, it's only a matter of time before I slide between those gorgeous fucking legs."

"Did you see that dress she wore yesterday?" my right wing asked, joining the other two. "I wasn't expecting her to have an ass like *that*. But, dude, it's just the kind of ass—"

"Walk." Landon's arm moved around my shoulders, his voice in my ear, blocking me from hearing the rest of what my right wing was saying.

"No, Landon," I growled. "I'm going to fucking—"

"Ignore them, Beck." The way he was guiding me forced my feet to move, and he directed me toward our lockers. "And wipe that look off your face."

I tossed my gloves on the floor. "What look?"

"The look that says you're about to end someone's life."

"But I am."

I pulled off my jersey and tossed it on the bench, along with my helmet. Now that my hands were free, my fingers automatically balled. That grip tightened as the trio made their way into the locker room, their comments about Jolie still coming in fast and hard.

"You're playing with fire, my man." Landon eyed my fists, pounding my shoulder, as though that would loosen them up. "You start this battle, and you're going to do everything she asked you not to do."

Why the hell had I confided in him and told him about my conversation with Jolie?

Because he wouldn't stop asking about what had gone down at my house—that was why.

Still, I regretted saying a goddamn word. Because the last thing I needed was him trying to talk any sense into me.

I blocked his fingers from tapping me. "She said nothing about fighting my teammates. Her worry is about them finding out. Me killing them? Shit, that wouldn't tell them anything."

He shook his head at me. "The thing is, you're fucking serious, and that's scary." He moved in front of me, hindering me from seeing the group. "How the hell would you explain why you'd shattered the nose of our second-string goalie?"

"You think it's only his nose I want to destroy?" I let out a deep chuckle. "It needs to be realigned anyway. Have you seen that fucking thing?"

He ran his hand over his buzzed head, shaved down for the start of the season. "Or why you knocked out our defenseman's teeth?"

"You mean, the rest of his teeth. He doesn't have a ton to begin with."

"Beck"—his hands went to my shoulders—"you need to tone it down, cowboy."

I moved out of the way and gripped the wall that separated our lockers. "I'm telling you, Landon ... I'm not going to survive this."

I didn't care that Jolie and I weren't together. The thought of her with these men and hearing them talk about her this way made me want to destroy them.

He nodded to one of the other players and said, "This is only the beginning. You know, when it comes to our team and women, things don't die down. They get worse over time."

I pressed my forehead against the wall and sighed. "I know. I'm telling you, someone is going to fucking die—"

"Beck, do you have a second?"

The question hadn't been spoken by Landon. So, I pulled my forehead off the wood and turned, seeing Mark standing at the mouth of the locker room.

"Yeah, I just have to shower, and I'll—"

"No need to shower," Mark said, adjusting the sides of his suit jacket. "Just get dressed and come into my office when you can."

I held the back of my neck, the sweat soaking my fingers. "You got it." I turned toward Landon once Mark was gone. "No shower? That man doesn't know what he's asking for."

Landon chuckled. "He must not know what hockey gloves smell like after a few wears."

"How would he? The dude's probably never even skated."

I unhooked my shoulder pads and stripped off the layers of equipment until I was down to my spandex shorts and grays. I took those off, too, using a towel to dry myself as best as I could.

"Is this your first meeting with him?" Landon asked.

I grabbed a clean set of grays—both shirt and shorts—from

my locker and put them on. "Second. The first lasted about two hours, I think. We went over everything."

"You're the captain. I'm sure he had a lot to say to you."

I tossed my wet towel at him. "And the things I couldn't say to him ..."

He laughed. "No shit." He threw the towel back and flipped me off.

I set it over my head, rubbing my hair. "You know, it's really easy to talk to the guy, and I like him—that's part of the problem."

"What's the other part?"

"I can't stop thinking about all the dirty things I want to do to his daughter."

He put his hand over one eye and shook his head. "Sir, that's a major fucking problem."

I put on a pair of slides and made my way out of the locker room to the elevator that would take me to the executive-level floor. Once the doors opened, I walked in, pressing the top button. As the doors were closing, with only a few inches to spare, a hand squeezed into the opening, causing them to reopen.

I recognized the painted nails at the ends of those fingers.

Fuck.

"Sorry, I ..." Jolie's voice trailed off once she saw that it was me. And instead of a smile as she stepped in, I got a smirk. "Hello, Beck."

"Jolene ..."

The doors shut, and we were alone.

She held a tablet against her chest, standing on the opposite side of me, her body halfway facing the door and me. "We haven't had our meeting yet."

Since I gave no fucks, I let my gaze slowly dip down her body. Today's outfit was electric blue, much brighter than the navy of our team colors. The pants hugged her delicious thighs, and the jacket hung open to show a tight shirt that was tucked in—one mostly covered by the tablet—and based on her height, I knew she had on heels.

"You haven't asked for one." I gradually locked eyes with her.

She moved a piece of hair behind her ear—an ear I fucking loved to kiss. "This is me officially asking."

"Yeah?" I lifted the bottom of my T-shirt to scratch the top of my abs. Jolie noticed. And when her stare returned to mine, I said, "When do you want me?"

She let out a layered laugh, filled with breaths. "How about in twenty minutes? I have to meet with Kirk first, and then I can squeeze you in right after." Her gaze fell again, this time going as low as my feet before making its way back up. "Unless you're busy?"

"I'm meeting with your father." I stroked my thumb over my bottom lip. "I can come to you after, although I'd prefer to take a shower first."

Her eyes narrowed. "Why?"

I chuckled, setting a hand on my damp hair. "So I smell better."

"I don't care about that, Beck. I won't be close enough to know whether you smell like a shower or a goat."

I gently banged the back of my head against the wall behind me. "That's too bad ..." I licked the lip I'd been rubbing, wishing it tasted like her pussy. "I was hoping that's why you were having me come in."

"To get close to me?"

"To let me fuck you on top of your desk."

She pointed at me. "You need to behave. Remember the talk we had at your house? Professionalism is our motto now."

The talk.

While I'd been kneeling on the rug in front of her. And just as I was about to tell her that I wasn't giving up, that I was going to do everything in my power to have her, she had jumped off the back of my couch and left my house.

I adjusted myself in my shorts, the sight of her making me so fucking hard. "I'd be professional about it. I'd even let you keep your suit on." I smiled. "The jacket anyway. Not the pants. Those I'd rip right off you."

"I can't with you."

I checked the monitor to see what floor we were approaching. "Relax, Jolene. I'm just messing with you. I know you don't want my mouth on your pussy again."

The doors opened, and she stepped toward them, looking at me over her shoulder as she said, "You should never tell a woman to relax."

I chuckled while she parted to the left, and I lingered outside the elevator for a few seconds, watching her ass and the way those pants were snug around each cheek. Shaking my fucking head, I turned and walked toward her father's office.

I gave the door a few knocks, and when I heard, "Come in," I opened it.

"Beck"—he waved me in—"shut the door and take a seat."

I did as he'd instructed, choosing the chair closest to the door.

Mark rolled the pad of his thumb over the top of his silver pen—the metal the same color as his tie. Although it wasn't necessary, considering the way all the players and coaches dressed, Mark was always in a suit. The colors varied, as did the ties. I was impressed with his sense of style and wondered how much influence his daughter had on it since her attire was perfect.

"I wanted to do a quick follow-up regarding our last meeting. You spoke about the travel schedule, and when there's more than one night in between games, you said your preference is having downtime in the city you just finished playing in versus immediately flying out to the next stop."

I nodded.

The end of his pen briefly went into his mouth before he set it on his desk. "You mentioned the previous owner only allowed you to do that a handful of times, and it's something you would like to implement permanently."

Ironically, the first time the previous owner had allowed it was when I had the three-night stand with Mark's daughter.

I cleared my throat, trying to keep my focus on him and not the hard-on that was finally starting to die down. "I would like that, yes."

"I discussed the idea with our pilots and staff—the ones who will be traveling with the team, like Jolene—and they're in agreement. So, effective immediately, we're going to make the switch. The only time that won't apply is if we run into a situation with weather."

"Nice." I crossed my legs, holding on to the armrests. "I appreciate you taking my idea into consideration."

"I've told you from the start, I want to make your lives easier and comfortable. The most successful teams are those where every individual feels valued and heard." He leaned forward, his forearms resting on the desk. "That brings me to the next topic. As of now, I'm in LA full-time, overseeing the transition, assessing staff, and making sure the right channels are in place so this franchise operates effectively and efficiently." He smiled. "But I'm a Bostonian, Beck. My main office is there, and my city is calling to me." He gave me a nod. "So is my wife."

I chuckled. "I understand."

"When you fellas hit the road for your first stretch of away games, my plan is to return to the East Coast. I'll be back and forth, I'm not gone forever." He lifted a puck off his desk and rolled it between his fingers. "While I'm away, I need someone besides the staff to be my eyes and ears. Someone who isn't afraid to give it to me straight and tell me what's happening or what's needed." He huffed. "I don't always get that kind of honesty from people who are on my payroll. More times than not, I hear everything is perfect when I know it's not. Now, Jolene, she's different. I can count on her candor, but Jolene only sees one side of the coin. I need both sides covered."

I crossed my arms over my chest. "You're asking me to be that person ..."

"As the captain of this team, yes, I want you to be that person. I want to be able to trust you. And I need to know that you're willing to come to me, given whatever the circumstance is."

This situation was getting more fucked by the second.

I would have gotten his daughter naked in that goddamn elevator. I would have hit the Stop button, causing it to halt mid-floor. And I would have fucked her against one of the walls, coming inside that tight little pussy.

And now Mark wanted me as an insider? Someone he could trust?

"I can do that." I nodded to emphasize my point.

"Good." He leaned back in his chair. "I won't keep you any longer. I'm sure you're ready to get home."

I thanked him and stood.

As I was heading for the door, he said, "The first stopover is going to be in Vegas. You're there for two nights. I'm counting on you to make sure things don't get too rowdy."

"My family and I own a few restaurants there. Some superb meals and relaxation—that's what I'll be focused on. And that's what I'll encourage the team to focus on."

"Excellent."

As I approached the door, I paused and said, "Out of curiosity, what happens when you get back to Boston? Are you going to give up those season tickets?"

He stared at me blankly for several moments, and then he leaned even further onto his desk. "Are you telling me you have a buyer?"

"Nah, nothing like that. But you've got to be feeling a bit torn between the team you grew up rooting for and the team you now own."

"Ah, yes." He shifted his gaze to the puck in his hand. "If I'm being honest, it's going to be challenging to attend those games without my daughter. She must have told you it's something we've done together since she was a little one?"

Fuck.

Had Jolie mentioned that during her speech to the team? I couldn't remember the details; my head had been all over the place at the time.

But he knew that she was meeting with us individually, so I figured it was safe to say, "Jolie spoke really highly about the games she went to with you."

A smile grew across Mark's face. "I bet she did."

I gave him a nod and closed his door behind me, and as I was walking to Jolie's office, Kirk, one of my defensemen, was just coming out of it.

The motherfucker's grin was far too large for my liking.

And I knew—I fucking knew—it had something to do with her.

My patience was gone.

I slowed as I got closer to him. "What the hell are you smiling about?"

"Jolene." His approval came out in a hum. "I just spent the last fifteen minutes mentally stripping off the blue suit she's wearing, and I couldn't stop envisioning myself fucking her on her desk." He whistled. "Jesus, Beck, someone needs to get in her pants and get a sample so we know what she tastes like."

I was fucking done. I'd had it.

My fingers clenched. My jaw immediately tightened.

"Hopefully, you have better luck than me—"

"Dude, fucking stop." My voice wasn't as loud as I wanted it to be, but my tone was sharp. "I'm trying to go to a goddamn meeting. I don't want to walk into a fucking room where you've just been mentally beating off and sit in a chair that's wet from your ass sweat."

He was lucky I wasn't slamming him against the wall and cutting off his air so he couldn't say another word.

He halted directly in front of me. "What the hell has gotten into you?"

"Motherfucker," I groaned. "Get your dick out of your hand and focus on some fucking hockey."

I continued past him and pounded my fist on Jolie's door, waiting for her to tell me to come in before I walked inside. Once I shut the door, I put my back up against it.

I'd been in this office plenty of times, but not since Jolie had taken it over.

It wasn't the pillows and plants and girlie shit that caught my attention.

It was the three framed posters on the wall. One of the entire team. One of Landon during the final game of last season.

And one of me, holding the Stanley Cup in the air over my head.

"Beck ..." She studied my face with concern etched across hers. "I can't tell if you're about to strangle someone or tear these clothes off my body."

The anger instantly started to dissolve. "If I told you it was the latter ... would you stop me?"

TWENTY-FOUR

Jolie

"Beck ... I can't tell if you're about to strangle someone or ..."

Angry, worked up, and feral. That was the only way I could describe Beck as he burst into my office, huffing and puffing by the door.

Something had irritated that man.

Or someone.

Or maybe I was reading him all wrong, and it wasn't anger on his face. The emotion I was seeing could be the result of our brief run-in in the elevator and the man was on the verge of stripping off my clothes. Just in case I was right, I moved my chair out from under my desk and wheeled toward the wall a bit. I knew that wasn't creating any real distance between us, but I also knew that, within a few steps, he'd be able to reach me ... "or tear these clothes off my body."

When his expression changed to pure, unfiltered lust, his

lips stretching in the most seductive smile, I knew my first assumption had been correct.

"If I told you it was the latter ... would you stop me?"

"Yes." I pointed at one of the chairs on the other side of my desk. "Now sit."

"Giving me orders," he groaned, but he still took a seat.

When he did, his scent drifted over to me. I'd think it would be salty from the glaze of practice that was slick on his skin. And there was a tad bit of that—a saltiness that came from overworked, strained muscles, like during the hours we'd had sex, a scent that was so utterly sexy. But then there was the spiciness of his signature smell, and that was far more dominant than anything else.

I slid my chair back to its original position. "Do you want to talk about it?"

"Talk about what?"

"About what's got you so hot and bothered?"

"Hot—I just got out of practice, and I desperately need a shower." He glanced down and pulled the T-shirt away from his chest, the sweat seeping through the thin fabric. The best part about grays was that the material was clingy, and even without the sweat, it stuck to his chest, showing the outline of his muscles and the broadness of his shoulders. "Bothered—I don't like to be denied."

"You were bothered before I denied you. Try again."

"Fuck, when did you go from fun girl to this professional with *all* the confidence?"

"When? Come on, Beck. We both know I'm no longer that girl you took back to your hotel room in Boston. She had to grow up at some point."

He released his shirt and put his hand on the edge of my desk. "You know what I don't like? You won't let me touch this version of you."

"By the way you look right now, I highly doubt that would change your mood."

"Believe me, it would change everything." He gave me that achingly beautiful smile. "Let me touch it, Jolie."

"Touch what?"

"Your pussy."

"Beck!" I slapped my hand on my armrest, and as soon as I did, I jolted from the feeling—not the stinging of the slap, but the wetness between my legs. "I told you! Professionalism! Don't make me kick you out of my office."

He held the side of his face, and as he looked at me, it appeared like he was taking all of me in. "All right. What do you want to talk to me about, *boss*?"

"Our opening home game." I placed a sheet of paper in front of him. "This is your pregame schedule. I need you prompt"—I positioned my finger next to the top line—"for this" —I moved it down to the second line—"and for this. As the captain, the media is going to be focused on you." I pulled my hand back. "How good are you at being on time?"

"Have you seen me late for practice?"

"I wouldn't know."

He laughed. "You wouldn't know? You've been watching the first twenty minutes of our practice every day."

"I'm not looking for you on the ice. I'm—"

"I think we both know you're looking for me."

My eyelids tightened, and I drew my arms in against my chest and folded them together. "One, you're unbelievable."

"You've told me that multiple times. Normally, it's in reference to my tongue, which I think you're probably referring to again right now."

My head fell back.

He was never going to stop.

"And two"—I let my chin drop so I could look at him—"I

need you to take this seriously. I need you to be on time. We're going all out on marketing, and I'm counting on you in major ways. Please don't let me down."

"I would never."

He glanced at the poster of himself on my wall—something I hesitated framing and putting up, but the picture was just too perfect, and in some ways, it was my vision board for this season. It would be incredible to win the Stanley Cup the first year my father owned the team.

"What else can I do for you, Jolie?"

"You can stop calling me that—" My voice cut off when there was a knock at the door. I sucked in a deep breath. "Come in."

The door opened, and Ginger popped her head through the crack, smiling and singing, "*Hiii*." Her eyes widened when she realized I wasn't alone. "Oops. I'll come back. I'm so sorry to bother you guys."

"Don't be silly." I waved her over. "Beck and I were just discussing his responsibility for our opening game." I smiled at Beck. Not like the woman who had seen him naked and knew all the different ways he could make me moan. I smiled at him like I was his boss. Because I was. "But our meeting is over."

"You're done with me already? It feels like we were just getting started." Beck chuckled as he stood. "Ginger, I'd give you a hug, but I'm all sweaty from practice."

Because I knew my best friend better than anyone, I could tell she was positively dying on the inside.

"I love that we're on a hugging basis now." She smiled at him.

"Well, we have something in common."

"We do?" Ginger asked him.

He nodded toward me. "We both have strong feelings for

her." He patted Ginger on the shoulder, and he let himself out of my office.

Even after he was gone, I continued staring at the closed door.

"I'm dying." Ginger plopped down where Beck had been sitting. "Like *dyiiing*."

I finally looked at my best friend, and I collapsed on top of my desk, holding both sides of my head. "Do not let me cave to that man. Whatever you do."

"Jolie—"

"I'm not kidding, Ginger. Work-wise, it would be catastrophic."

"And personally?"

I let out a long breath. "It would be the best thing that's ever happened to me."

TWENTY-FIVE

Beck

Practice wasn't for another few hours, which meant I had plenty of time to close my eyes and get more sleep. But for some reason, my eyes wouldn't shut. I was fully awake, and sleep was the furthest thing from my mind as I faced the opposite side of the bed, staring at the empty spot.

The place where Jolie should be lying.

It didn't matter if she was in front of me or only in my fucking head; the thought of her, like the sight of her, made my dick throb.

It made me painfully hard.

One of the images I couldn't get out of my head was when I had been in her office a few days ago and I was teasing her with my words, knowing every one I spoke was working her up even more.

When I begged to touch her pussy and she acted as though she didn't want it.

When we both knew she did.

She probably didn't even realize that her jacket had fallen open, the shirt underneath that was tight against her body showing her nipples—and they were as hard as my dick was right now.

She wanted me to lick them.

She wanted me to bite them.

She wanted me to pull them with my teeth.

And while my mouth was on her body, she wanted me to touch her cunt.

She'd wanted me to slide down her stomach and stop at the top of her clit, massaging that tender spot with my tongue. And as I got that little bead hard and wanting and desperate to come, my finger would slip inside, arching up, the end of it grazing her G-spot.

Fuck me.

I needed her.

Since I slept naked, I rolled onto my back, moving the covers off me, the cold air in my room doing nothing to tame my cock; all it did was make me crave her mouth even more. I stretched my fingers around my dick, the instant friction causing me to moan, "Fuck."

The tightness of my palm sent the top of my head into the pillow behind me. Within a few strokes, my toes were bending toward the end of the mattress.

I saw Jolie behind my closed eyelids. The outline of that gorgeous body. The way her hips briefly jutted out, rounding to her ass, and how those cheeks cinched up into the most perfect-shaped heart.

I released my dick just long enough to spit on my hand, and I resumed the same movement—going from base to tip, rounding across my crown, and down the other side, a constant U formation.

Fuck, it felt good.

But her mouth would feel so much better.

So would her ass as I glided between her cheeks, teasing that forbidden hole, getting even the smallest taste of it, before plunging into her pussy.

I wanted that tightness.

I wanted to get soaked in her wetness.

My heels pushed into the mattress, my body swaying to the rhythm of my hand. The harder I stroked, the faster I pumped, the deeper I moaned, "Jolie."

I saw her.

I fucking felt her.

Hell, I could even smell her.

It was that combination that had me thrusting my fist over my cock as quickly as I could go, my fingers squeezing, trying to mimic her cunt. That was what sent me straight to the edge, forcing the cum toward my tip.

But what really brought me there was her.

The sound of her begging in my head. The sound of her pleading for more. The sound of her desperate to be fed my cum.

She was taking it. Every fucking inch.

Sucking it.

Urging it out of me.

Right at that moment, when the intensity was moving through me, the little fucking tingles that started in my balls and burst through my shaft, peaking, I shouted, "Fuck yes."

And behind my eyelids, Jolie's eyes locked with mine.

There was something so perfect about a woman holding your gaze when you filled her with your cum. It was that eye contact, the way you weren't just giving her something you wanted, but she was taking something she had asked for that was so fucking sexy.

And Jolie always asked for it.

I didn't block the stream as it shot from my tip. I didn't try to catch it.

I just slid my palm up and down my dick, twisting out the cum, letting it hit my stomach, reaching as high as my chest.

Each load that landed, I moaned, "Jolie," as though she were the one milking it out of me. And I didn't stop until the very last drop was drained. "*Mmm.*"

My hand gently released my cock, my feet went straight, my arm reached back to grip the headboard, and I pulled myself up, glancing down my body to see the aftermath. There were drops of white everywhere, some creating small puddles as they rolled into the valleys between my abs.

I needed a shower.

I released the headboard and lay flat, waiting for the satiated feeling to take over, the calmness that normally came after I got off.

But it wasn't there.

There was no fullness and no quietness.

It didn't matter how much cum I beat out; unless Jolie was the one doing it, I was never going to be satisfied.

"I'm guessing you're on your way to practice," my sister said as I answered her call.

I turned down the volume of the speakers—a volume that had been perfect for music, but far too loud for Eden's voice.

"What, are you tracking me?"

"Maybe." She laughed. "But, no, I'm not."

"What's up?"

"I'm just checking on you."

Of course she was.

I gripped the steering wheel and turned at the light, shaking my fucking head.

Through text, I'd filled my family in on the Jameson bomb. Not a single one of them could believe that Jolie and her father were the new owners of the Whales. They hit me with a slew of questions, but the one that was asked more than once was what would happen to us—and if there would be an us. I told them about the conversation Jolie and I had at my house, and their questions had seemed to die down a little.

But I knew it was only a matter of time before they started back up.

"Were you delegated to be the one to call and ask about Jolie?" When she didn't say anything, I added, "I'm sure you're all wondering how it's going. I haven't said much in the family text thread."

"You haven't said anything."

"Because there's shit to say." I sighed. "I haven't brought her over to the dark side yet."

"Do you think you can?"

I let out another long breath. "I sure as hell hope so. Every day feels like this endless fucking tease." Two cars ahead of me was a black Wrangler with chrome running boards, and I chuckled to myself. I couldn't escape her. "I get why she would have reservations, and it would be complicated in the beginning—the team would eventually find out, her dad might have issues with us being together. I'm not sure. But, Eden, I don't know how much longer I can take this."

"Is her being there affecting the way you're playing?"

She was the only one of my siblings I'd told about the Boston game and how badly I'd played and how I'd let it all get in my head.

"Not yet," I told her. "But it'll be interesting to see what happens when we start traveling." I slowed down for the light.

"What's that going to look like?"

"Dude, fuck if I know. Torture? Yeah, I'm going with torture."

"Remind me, do the coaches and staff stay in the same hotel as the players?"

I was getting restless just thinking about it. "Same hotel. My luck, she'll be on the same floor as me."

"Your luck, she'll be in the room next door."

"Don't put that out into the universe. I won't sleep a goddamn second if I know she's on the other side of my wall."

"Knowing you and how you work, I give it a few weeks. Maybe less, assuming she's feeling the same way as you. You can only be strong for so long before the temptation takes over, and you two being around each other that much, I think it's going to be impossible for her to resist you. Unless she has no feelings—then that's a completely different situation."

"She has feelings."

I was fucking sure of that.

At least ones that were physical. But if she was worried about the way her father would react and the future of her job and if the team was going to respect her, that could certainly affect her emotionally.

And it could put a giant roadblock between us—bigger than the professionalism motto that she'd been chirping about at my house.

Would I ever get her to move past professionalism and officially get her to be mine?

Did she even want that?

"I'm sure she does have feelings," Eden said, tearing me out of my thoughts. "But still ... Beck ..."

"What?"

"It's nice to see this side of you. I wasn't sure I'd ever see it.

You, like all the others in this family—aside from Hart—have been so anti-relationship and—"

"Wait. Are you really talking to me about being anti-relationship? When I don't think you'll ever date?"

She turned quiet.

I wasn't surprised.

When it came to this topic, Eden could dish it out, but she couldn't take it.

And I understood why, but I wasn't making digs at her; I was simply stating the obvious.

Because I knew she wasn't going to say anything, I added, "You know, there are moments when I agree with you, and I think it's just a matter of time. And then there are moments when I think she might not choose me." My thumb was tapping the steering wheel as the honesty poured right out of me.

"And if she doesn't choose you?"

The cars in front of me had either changed lanes or turned, which put me directly behind Jolie. I could see the outline of her hair and shoulders through her back windshield.

"I don't know ..."

"If she doesn't, being around her every day during the season would be tough."

Tough?

No.

It would be excruciating.

And I didn't know if I could do it ...

"Don't fucking remind me," I barked.

"Walker's calling. I'm going to merge us together instead of telling him I'll call him back. One sec." There were a few moments of silence before Eden said, "Walker, hi."

"Walker, my man," I voiced.

"What the fuck is happening?" Walker said. "I called Eden and got you too?"

"I was already on the phone with Beck, so I decided to stick us all together," Eden explained.

"While I have you, Beck, your season opener is next week," Walker said. "The whole family will be at the game. We need to talk about what we're going to do after. Should we celebrate at Musik? Or go somewhere else?"

When Walker said all, he meant my siblings.

But that didn't mean all of them would go out after.

"Musik is easy," I told him. "We'll get the privacy we need. We can get Charred to deliver whatever we want food-wise. And we can reserve the whole VIP area if we need to, given that I'll be inviting the entire team and staff." I paused. "Eden, you're going to come too, aren't you?"

She quickly replied, "To the game, yes. Out, no."

I expected her answer, but I still wanted to ask.

"Give me an estimated number of people who will be going to Musik," Eden said. "I'll make sure the rest is taken care of."

"I'll talk to the team today at practice." I pulled into the private lot directly behind Jolie. "Speaking of which, I just arrived, so I've got to go."

"Get me that number, Beck."

I groaned, "I'm on it," and I disconnected the call.

I pulled into the security gate, showed the guard my credentials, and headed toward the back side of the covered lot, closest to the elevator. Practice didn't start for another thirty minutes, so there were plenty of spots available.

It was no coincidence that I chose one close to where Jolie had parked. She was in the row directly in front of me, and she was standing outside her back seat, reaching in to grab something, wearing a long dress that wasn't nearly tight enough. She still looked achingly beautiful in green.

I got out, locked my car, and walked across the row toward hers. I was about halfway there when I saw she was struggling with whatever she was trying to take out of her back seat.

"Let me help." Those words were my warning before I appeared at her side, moving right in, lifting the box off the seat and hauling it out.

"You ... didn't have to do that."

"But I did."

Her slow speech, I assumed, was because she had just realized how close we were standing. The box was tall and wide, like a piece of artwork, and it was the only thing between us. Which meant several inches of cardboard were all that separated us.

That also meant I was getting blasted by her scent, my vision overwhelmed with the sight of her face, my imagination exploding from everything I wanted to do to those goddamn lips.

Why is she so fucking beautiful?

The silence was building between us. Her stare was moving from my eyes to my lips, and with each dip, she seemed to breathe a little harder, her chest rising faster.

What are you thinking about, Jolie?

"Beck ..."

"Yes."

She rubbed her lips together and glanced away. "Why does it seem like every time I blink, you're here—in some way or another?" Her voice was slightly above a whisper, but not by much.

I chuckled. "Trust me, I feel the same." A memory of this morning and that raging fucking hard-on was haunting me. "What is this? Another poster of me?" My teeth skimmed my bottom lip, and I nodded toward the box. "I'm just taking up all your walls, aren't I?"

She stared at me silently for a few seconds. "No, I—"

"I was joking." I smiled.

She nodded. "Of course you were."

"Come on. I'll carry this to your office. That's where it's going, isn't it?"

"Yes, but you don't have to—"

"I know I don't have to."

I started walking and heard the sound of her Jeep lock, and she rushed to catch up to me.

"So, funny story," she began as she reached my side. "Ginger and I ended up at Toro last night for dinner. Beck, I've got to say, it was amazing. We couldn't stop raving over everything we ate."

Our seafood and raw bar was one of our newest concepts, and it had exploded in LA, becoming one of the most popular restaurants here.

"And you didn't tell me you were going ..." I eyed her down, those red locks softening me. "I'm disappointed in you."

She smiled. "It was girls' night."

"I wouldn't have come." I laughed. "I would have sent over a round of drinks or my favorite dish."

"Next time."

We reached the elevator, and the doors opened.

I nodded at the entrance. "After you."

She stepped in and hit the button for the executive-level floor.

I stood against the back wall, holding the box against the front of me. "Listen, since becoming the captain, I host a little get-together—or whatever you want to call it—every year after the season opener. It's going to be at Musik, and most of the team will be there, I'm sure. The coaches will be invited and your dad too. You should come if you're free. Bring Ginger if you want."

Her arms were folded around her stomach, and they

seemed to tighten once my question lingered. "I'll ask her, but I'm sure she'll want to go. Thanks for the invite."

A reply that told me Jolie was going regardless.

Interesting.

The elevator opened, and she got off first, making her way down the corridor that had a direct view of the rink. The ice had just been cleaned and smoothed out by the Zamboni, and only a few lights were on, the stands, monitors, and scoreboards completely dark.

"I love seeing the arena like this."

She looked at me over her shoulder. "Yeah? Why?"

"I like the quiet before the storm."

"You are the storm, Beck Weston."

I laughed and followed her into her office. "Where do you want this?" I set it directly where she pointed and turned around to face her. "Do you need help hanging it?"

She lifted her bag off her shoulder. "No. I'm going to bribe the maintenance department to do it. Meaning I'm buying someone lunch if they say yes."

"Jolie, if you have a hammer and a nail, I can do it for you right now."

"You need to go stretch and get ready for practice. You've already done more than enough." She smiled again, this one smaller than before. "But thank you." She had a closet in her room, and she opened the door to put her bag inside.

I had to pass the closet on my way out. But instead of leaving, I stopped directly behind it. The placement put me only a pace away from her.

Less than a foot or so from her body.

A closeness I fucking needed.

And even though her scent was all I could smell and I'd gotten a little of the nearness I'd been craving in the parking lot, it wasn't enough.

I needed more.

She must not have realized my new position because when she turned around, she looked startled. Even after she calmed, she was still drawing in long breaths.

My fingers clenched at my sides. "I didn't mean to scare you."

"What did you mean to do, then?"

I touched her waist. I couldn't help myself. "I want to ..." I was scanning her eyes, trying to read them. My other hand went to her hip, and I was so tempted to pull her against me.

She just felt so fucking good.

"Beck ..."

I waited for her to push me away; it didn't happen. I waited for her to tell me to back up; that didn't happen either.

My arm lifted, my palm pressing against the wall above her head. The movement caged her in, but there was plenty of space for her to get out if she wanted to.

She clearly didn't.

"I want to kiss you so fucking bad." The hand that was on her waist wrapped around the back of her head, getting lost in her wild web of red hair. "Tell me you don't want me to."

I could feel her exhales, especially as my face got closer to hers. "I don't want you to."

Her eyes were saying something different.

"I don't believe you."

She turned silent and still didn't wiggle her way out of my hold. "Do you have any idea what this is like for me? How hard this is? My father is the owner of this team, Beck."

"And?"

"And—" Her voice cut off when her phone began to ring. She set her hands on my chest, holding them there, tapping my pecs, as though she was rethinking her decision or she was having second thoughts, and then she ducked under my arm and went to her desk.

"This is Jolene," she said as she answered, her eyes on me.

The moment was over.

Her attention ... lost.

Whenever she hung up, if I stuck around for that long, I wouldn't be able to get her back to that place.

So, I left.

JOLIE

I need some shots of you working out, so after today's workout, do you mind sticking around, and the video team will snap some footage?

ME

It's leg day. That means I'll be extra sweaty. Do you want me to shower first?

JOLIE

Please don't.

Remember the meme of you stretching that went viral? When they see your sweat, this will have the same result.

ME

You're using my sweat to sell our team ...

JOLIE

Don't be mad at it. Our audience is going to die when they see the footage.

I wondered if she was going to die when she watched me work out. Or maybe the better question was ... could I make her die?

I smiled at the thought and slipped my phone back into my pocket.

I was on the floor of the gym when Jolie walked in, the sound of her heels a dead giveaway. I was just finishing a round of abs, and as promised, there wasn't a dry spot on my body; the last set of crunches, balancing a thirty-pound kettlebell in the air, was only adding to it.

"I'll be done in a second," I grunted.

"No need to rush."

I sensed her by the incline benches, directly next to me, and a quick glance told me I was right. "Admiring the view?"

She laughed. "Asshole."

"Well, are you?"

"I'm checking to see where the best lighting is. You happen to be in my direct line of sight."

"Sure you are." I sat up and placed the kettlebell on the rubber flooring, noticing that Jolie didn't move, nor did she look away. "I told you I was going to be sweaty." There was a towel around my neck. I used it to wipe my forehead, and I ran it over my hair, flattening the strands when I was done. "Keep staring at me like that, and I'm going to think you want to lick this sweat off me."

Her eyes widened. "What if someone heard you say that?"

"If there was someone in here other than us, I wouldn't have said it. But if there was someone in here, I suggest you stop looking at me that way."

"I'm not looking at you any differently than I normally do." She shifted her weight.

"Jolie, the expression you have right now, it's the same one when my face is between your legs and my tongue is on its way to your pussy. Any idiot could guess what that look means."

"Oh my God."

"Did I make you wet?"

Her head dropped. "I simply can't with you."

Pleased, I stood and brought the kettlebell back to its home, a spot not far from where she was. "Where's the film crew?"

"They'll be here at any second."

"Where do you want me?"

She pointed to the other side of the gym, toward the rack of free weights. "I think the lighting is best over there."

I stretched my arms from one side to the other and then over my head. "What do you want me to do?"

"Lift, like you normally would." She wasn't smiling, but her eyes were.

"Any specific body part?"

Her lips finally moved into a grin. "Whichever one you think will have the biggest effect."

"You mean whichever exercise will make the women lose it and die …"

"*Mmhmm.*"

I held my hips. "When you were filming my other teammates, did you say these kinds of things to them?"

"Heck no. I just have a … different relationship with you."

"We have a relationship now?" She went to say something, and I cut her off with, "I see we're still rolling with the professionalism."

She crossed her arms. "Are you kidding me? First, you try to kiss me in my office. Now you're talking about licking me. And I'm the one who's not rolling with the professionalism?"

"I also see you're avoiding my question."

Her head fell back.

And before she could answer, the door opened, and the two-person film crew walked in.

When her eyes locked with mine, I gave her my cockiest smile, and I made my way over to the free weights. My legs were toast after today's workout. They were going to have to settle on arm exercises.

The film crew—a man and woman—came closer. The woman pointed the camera at me as I lifted the forty-pounders off the rack, and the man positioned a microphone not far from my face.

"We're not going to ask you any questions," the man said. "We just want to record your movements and catch any sound you make. We're ready whenever you are."

I didn't look at the camera.

My focus was on Jolie as I curled the weights. But after a few reps, my grays were really sticking to me, the sweat acting like fucking glue. So, I set the weights down and peeled off my T-shirt.

Now shirtless, knowing the weight and repetition would cause a pump through my muscles, making my veins pop and my biceps bulge and my pecs tighten, I looked fucking ripped for this shoot.

And Jolie noticed because there was an instant change in her expression.

A redness spread across her face; her lips parted, like she wanted to say something or she needed them open to breathe. Whatever the case was, she stayed silent. I was sure that was due to the fact that we weren't alone. And since she was standing behind the film crew and had nothing to hide, she didn't just watch me; she gawked.

Before I even finished a set, she was shaking her head and putting her back to me, walking to the other side of the gym.

Someone couldn't handle what she was seeing.

Someone was fucking dying from the view.

And someone was trying to maintain the utmost professionalism.

But I saw right through her.

TWENTY-SIX

Jolie

"**B**eck! *Gooo!*" I screamed through my cupped hands as I looked out onto the ice from our owner's box, one that we'd taken over when my father bought the team.

Of course, we weren't directly on the ice, so we couldn't see the players' faces or hear the shit talking between them, but from up here, we could see the game as a whole. Beck was charging toward Montreal's goalie, and when he couldn't get a clear shot, he passed the puck to the other wing, who then sent it right back to Beck. Beck was looking for an in—a few inches was all he needed for the puck to fit—and the man was an expert at finding one.

"Yes! Get it!"

Beck's arm reared back, telling me he'd found that in, which then caused the goalie to prepare to block. But at the very last second, Beck sent the puck to the right side of the ice, the other wing immediately slapping it into the net.

"Goal!" I shouted, jumping from my seat. "*Ahhh!*"

There were only five minutes left in the game, and we were now up by two. Of course, Montreal could pull their goalie, and with six men on the ice, the stakes would technically be in their favor to score. But our defensemen slayed at their job, and even outnumbered, I still didn't think Montreal would have a chance.

As Ginger's fingers squeezed mine, I looked at her and smiled. She knew just how I was feeling about this win. All the hard work my team and I had put in, and the season opener had been a success in so many ways. The media buildup had gone exactly the way I'd wanted; the video of Beck working out had been shared over four million times, and memes of him were owning the internet. The entire stadium was sold out, and the cost of resale tickets was breaking records. After the first period, I'd checked in with merchandising and food and beverage, and both sales were higher than some of the playoff games last season.

LA was the team to watch.

And as I glanced at my father next to me, the satisfaction on his face told me he was pleased with everything he'd seen this evening.

His arm slipped around my shoulders. "Now that was one hell of a goal."

"And an assist," I threw in.

"That assist, yes. He's impressive, isn't he?"

Whenever I discussed Beck with my father—a topic that came up constantly, given that he was our star player and the team's captain—I always proceeded with caution. I never wanted to sound like I spoke about him more than the other players, that I was favoring him for any reason, or that I was personally interested. I also didn't want to come across as if I wasn't giving him enough attention.

But I also knew I was overthinking it and being far too sensitive due to our past.

Because Beck should be focused on—and not because I'd slept with him or had feelings for him, but because he was the highest-paid athlete on the team, the top scorer, and one of the best, most sought-after players in the league.

"Dad, he's a legend. We're so lucky to have him on our team."

The arena was exploding; posters were held up in the air, flags were waved, cowbells were going off. Our spectators were yelling and applauding, their sounds getting even louder when the announcer came through the speakers to acknowledge the player who had scored the goal, the roars growing when Beck's name was called out for the assist.

If I glanced at Ginger, I knew she'd give me a look—a look that would have everything to do with Beck—and I was avoiding that as much as possible while my father's attention was still on me.

"We just need to keep him healthy," my father said. "Healthy and focused. We don't have time for injuries, and we certainly don't have time for distractions. As owners, we have a lot to prove this season."

"And we will." I nodded.

"With Beck's help."

I tried to read his expression, curious as to where he was going with this. "Dad, we're not losing Beck."

"I sure hope not."

I turned away to watch the face-off. "Are you going to Beck's get-together tonight at Musik?"

I knew my father had been invited; we'd discussed it earlier in the week when Beck's email went out to the staff.

"Your mother and I will be going home after the game."

Home was the condo he'd purchased not far from the arena

—a four-bedroom penthouse that suited his needs while he was in LA. But home, to him, would always be Beacon Hill—the townhouse I had grown up in, nestled within Boston's elite and in a historically significant part of the city.

I leaned forward to look at Mom, who sat on the other side of Dad. "You don't feel like going clubbing tonight?" I smiled.

"Pumpkin, I retired from clubbing the moment I found out I was pregnant with you." She laughed.

I gave her arm a squeeze. "Fair."

"I let Beck know during our meeting this morning," my father added.

I followed the puck, holding my breath until our defenseman shot it away, and said, "You guys have been meeting a lot."

"The season has officially started, Jolene. I'm putting some heavy responsibility on Beck's shoulders, and with that, there's much to discuss."

The more time my father spent with Beck, the more I tried to fight off his flirting. And the more I tried to fight off his flirting, the more I attempted to convince myself that we could never happen.

How could I consider a future with that man?

The captain of my dad's team?

But Beck was making that decision impossibly and painfully difficult.

And there were times I failed when I tried to be so strong.

"One of the things we've chatted about at great length is my return to Boston," my father voiced.

I gave him a quick glance. "Is your plan still to take off as soon as the team leaves for the Vegas game?"

"That's not changing"—his eyes hardened as he looked at me—"unless something comes up and prevents me from going."

I felt my brows rise. "Nothing like that is going to happen,

Dad. I promise. My team and I have everything under control. You have the perfect management in place. The players are one giant family and seem to get along great. What could possibly happen?"

"Any hiccup can send an organization spiraling. I've seen it occur far too many times. And in many cases, they aren't able to recover, and that's when I come in and buy the company." He brushed a hand over his freshly shaven cheek. "I won't have that happen to one of my businesses."

I was that hiccup.

I was what could cause that spiral.

I was what my dad didn't want to happen to the Whales.

I swallowed, the spit burning as it traveled down my throat. "It won't happen. You need to trust me."

Why had I said that?

And why were those words making me feel sick?

"I do. Implicitly."

He searched my eyes, and I felt the entire arena dissolve, the background morphing into a courtroom and I was suddenly delivering my testimony. I couldn't imagine what my face looked like, but I could feel my breathing, and that was far too labored.

"I want to ask you something."

I nodded. "Okay."

"Do you allow anyone on the team to call you Jolie?"

Where was this coming from?

Why would he even ask this?

Did he know something?

Was he testing me?

Was I reading too much into this, like I did with everything else?

I smiled because, surely, that would cover the anxiety I was riddled with. "No one on the team even knows my nickname." I never said it to anyone besides Beck. It wasn't part of my email or signature. It wasn't listed anywhere aside from my social media. "Unless someone looked me up on Instagram—but that account is set to private, and I highly doubt anyone would be searching for me." I paused, my heart pounding so hard that I felt nauseous. "Why do you ask?"

"Just wondering." He continued to stare at me, his gaze as unreadable as his expression. "You know ... I want you to always maintain a professional front, especially with the position you have."

"Of course."

The buzzer went off, signaling the end of the game.

The Whales had won.

I could feel Ginger celebrating next to me. I even heard my mom clapping.

But I didn't tear my eyes away from my father. I kept my grin wide, reinforcing that choosing me to be his head of marketing for his newest baby was the absolute right decision.

And no matter what, I wouldn't let him down.

He patted my shoulder. "You're doing a great job, Jolene. I don't tell you that enough."

TWENTY-SEVEN

Beck

I looked around the private VIP area of Musik, where most of my teammates, coaches, staff, and my family were all hanging out, and I raised my bourbon in the air. "To the winners!" An eruption of applause came from the room, and once everyone quieted, I added, "And to one hell of a season that's going to bring us straight to the playoffs and finals." I didn't mention the Cup—we were too superstitious to say that word out loud. But everything else was free rein. "And to the Jamesons ..." I was well aware of where Jolie was sitting—a spot on the couch, mid-room, nestled up next to Ginger. With a smile already on my face, I connected eyes with her. "I'm speaking for the whole team when I say you guys are doing a hell of a job and we're grateful to have you as owners."

Jolie gave me a grin and quickly turned toward the rest of the team, holding her glass high in the air. "To an incredible season, and may we end up on the very top." She laughed.

THE WILDEST ONE

In response, everyone hollered and clapped and cheered, "To the very top!"

I took a drink and turned toward Walker, who had moved in next to me. "Glad you came, buddy."

He clinked his glass against mine. "Fuck, that was a good game. You played well. And that assist? Shit, I thought you were going to take that goal all for yourself."

"I would have if I could, but the goalie was all over me, blocking me hard. I knew if I could fake him out, my right wing could get the puck in the net. Just like he did." The bourbon was going down easy, the burn a refreshing feel after the beating my muscles had taken tonight. Practice made me sore, and game play made me ache something fierce. "Overall, the game was a solid start to the season. We play Florida at home next, and they're going to be tougher than Montreal. Then we hit the road for ten days."

"Your first away game will be Vegas?"

I nodded. "And we'll be there for three nights."

"Three fucking nights in Sin City?" His head fell back as he laughed. "What the hell are you going to do with all that time off?" He waited for me to respond and then said, "You know, trouble is easily found in Vegas. And if I know you, you're bound to find some."

"Nah, man, I'm going to be good." I glanced toward Jolie. My backup goalie was sitting on the table in front of the two women, talking to them. Far too fucking close for my liking. "Pool time, lots of relaxation. I'm going to eat at Charred. And I'm going to sleep. I'm not going out."

His brows rose as he smiled. "Isn't *she* traveling with the team?"

The emphasis wasn't missed.

I nodded. "She'll be at every game, staying in our hotel, attending each team meal."

"Jesus."

"I know."

His green eyes moved in the direction of where Jolie was sitting. "Which one is she? Wait, she's the redhead, right?"

"You didn't meet her?"

Eden, Hart, and Colson had come into the locker room before the game, and I introduced them to Jolie, who was in there with her father. Walker didn't come until after the game started since Charred had some large parties tonight and it was hard for him to get away. I just assumed at some point, maybe in the locker room after our win, they'd been introduced.

"I know the others did," he said. "But we haven't crossed paths yet." He stayed looking at her. "You know, she might just be the trouble I was referring to."

"Tell me something I don't fucking know."

He put his hand on my shoulder. "Any breakthrough?"

I huffed, "No. I mean, nothing concrete. There's no question she wants to fuck me. You should see the way she looks at me."

His stare left mine for a moment, and when it returned, he said, "Oh, I'm seeing that right now."

I didn't glance at her since I didn't want her to know we were talking about her and continued, "But anything beyond that, there's been nothing. I have no idea where her head is at. Aside from thinking it's all a bad idea."

"She's right. It probably is."

I went to take a sip and stopped midair. "What would make you say that?"

"Can you honestly say to me that she's *the one*? If that's where *your* head is at, then it's the best idea you've ever come up with. If she's just going to be someone you're with for a little while and get bored with, then don't mess with that, brother. There's far too much overlap between your professional and personal life, and you don't need that kind of drama."

I finally took a drink. "You do know how long this has been going on for, don't you?"

"That doesn't answer my question."

"But it should."

I gazed toward the couch, and she was talking to my right wing, the one who had scored tonight's final goal. The way he was staring, the way he was so engaged—it was like she was a puck, and he was fucking mesmerized. I didn't like it. Not at all.

"When have I ever spoken to anyone for any length of time? When have I ever made the effort to reconnect with someone I hooked up with on the road? I invited her to Paris, Walker. And Africa—at least I attempted to. Have you ever known me to do that?"

"You've been able to have anyone you ever wanted. Except her. But what happens when you get her—saying you do? Will you still want her? Or will she become something you've conquered and you'll want to move on?"

"Fuck yes, I'll still want her."

"And how do you know that?" At some point, his hand had lifted off my shoulder, and his arm was now crossed over his chest, the other holding his drink near his collarbone. "And how are you so sure?"

"That's easy." I felt my lips drag into a smile.

"Yeah?"

She was now speaking to Ginger, the two of them whispering about something.

"I think about her as much as I think about hockey."

Walker let out a mouthful of air, slowly shaking his head back and forth. "Hockey's your one true love."

"And now it has competition."

His head went from shaking to nodding. "That's some deep shit right there."

"Does that answer all your questions?"

"Sure does."

Since the filming in the team's gym, the teasing between us had been amplified. We seemed to arrive at the arena at the same time every morning, and I had to endure the torture of sharing an elevator with her. Every time I met with her father, I was somehow passing her in the executive hallway. Whenever I left practice, she and her team were always needing something from me—an interview, a photo, an extra skate around the ice for the team's social media channels.

And every time, I wanted more—more of her attention, more of her eyes on me, more of her words—and I couldn't get any of it.

But I was going to change that right now.

Jolie was leaving the couch area and walking to the hallway that led to the restrooms.

I handed Walker my drink and gripped his shoulder, leaning in to whisper, "I've got something I need to do. I'll be back."

"It'd better be her."

"Do you think I'd give up my cocktail for just anyone?"

He laughed. "That's my man."

The ladies' restroom in the VIP area had two stalls, which meant there was a good chance Jolie wasn't in there alone. With the men's restroom directly next door, it didn't look suspicious for me to be headed there. But rather than going all the way down the hallway, I stopped halfway where the manager's office was located and hit the numbers on the pad to unlock the door.

I went inside, keeping the light off, and I held the door open just wide enough to see who was coming down the hallway. The sound of Jolie's heels was the first sign of her; the scent of her was the second. Once I made sure she was alone, that no one else had entered the hallway from either side, I waited until she was within reach, and I slipped my arm around her.

She gasped, "What the fuck?" as I pulled her into the office.

I immediately flicked on the light so she knew it was me.

"What in the hell?!" She banged her fist against my chest.

I laughed.

"It's not funny, Beck. You just scared the shit out of me. I swear, I just lost ten years of my life."

My hand went to the door, directly above her head, where she stood. "I didn't mean to scare you. I just need to be alone with you."

She scanned my eyes. "What are you doing?"

I had her right where I wanted her. And, fuck me, she looked gorgeous, wearing a tight black skirt that went all the way to her ankles and a shirt that ended above her waist, giving just the tiniest peek of her navel.

"In here, there's no phone that can ring and interrupt us. There's no camera crew that's about to walk in. We're alone, unlike most of the elevator rides we've recently taken together." My hand moved higher on the door, and I leaned toward her. "So, the only person who can stop this from happening is you."

She looked so small and petite against the entrance, her hair spread out like she was lying on my pillow. "Stop what from happening?"

"What I've been dreaming about doing for fucking weeks." My other hand went to her side, and my face dipped into her neck. I hesitated for just a second, listening to her breathe before I kissed the soft skin below her ear. "I fucking need you, Jolie—"

"I can't." Her hand went to my chest again. It didn't push—it was flat—but there was strength in her fingers.

"Can't?" I kissed lower, toward the base of her neck.

"Yes, can't. You ... have to stop."

I pulled my face out and looked at her, my hand dropping into the air. "You want me to ... stop?"

She said nothing.

"Jolie, what the fuck is going on? We've been at this game for weeks. You want me to flirt with you, and you flirt back. You never stop looking at me. I feel your eyes on me at practice, in the gym, anytime I'm around you—even tonight at this club. And suddenly, you don't want me?"

There was emotion in her eyes. She was fighting it. I could see it.

"It's my dad."

"He knows?"

Her head shook against the door. "No. But he said something to me while we were watching the game in our box."

"What the hell did he say?"

She rubbed her lips together, the whites of her eyes turning red. "He said, 'I want you to always maintain a professional front, especially with the position you have.'"

"And you think that applied to us?"

"I think that applies to everything, including us."

My fucking blood pressure was skyrocketing.

"Are you telling me your father is the only thing that's stopping you from being with me?" My hand, pressed against the wooden door, balled into a fist. "That if your father knew about us and he approved, you would be mine?"

"Yes."

The anger was wrapping its way around my fucking throat, and I turned around and went deeper into the office.

I couldn't believe this.

I couldn't fucking understand it.
I didn't care if—
"I want to be yours."
My feet halted at the sound of her words. My heart stopped throbbing.
I backtracked and faced her. "What?"
"I care about you, Beck. I think about you nonstop. God, I even dream about you." She held her chest, her fingers shaking. "The whole reason you brought me in here is because you know I'm positively wild about the wildest one." She gave me a soft smile. "But my entire life, I've wanted nothing more than to work for my father and make him proud. To one day take over his company." She banged her head against the door, and when she did it again, I realized it was on purpose. "How can I do this to him? How can I disappoint him this way?"
I gripped both sides of my head. "I can't believe what I'm hearing right now."
"This is the hardest thing I've ever done. The hardest thing I'll ever do."
"What is?"
Her eyes were completely filled, and the first tear dripped. I went to step closer so I could wipe it from her face, and she said, "Walking away from you."
Then the door opened, and she was gone.

TWENTY-EIGHT

Jolie

That smile. The slicked-back chestnut-brown hair. His beard, just starting to really thicken since it had been shaved at the start of the season. The most alluring hazel gaze. A body, professionally conditioned, capable of doing absolutely anything and everything to mine.

That was what I saw every time I closed my eyes.

I wasn't sleeping.

I wasn't focused on work the way I should be.

It was as though my doctor had written me a prescription: *Stare at Beck Weston during the day to entice you, to turn you on, to torment you into full misery mode, fantasize at night about what he can do to you, and live vicariously through those dreams.*

I was taking that prescription every day.

And every day, it was an internal battle to stay strong and not throw myself into his arms or reach for his hand or slam my lips against his.

But each day proved to be harder.

When the team had beaten Florida during the second home game, I'd gone into the locker room after with my father, and Beck was shirtless, celebrating with the guys. I wanted nothing more than to put my hands on his hot, sweaty, chiseled chest, wrap my legs around him, and have him carry me straight into the shower with him.

Instead, all I could do was admire. Tell him how well he had played, that the goal he'd scored was outstanding.

While deep down inside, I had secretly been losing it.

Each practice that followed, the same tension seared through me. The same needs pulsed while I looked at him. The same words, the ones that lived on the tip of my tongue, wanted to be admitted.

His weight training sessions were no different.

Neither were the run-ins in the parking lot.

And the elevator.

I swore, this man was making me suffer on purpose.

And now, on the plane to Vegas, I was so spun up on him; I was barely functioning. I'd taken a seat near the back with the rest of the staff, the players up front, giving me the perfect view of Beck. Every time he looked across the aisle to speak to a teammate, I got the sight of that delicious profile. And when he was turned straight ahead, I got the broadness of his shoulder and his wide neck, the way his shirt and suit jacket hugged it from the back.

I needed to stop staring.

I needed to concentrate on the screen of my laptop and get some work done.

I needed—

The vibration of my phone startled me out of my thoughts, and I glanced at my cell, which just happened to be resting in my palm.

DAD

Remind me again about the pink jerseys and what you want to do with them.

ME

It's Breast Cancer Awareness Month. I think we should donate our half of the 50/50 raffle toward breast cancer research. In addition, have the guys wear pink jerseys for a home game. They can sign them at the end of the game and auction them off to raise more money to donate.

DAD

Your team can handle the logistics?

ME

Of course. I wrote out a marketing plan in hopes that you'd say yes.

DAD

How quickly would you need to order the jerseys?

ME

Today. Tomorrow at the very latest.

DAD

Discuss this with Beck. Make sure he's on board. If it's a go, order them today.

ME

On it.

Once the plane landed, we would be checking into the hotel, and the guys would have a little time to rest before we had to head to the arena for the game. I didn't know if I would have time to chat with Beck beforehand.

I had to have the conversation with him now.

The anxiety started to trickle in as I slipped my phone into my bag. Taking a haggard breath, I unbuckled my seat belt and stood, making my way down the narrow aisle. When I reached his seat, I held the top of the cushion to steady myself even though there wasn't even the slightest bump in the air.

Since he didn't look at me—he was staring at his phone—I said, "Beck, can we talk for a second? I just need to run something by you."

As soon as his eyes began to take me in, it became even harder for me to breathe.

He popped out his white earbuds. "What's up?"

He hadn't heard me.

"Do you have a second to talk?" I repeated.

His stare didn't stay on my face. It gradually moved down my entire body—something he dared to do because I was blocking the aisle, so no one aside from me could see him.

"Okay. Talk to me."

I couldn't imagine this type of tension lasting all season.

I either needed amnesia or Beck needed to be traded to Antarctica.

"Do you want to come to the back of the plane to sit ... or ..."

"Why don't you join me right here?" He patted the empty seat beside him.

In order to get into the seat, I had to move past him in that tight, tiny walkway. With the way he was sitting, our knees would brush, and even the slightest movement of the plane would send me straight into his lap.

He had known exactly what he was doing when he asked me to sit.

Professionalism, my ass.

"I'll help you." He held out his hand.

I grabbed his fingers, an instant jolt of electricity going through me—to my chest, to my stomach, to that throbbing spot between my legs—and I hurried past him. I tried not to pay attention to the way it felt when the side of my leg grazed his or how his cologne was triggering memories of the way his skin had tasted when I licked it. But I was going so fast that I was moving awkwardly, and I flopped down in the seat, my landing anything but graceful.

"You all right?" He chuckled.

"Yeah ... yeah."

He crossed his legs. "What do you have for me?"

Me.

That was what I wanted to say anyway. Rather than admit the truth, knowing the heap of hell it would get me in, I gazed across the aisle, reminding myself that I was surrounded by ears.

"After we get back from this stint of away games, we're going to pick a home game, and our half of the raffle earnings will be donated to breast cancer research. For that game, I'd like to have custom pink jerseys made that you guys will wear and sign at the end. Those will be auctioned, and the proceeds will be donated too."

"And you're telling me this because you want my approval?"

The way he looked in a suit should be illegal.

The crispness of the white shirt with the dark gray jacket. How the edges of both bordered his face and neck. The way each accentuated his eyes.

Dear God.

I cleared my throat. "It would be a change to your uniforms. So, yes, I was told to run it by you."

"I would never say no to charity. I also think I look sexy as fuck in pink."

I laughed.

"You don't believe me? Just wait and see." He smiled.

I wished he wouldn't.

It was too beautiful.

He occupied the armrest between us and leaned in a little closer. "Who's going to be collecting the jerseys after we wear them?"

"Probably me. Why?"

"I know how you feel about my sweat."

He was unbelievable.

Before I could respond, he continued, "I wouldn't want to cross any lines by giving you more of that sweat ... you know, professionalism and all." His voice had been as soft as a whisper this entire time, and now it was even quieter.

"That would be so out of character for you." I rolled my eyes.

He stroked his lip with his thumb. "That's why I think it should be a job for your assistant—so when I strip off that jersey, you don't have to touch it or see what's underneath."

I wanted to scream, "You make nothing easy, do you?" but I said it in a hushed voice instead.

"Would it be better if I was this raging asshole who gave you every reason to hate me? That way, the decision, which you've already made, wouldn't be difficult for you?" He paused, his eyes narrowing. "Is that what you want from me, Jolie? Because I can be that person."

"No."

"Then this is the side of me you're getting."

I held my cheek. "But this doesn't make it easy on me either—"

"You can't have it both ways."

"Can't you at least respect me?"

His expression was like I'd slapped him. "And you think I don't?"

"I think you're just trying to make this harder on me."

He bent his arm on the armrest, making me think he was going to touch me, but he kept his elbow balanced and his hand in the air. "If you consider this hard, I'd hate to see your reaction if I was actually trying to make you regret your decision."

"You're not?"

His teeth went over his bottom lip, and he dragged them across it. "If I was trying, this hand"—he moved his fingers, pointing at me—"would be reaching under your dress right now, climbing until it reached your pussy, and I would finger you until you were coming in this seat. But I'm not. Because I respect you. Therefore, my hands are in my lap"—he moved them there—"like a good fucking boy."

I hate you.

And, damn it, I love you.

"Fuck me ..." Beck groaned.

I was holding the key card in front of the reader outside my suite, trying to open my door, when I heard Beck's voice. I glanced down the hallway, and he was walking toward me.

"What are you doing?"

"I'm going to my room."

The *fuck me* told me he was as unpleased as I was.

I drew in some air, my lungs suddenly screaming. "Don't even tell me ..."

He stopped at the door next to mine. "My sister fucking said this was going to happen."

I'd met his sister at the first home game, along with two of his brothers. Each of them was so beautiful in their own way, and even though the introductions were brief, I'd felt like I was getting handed another piece of the Beck puzzle.

A puzzle I could never complete.

"First off, I cannot believe you're going to be staying in the room next to mine." I didn't know whether I should throw up or buy extra batteries for the vibrator I'd packed since I had a feeling I was going to be using it a lot during this trip. "And second, what do you mean, Eden said this was going to happen?"

"We were talking about my travel." He waved the key in front of the reader and opened his door, pushing his suitcase inside before he leaned in the doorway and looked at me. "She thought it would be real funny if we ended up as neighbors." His stare dropped down my body, and I could feel every inch it traveled. "And somehow, we did."

Why was my chest aching from this news?

Why did I want to be a fly on the wall when I was the topic of conversation with his sister?

Why did any of this matter?

It shouldn't.

But it did.

"You talk to Eden about me?"

"Don't you talk to Ginger about me?"

He had me there.

"Beck, we're at this hotel for three nights." I swallowed. "THREE." How was I supposed to sleep? Breathe? Function? With him this close? "I'll ... change rooms. I'm going to go to the front desk and—"

"You can't. My assistant already tried to upgrade me into a larger suite. She was told by management that the entire hotel is sold out."

If there was air in my body, it was gone. "You're telling me I'm stuck in this room?"

"Come on. It won't be so bad. Besides, you're the one who doesn't want anything. So, where I sleep, whether it's on a different floor or on the other side of the wall as you, shouldn't affect you at all."

I snorted.

The sound, I assumed, made him smile.

"Sorry to torture you, baby." He went into his suite, and the door closed behind him.

GINGER

OMG, that game. You guys crushed Vegas!

ME

It was intense, wasn't it? I swear I held my breath the entire time.

GINGER

Beck was on fire. I mean, the man was angry out there. He was hitting that puck like he needed to get something out.

ME

That's because he is angry.

GINGER

At you?

ME

My decision. Our situation. How there's nothing but this scorching chemistry between us and we're on the verge of exploding from it.

GINGER

You know, it seems like he'll do anything to have you.

ME

It's bizarre to hear you say that—or type that, whatever.

GINGER

You do realize it though, don't you?

THE WILDEST ONE

ME

He's made it clear how much he wants me, which I honestly still can't believe. But I think I've made it clear that it can't happen.

I don't know, Ginger. This is so hard ...

GINGER

It has to be so tough to be on the road with him, seeing him so much in addition to thinking about him. It's like you don't get a break.

ME

I'm angry. Just as angry as him and for all the same reasons.

And we're only at our first stop, and our rooms are directly next to each other. I guess I shouldn't be surprised that happened.

But is the world trying to punish me?

Seriously, Ginger, did I piss someone off? Did I fuck up somehow?

GINGER

Do you want my honest answer?

ME

Please.

GINGER

The man you've been thinking about since our sophomore year in college is madly and wildly obsessed with you. BE WITH HIM. We'll figure out the consequences later.

I heard the sound of a door opening, and I sat up in bed to check my own. It was dead-bolted, so of course it couldn't be mine. And because I was in the last room in the hallway, that meant there was only one other it could be.

Beck's.

I got out of bed and moved to the wall, putting my ear against it, trying to listen to what he was doing on the other side. There was running water and the clearing of this throat and—

What the hell am I doing?

I crawled back into bed.

ME

I'm not even going to tell you what I just did. You're going to think I'm bananas—because I am.

GINGER

Tell meeeee.

ME

I heard Beck return to his room, and I put my ear to the wall to listen. Like it matters what he's doing. What is wrong with me? When did I become this person?

GINGER

I don't blame you for doing that. You're making sure he's not with another girl. And if he is, you go over there with a flamethrower and set that room on fucking fire.

ME

What? Why would you even say that? Why would you even put that thought into the universe?

GINGER

Does the thought bother you?

ME

It makes me feel ill. The kind of ill where my heart aches, and my hands shake, and my stomach turns to knots.

GINGER

Good.

Now do yourself a favor, go be with that man before he DOES bring home another girl.

He's not going to wait forever, Jolie.

DAD

Have you seen the team this morning?

ME

Yes, at breakfast.

DAD

Any idea what they did last night after the game?

ME

I think they grabbed some food at Charred—Beck's restaurant.

DAD

Do you know what they're doing today?

I moved over to the window in my room, gazing down at the pool. My suite was so high up, it was impossible to see any of the faces below, but I'd heard the murmurs at breakfast that a bunch of them were going there, and someone had mentioned there was a volleyball net and they should have a game in the pool.

ME

I believe they'll just be hanging out at the pool.

DAD

I'd like you to be there too. I want you to keep an eye on things.

ME

Why?

DAD

Just to make sure nothing happens.

ME

Dad, these are grown-ass men. Some are married with children. They don't need a babysitter.

DAD

Jolene, these aren't just men. They're the representatives of our team.

I'm not asking you, I'm telling you to be there.

Times like this, I wished my boss weren't my father. As his daughter, I felt I had every right to talk back and tell him exactly how I felt about what he was asking of me. As his employee, I didn't. I had to just do what he said.

But, my God, his order was making me furious.

I needed a break from Beck. That was why I'd only popped into breakfast, grabbed a banana and a coffee, and quickly left to hit the gym. That was why I'd spent the rest of the morning at the spa. And that was why, once I showered and got dressed, I planned on walking the Strip this afternoon, getting lost within the chaos of pedestrians and doing some massive retail therapy.

The pool wasn't on my agenda.

Beck amnesia was.

Yet my dad was making that impossible, forcing me to face a reality that I was beyond tired of looking at, just like he'd done to me on the plane. A reality that continuously repeated in my head, *You can't be with him.*

> ME
> I'm headed there right now.

"Would you like a refill?" the server at the pool asked as I set down my empty whiskey sour on the small table beside my lounge chair.

I would like ten.

Make that twelve.

And hold the sour mix.

But instead, I smiled at him and replied, "Please," and returned my gaze to the tablet in my hands.

At least I was attempting to read. The book was loaded onto the screen. Except I would skim a line or two and immediately glance up to stare at Beck.

Fucking Beck.

He was in the pool, not more than fifteen feet from me, hanging with a bunch of the players. They'd just finished a game of volleyball. Which meant I'd had to endure almost an hour of his arms lifting in the air, his triceps contracting from the movement, his shoulders flexing, his back muscles tightening, his pecs bulging. And when he jumped to spike the ball, I had a clear shot of his abs, etched like someone had used a spade and dug an outline around the perimeter and middle of his abdomen, each one ripped from the tension.

But that wasn't the only thing that had me completely worked up.

His whole attitude was doing that too—the way he was laughing with his friends, smiling, the sly glances, the flirtatious ones. With his sunglasses being so dark, I couldn't tell if at any point he was looking at me.

But did it matter?

Ugh, this was excruciating.

And all it did was make me angrier at my father.

I'd been down here for almost two hours. That was more than enough.

The guys were fine.

They didn't need someone watching over them.

Besides, I simply couldn't take another second of this.

I waited until the server returned with my drink, and I closed out my tab and downed the last cocktail he had delivered. I then grabbed my cover-up—an old white button-down of my dad's that I let hang open. I tossed my bag over my shoulder and walked toward the entrance of the Cole and Spade Hotel.

The second I got inside, I was blasted with a breeze of the freezing air-conditioning. I didn't even shiver; the cold air was needed. Not because the desert sun had steamed up my skin—although there was that—but because Beck had.

I moved through the lobby and passed the archway of the casino. I wasn't a gambler. I worked hard for my money. I didn't like the thought of wasting it on something that could gobble it up with one pull, but for some reason, the sound of the machines and the lights and music were calling to me.

The first row of slots I came to had large decorative coins hanging from the ceiling above them, along with massive four-leaf clovers. There were digital leprechauns dancing across the screens.

I didn't feel like luck had been on my side lately.

Maybe the slots could change that.

I grabbed a five out of my wallet and fed it into the opening near the center of the machine. I had absolutely no idea what I was doing. I searched for a handle to pull, but there wasn't one. But there was a button labeled *Spin*, and I hit it. The wheels inside turned, and when each one landed, I waited for a noise, a siren—anything.

There was nothing.

I did it four more times with the same result, and when I located the box that listed how much money I had remaining, it showed zero.

I hadn't won a single round out of five?

Fuck my life.

I made my way out of the casino and into the elevator that brought me to my floor. Once I got off, I went down the hallway, and in front of my suite, I dug through my bag for the key card. My fingers touched the sunscreen and tablet and wallet and bottle of water before I found the small rectangular piece of plastic.

Just as I was waving it in front of the reader, I heard the sound of flip-flops.

I glanced down the hallway, the same way I'd done yesterday when I was checking into my room. And just like last time, Beck was there.

Oh God.

He had on a pair of swim trunks and a short-sleeved button-down that was open, his skin glistening and already tan.

And those muscles ... they tightened as he walked.

He was heading to his room. Because of course he was. The one that was regrettably next to mine.

Would I forever have to fight these temptations?

And my feelings?

What about what Ginger had said to me? How eventually Beck would get tired of waiting for me and be with another woman.

Would I be able to handle that?

Would I live with a lifetime of regret?

I turned around and pushed my back against the door, watching him get closer.

My body was warming again despite the hallway being as

cold as the casino. My skin was actually tingling. That spot between my legs, throbbing.

There was only one man whose arms I wanted to pull me against him.

To kiss me.

To touch me.

"Locked out of your room?" he asked.

"No."

"Then what's going on?" He stopped at his door, his hand on the knob, the other one holding the key card. His gaze eventually became fixed on mine. After a few seconds of silence, he said, "Do you have something you want to say to me?"

I nodded.

"What is it, Jolie?"

Was I putting off the inevitable and wasting moments that I could be spending with him?

Yes.

Would I have to deal with the consequences, some that could be catastrophic?

Yes.

Would I regret this decision?

No.

"I want you."

TWENTY-NINE

Beck

"I *want you.*"
Three words I'd been dying to fucking hear.

I didn't waste a second before I pulled Jolie into my arms, my mouth immediately devouring hers. God, she tasted so good. There was a hint of whiskey on her tongue from what she'd been drinking at the pool, and the scent of the sun was on her skin, and there was a desperate, rabid, starving feeling coming from her body.

It was as though I'd spent hours bringing her to the edge and never letting her come. I could feel how much she was craving this, the longing in her fingers as she gripped me, the moaning in her breaths.

I pulled my mouth away just long enough to growl, "Open your door, Jolie."

She handed me the key card, and the moment the lock freed, I lifted her into my arms and carried her inside, tossing her on the bed. While I stood at the end of the mattress, I spread her legs around me, holding her knees as I gazed across that perfect body.

She was in a red bikini with a men's white button-down shirt that I assumed was to cover her up, but it was hiding almost nothing. Most of her body was on display. And the parts that weren't—the triangles that wrapped over her pussy, ass, and tits—were thin and narrow, hinting at the spots beneath.

"When you put on this bikini and came down to the pool, did you think to yourself, *I want Beck to see me in this?*" I traced around each tit. "*I want Beck to look at me and fantasize about all the places he wants to slide his dick in?*" My fingers crawled down her stomach. "Don't lie to me, Jolie."

She ran her hands through her red locks, spreading the curls over the comforter. "Yes."

I fucking knew it.

The two times she'd pranced around that goddamn pool deck, I could tell by the way she was shaking her ass that she wanted someone to look at her.

And that someone could only be me.

"You know, by wearing this, you let my entire team and the Whales staff and every man at the pool see you."

"What was I supposed to wear? A one-piece? I don't own one of those, Beck—"

"That's not the question I asked."

She smiled. "Yes. I let them see me."

I moved my hands to her thighs. "But this is mine, Jolie." I focused on the bottom of her bikini, knowing under that fabric was a wet, hot, beautiful pussy. I pulled at the strings on each side, the material falling open, making my dick throb and my exhale come out in shudders. "Do you know what it was like for me while I was in that pool, knowing any of those motherfuckers could be looking at you? And they were, trust me. I heard the comments." And I'd wanted to rip every one of their faces off.

"But they were just looking."

I let my shirt drop to the carpet. I did the same with my shorts, and I fisted my cock while I looked at her cunt, pumping my hard-on. "They were doing more than just looking, Jolie. They were dreaming about putting their dick right here." I swiped my finger through her wetness and stopped at the base of her pussy, sticking it all the way in and arching upward, earning the loudest moan. "Do you know I want to knock out every single one of those bastards for having those thoughts?"

Her head was back, her mouth open as I fucked her with my finger.

"But it's yours." She began to rock against it. Meeting me. And the way she was getting wetter told me she wanted more. "They can look all they want. But they can't touch, and they can't have."

"That's what you think?" I pulled my hand away, and she gasped from the absence. I leaned toward the edge of the bed and placed my face in front of her pussy. "That they're allowed to look at what's mine?" I wasn't speaking directly to Jolie; I was whispering to her cunt. "That they can fantasize about what's mine?"

"No."

Happy with her answer, I gave her a lick. Just one. But it was a long one.

"Please, Beck." Her legs fell open, as though giving me more room would up her chances of getting more tongue. "I need you."

I chuckled.

Those words were as sexy as *I want you.*

"You've made me wait a long time to have this."

"I know." She glanced down, and our eyes locked. "I'm sorry."

"Maybe I should make you wait just as long to get off." I rubbed my nose over her clit, my skin soaked from the contact. I could tell she enjoyed the friction because she arched into it.

"*Mmm.* You wouldn't dare."

"But I would." I gave her some of my tongue, and I pulled it away, showing her just what she'd been doing to me over the last few weeks. Goading, teasing—it had been fucking endless. But the taste of her was just so good; it was as much of a punishment to her as it was to me. "The problem is, I need you just as badly." I was smiling as I smelled her. That was what her scent did to me. It made my dick harder than stone, and it put a goddamn grin on my lips. "Jolie ..." I kissed her clit. "Baby, don't ever give this pussy to anyone but me."

Her moans rang in my ears as I licked upward, stopping at that highest peak, flicking it horizontally with my tongue as my finger slipped right in. I continuously changed up the motion of my mouth, switching from licking to sucking, assessing which she needed the most.

And my hand twisted, turned, and with each plunge, I heard, "Yes!"

God, I'd missed this.

The feel of her on my lips.

The taste of her on my tongue.

The sounds of her nearing an orgasm.

Like she was doing now.

When I knew she was on the verge of having one, her legs shaking, her hips bumping up and down, her breathing becoming faster, I pulled back and earned myself an, "Ah!"

She stared down at me, her hair wild, her lips ravenous.

"Are you trying to kill me?" She waited. "Seriously though ... or maybe you're really trying to torture me."

I got up from the edge of the mattress. "I know how close you were. Don't forget, I know your body well." I grabbed her ankles and rolled her onto her stomach. "You're going to come. Don't you worry." I lifted her ass to get her onto her knees and into doggy style, my palm gliding down the center of her back as my tip found her pussy. "But when you come, instead of feeling it on my tongue, I want to feel it on my dick."

I gave her one slow thrust. A reminder of what she'd been denying me and a promise of what was to come. "*Fuuuck*."

"Beck!"

There was nothing that felt better than this.

It was impossible.

"You like that?" I knew she did. I just wanted the satisfaction of hearing her confirm it with words instead of sounds.

"Yes!"

"Do you want more?"

She looked at me from over her shoulder. "Please! Now!" She backed up, trying to hurry me. "Harder!"

That begging. Why was it so fucking sexy?

I held on to her waist, using it to steer me, only going in as far as my crown. From there, I didn't move any further; I just pulsed. But dipping in those few inches was so powerful, almost enough to get me off.

My head fell back as each mini-stroke sucked the end of me, working me closer. "Damn!" And when I couldn't hold off anymore, I thrust all the way in. "How are you so tight?" I placed my left foot on the bed while the other stayed on the floor, and as I pounded into her, my balls banged against her. "You feel so fucking good."

"Yes," she cried. "More!"

Her upper body lowered to the mattress so her ass could point up higher in the air, and her legs spread further apart. What that did was give me all access, and I took it, ramping up the pace, my hands wandering over her body since I didn't have to hold any of her weight.

The first thing I did was pull each nipple.

"*Wooow*," she hummed.

I wanted her to feel the pain of the tug and the pleasure of me rubbing it after.

"Don't stop," she ordered.

I'd slowed, this time because I knew she was nearing an orgasm. It wasn't that I didn't want to give her one. I wanted her fucking screams to fill my ears. I wanted her shuddering on my dick. But what I also wanted was for it to be the most intense one she'd ever had. To make that happen, I needed her body overwhelmingly worked up. I needed her so goddamn desperate that she'd be willing to do anything to get off.

And she was almost there.

So, I pulled out and grabbed her from behind, moving her with me to the end of the bed. As I sat on the very edge with my feet on the floor, I set her on my lap, facing away from me.

"Another one I've never tried." She was lifting herself up to put her pussy on the tip of my dick. Once it was in, she moaned as she sank down my entire shaft. "My God. Each position feels so different, and this one ..." She took a loud breath. "This one is wildly perfect."

I reached around her and rubbed her clit.

"*Ohhh* shit, Beck."

I knew it was only a matter of seconds before she came.

Her clit was already hard, her wetness thickening.

But having her like this meant we could move together, and with her back against my chest, every part of her body was easily within reach.

I wrapped an arm across her chest, pinching her nipple, and with my other hand on her clit, I rocked forward.

"Argh!" she shouted.

I sucked her earlobe into my mouth, releasing it to moan, "I'm going to come in you."

"I want you to." She turned her face to the side, giving me her cheek. "I need you to."

I gave her several more pumps before I ordered, "Balance your feet on my thighs."

She did as instructed, and it set her a little higher in the air, allowing me to drive in harder and punch even deeper.

"You get one finger, Jolie. When you come, do you want that finger on your clit? Or do you want it in your ass?"

"Ah!" She was lost. I could tell by every sound she was making.

So, I grazed her nipple, urging a response from her, and said, "Tell me."

"My ass."

Good fucking choice.

I rotated my hand around the back, using some of the wetness from her pussy to coat my skin, and when she was on her way down to grind against my dick, my finger was there.

Waiting.

Ready.

And it skated right in, filling her ass the same way my dick was filling her pussy.

"Beck!" She immediately tightened around my shaft, and that ass—it was wet, and it was fucking needy.

"Are you ready to come?"

Her scream was her answer, and it was even louder than I'd anticipated.

With her body bucking against mine, both of her spots

brimming with pressure and friction, it only took a few lunges before the tingles were setting into my balls.

"Jolie," I hissed, "you're going to fucking get it."

"I want it!"

The speed and power I'd been reserving for this moment took over, my finger moving just as fast as my dick. And with each stroke, she was drawing me that much closer, pulling the cum toward my tip.

"That's it." My mouth was now behind her ear. "That's fucking it."

She was shouting my name, sucking in air, only to yell it again.

Those sounds, the feel of her, the desire that was burning through her and into me—I couldn't hold off.

Her hips rocked up and down, giving me exactly what I needed, and I fucking lost it.

"Fuck! Me," I roared, each movement causing the cum to shoot from my tip, our stomachs shuddering. "Jolie!"

She finally reached her peak and was on her way down, and after burying my dick a few more times, I joined her, emptied and still. Following some heavy breaths, I gently pulled out my finger, but I left my dick in, and I wrapped both arms around her.

"I feel half dead," she panted.

I chuckled. "A shower will fix that."

"I can't believe I was doing everything to stop this from happening." She rested her head in the crook of my neck. "I wanted this more than you can even understand. But I avoided it because I knew what would happen."

I kissed her hair. "What would happen?"

"The second I gave in, I'd have to admit, to you and myself, how much I truly care about you."

I let out a deep groan of approval.

She was giving me everything I wanted.

But there was a time to have that talk, and it wasn't now.

"Let's save that conversation for the morning."

"What do you plan on doing with me until then?"

My teeth went to her neck, and I gave it a tender bite. "You mean, what I *am* going to do to you, which is make sure you don't leave this bed."

THIRTY

Jolie

"Good morning." Those were two words I hadn't expected to whisper toward the other side of my bed while I was in Vegas.

I also didn't think that what had gone down yesterday afternoon, once I left the pool, and what had followed into the evening and the very early hours of the morning would happen either.

But as I lay under the comforter, facing the opposite end of the mattress, all I saw was Beck.

A sight that made me the happiest girl alive.

His arm was extended across the little space between us, his hand holding my cheek, his gaze still as hungry as when he'd carried me into this room. "Morning."

That gaze—my God, I couldn't get enough of it. The way it made me feel, the confidence it triggered inside me, the warmth it spread over me. I hoped he never stopped looking at me.

But as I rubbed the sleep from my eyes and the silence began to tick between us, I knew a conversation had to happen.

Yesterday had changed everything. When I'd leaned my back against my door and watched him walk down the hallway, I had known that I wasn't just making the decision to sleep with him. I was giving myself to him.

And the last thing I wanted after mentally making that commitment was to hang in this unknown place full of questions.

I'd lived far too many years with those eating away at me.

"I want to talk to you about something."

I massaged the outside of my chest, trying to calm the beating inside. Anxiety was so fickle. I never knew when it was going to appear, how it would morph, what face it would wear, if it was going to seep in or pour out.

Right now, not only was it living in my chest; it was digging a hole in my stomach.

"Talk to me."

"It's about this …" I added more volume to my voice and traced the air between us when I said, "Us."

He bent his arm behind his head and sat up a little. "Are you going to tell me it was a mistake? That it can't happen again. That professionalism bullshit you've been saying on repeat—"

"No."

"Jolie, you've been playing this game with me for weeks. Giving me a little and backpedaling. You want me to flirt with you, and then you seem to regret it. You love when I fight for you, and then you don't give in."

He was right.

About all of it.

But it hadn't been a game.

That was me struggling between wrong and right. That was me trying to weigh which side of regret would cut deeper.

That was me trying to do what my father would want and attempt to completely ignore my heart.

"But I gave in yesterday, and I told you, when that happened, I'd have to admit to you and to myself how much I truly cared about you."

He chuckled. "A lot of people say a lot of shit the night before. It's what they say in the morning that matters."

I sat up, pushing my back against the headboard, and pulled up the comforter to cover my bare chest. In the process, his hand left my face. "Yesterday was a long time coming."

"So was putting my face between your legs. But that doesn't mean you want me to do it again right now. Or that you want to spend the rest of the morning with me or the afternoon or wake up tomorrow in my arms."

"But I do." The anxiety was coming in thicker, running sprints between my chest and stomach. "That's what I want to talk to you about."

I didn't know why this was so hard for me to say. Was it because it felt like things had been dragged out for so long between us? Or my role with the Whales? Or the thought of having a chat with my dad about this and how it made me want to dry-heave?

"I want more, Beck."

"More." He said that like he needed to test how the word would feel coming through his lips. "Explain what that looks like to you." He stretched his arm up, the blanket falling to his stomach.

"It would be everything I've always envisioned for us." I paused. "I'm not talking about just the physical stuff. I'm talking about all of it."

He wet his bottom lip with his tongue while he listened.

"Being together. A ... relationship."

He stroked the outside of my thigh. "You know that's what I want." He gave me a small smile. "And you know it's what I've been waiting to hear you say. But why now? Why during our first week of travel?"

"I literally couldn't take another second of being away from you. I was fighting against what I wanted and making myself miserable in the process." My eyes closed for just a moment. "You're all I've ever wanted, Beck. Since my sophomore year of college, it's only been you."

He leaned across the bed and put his mouth by my ear, breathing me in before he kissed my cheek. "You're making me so fucking happy." When he pulled back, his eyes changed. "But what about your dad, Jolie? The team. Everything you've been worried about. You're telling me none of that matters to you anymore?"

As my anxiety jolted, I drew in some air and patted the center of my stomach. "I'm filled with worry about it." I rubbed several circles over my navel and relocated my hand to my chest. "I have no idea how Dad is going to react. I worry I'll lose the respect of the team when they find out I'm sleeping with their captain. I—"

"I'm going to stop you right there. That team—those boys—they're my family. If they're told we're in a relationship, they will know the gravity of the situation. You being mine is a very serious thing, Jolie, and they will treat you with nothing but respect." He slid his hand behind my head.

That part was a relief at least.

But my dad was an entirely different beast that I was not looking forward to tackling.

"What if my dad doesn't allow me to work for the team anymore?" Things were tightening within me, and I didn't like it. "What if I get reassigned to my old accounts and I have to move back to Boston? What will happen to ... us?"

"I'll talk to him."

I laughed. "You're funny."

"I'm not joking." He rolled onto his side and moved his palm to my stomach. "He's the owner of my team, and that puts me in a position where I need to have a conversation with him. And I'll explain to him that we're not new. Things started long before you worked for the Whales." He moved his thumb around my belly button. "Once he hears that, I'm hopeful he'll look at things differently."

The thought alone had me sitting up straight. "So, you think it's a genius idea to drop the *I slept with your twenty-year-old daughter* bomb on my father? That I moved into your hotel room and we had a three-night sexfest during one of your stopovers in Boston? You think he's just going to smile and nod and say, *That's my girl?*" I waited for him to voice something as the nausea hit me and then added, "Are you high?"

"What does being twenty have anything to do with this?"

"I was a baby."

He winced. "You weren't a fucking baby. You weren't even living at home anymore. You were working and going to school full-time."

I crossed my legs in front of me. "You're saying never once in your mind did you think, *Holy shit, am I really into a twenty-year-old who lives in a dorm?*" I waited for him to respond. "We both know I just won that round."

He moved in closer, locking our stares. "Regardless, we need to have a conversation with him. There's no way around it. I don't know what details will be included in that talk, but I'm sure as hell not mentioning a three-day sexfest."

"You just ... don't know my dad." I focused on my hands as they fidgeted with the comforter.

"That's true. But I've gotten to know him decently well since he purchased our team. We meet almost every day. We have conversations that aren't always about hockey. Things are good between us."

I glanced up. "They are now. But just wait."

He put his hand over mine. "Listen to me. We're going to deal with this. We're going to figure it out. Whatever happens, it's going to be okay." He raised his hand into my hair. "The most important thing is that you're mine."

When I nodded, he pulled me toward him, and I rested my face on his chest, my arm wrapping around him. "I don't want to leave this spot right here. Our very own little bubble. Where no one knows and it's our secret and everything feels perfect."

He pulled my fingers up to his mouth and kissed each tip. "It will be when they all find out too. Stop stressing about this." As I was letting out a deep sigh, he said, "Is that your phone blowing up?"

My phone was on vibrate—that was how I usually kept it—but Beck was right; I could hear the pulses rattling against something. And that something had to be one of the many items inside my purse.

My purse?

I really hadn't checked my phone at all since Beck had carried me in here yesterday?

No.

I hadn't.

A realization that was suddenly slapping me back into reality.

Shit.

"It's probably one of my assistants. I should go look." I glanced up his chest and smiled. "Do not move." I slid out of bed and found my bag on the floor by the entrance, reaching inside to get my phone.

The screen showed over thirty missed calls.

More than fifty texts.

And an explosion of social media notifications.

What the hell?

My thumb shook as I swiped it over the screen, scrolling through each of the missed calls. The phone calls had started at around ten in the evening and went straight through this morning, an equal number from Celeste and Joel—my assistants. The last call that had come in a few seconds ago was from my father.

Oh God.

I went to my texts, and the first one I pulled up was the group chat I had with my assistants.

> CELESTE
>
> Jolie, the second you see this, I need you to call me.
>
> JOEL
>
> She still hasn't called?
>
> CELESTE
>
> No.
>
> JOEL
>
> Where is she?
>
> CELESTE
>
> I have no idea.
>
> JOEL
>
> I just knocked on her door, and she didn't answer.
>
> CELESTE
>
> I don't want to make a decision without her, but someone needs to do something.
>
> JOEL
>
> Do we call Mark?

CELESTE

I'm shivering at the thought.

JOEL

Same.

CELESTE

If we don't hear from her in an hour, I'll call Mark.

CELESTE

Still no word from Jolie ... I'm calling him.

CELESTE

Jolie, don't hate me. I swear I'm doing this because I have to, not because I want to.

JOEL

Oh boy. Keep me posted.

CELESTE

Mark's aware of the situation, he told me to send all the info to the PR crisis team. They'll be calling me in the next hour.

JOEL

I'm at the hotel. If you need me, I can meet you, and we can take the call together.

CELESTE

Yes, come to my room—252.

JOEL

The memes have started. Social media is exploding. It's a fucking shitstorm.

CELESTE

I'm too afraid to look. Bring wine when you come.

JOEL

No, I'm bringing vodka.

"Oh my God." My hand slapped against my heart. If I

didn't add pressure to it, I was positive it was going to burst straight through my skin.

I exited out of the group chat and scrolled to the next message.

> DAD
>
> I've never been more disappointed in you in my entire life.

"Jolie, what's wrong? Why do you look like you're on the verge of throwing up?"

My gaze slowly rose and locked on Beck's. He'd gotten out of bed and was standing not far from me.

"Something happened ..."

"What do you mean, something happened?"

My head shook. "I don't know. I missed it all. Because I was in here ... with you."

THIRTY-ONE

Beck

The conference room at the Cole and Spade Hotel in Vegas was currently as loud as a locker room, the guys in various states—some hungover, some still buzzed, only a few, like me, completely sober. But that hadn't stopped me from tearing into those motherfuckers.

I didn't care if it was one person's mistake; we were a team. When one fucked up, we all fucked up.

By the owner, by the staff, and by the public, we were viewed as a whole.

And what this team had done yesterday while Jolie and I were ravishing each other's bodies was inexcusable.

Since I was the captain, they first needed to hear it from me.

But I was only a small part. Jolie and her assistants would be here at any second, and I assumed the guys were going to hear it all again.

"Dude, you need to go on Instagram and type in Kirk Clark

and see all the shit that pops up," Landon said from the chair next to me.

"I don't do social media—you know that," I told him. "Besides, if I saw a meme, or whatever those things are called, with our defenseman's face on it, I might lose my shit on everyone again."

I glared at Kirk, who was on the other side of the room. He was reclined in his seat with his arms crossed, a smug look on his face. If he was feeling remorse—and on some level, he had to—he wasn't showing it, and that only made me wilder.

"You mean like this one?" Landon tilted his phone toward me.

"This isn't funny, fucker."

"I'm not laughing." He swiped his screen several times. "But look at this one."

"I'm going to fucking kill you, Landon. Put your goddamn phone down and stop adding to the views."

"My views aren't making a difference—I promise that." He turned his Whales hat backward. "According to one site, Kirk's name has been viewed over twelve million times. And you know that's not all from hockey." He smiled. "I'm just thankful it was him and not me. I'm the king of bad decisions."

I slumped down in my chair and pulled my hoodie over my head.

This was a fucking mess.

And now it had become Jolie's mess. I couldn't even imagine how this was affecting her. Aside from a text about thirty minutes ago that told me to round up the guys and have them come to the conference room, we hadn't spoken since she'd run out of her suite three hours ago.

But I knew the fallout was going to be a PR nightmare, and she would be in the center of it.

The door opened, and Jolie and her two assistants walked

in. The stress was evident on her face—bags were suddenly under her eyes, her hair messier than usual, like she'd been pulling at her strands. I could almost see the headache pounding behind her eyes.

My baby.

I just wanted to take care of her.

I just wanted to take her away from this mess.

She stood at the front of the table, holding the top of the vacant chair that I'd reserved for her, her knuckles white as she looked at the faces around the room.

"I'm assuming you're all aware of the incident that occurred yesterday at the pool." She took a deep breath. "An incident that has now gone viral. Our team's name is being dragged through the mud with the help of every news channel and social media site." She pulled at her sweatshirt—the first piece of clothing she could find in her room, which she had thrown on before she flew through the door. "Our crisis PR team is on their way to Vegas. They've already drafted a statement that will be released to the press. Kirk will have one as well, just slightly different, and he'll release his at the same time. At some point this evening, they're going to have a meeting with you all and discuss this in more detail."

She folded her hands together. "In the meantime, I would appreciate it if the rest of you stayed silent. Don't engage with any posts. Don't offer any comments if the media reaches out to you. Don't make your own statements. Our team will handle this. Not you."

She glanced toward the seat of the chair, her hands rubbing back and forth across the cushion.

Kirk. I wanted to strangle that man. Not because of what he had done—although that was fucked up. But for putting Jolie through this. For causing the stress on her face. For causing these emotions to be running through her.

"I want you to hear me when I say that everyone in this room represents the Whales as a brand. You're public figures. Every move you make has the potential of being captured on camera and shared across the world, as we witnessed yesterday and as we're still witnessing today, unfortunately."

She was avoiding my gaze, and I wondered if that was on purpose.

"You're all adults. You know the difference between right and wrong. I don't want to scold you like children, and I don't want to treat you that way." She backed up a few feet and crossed her arms. "I'm going to remind you that during the season, while you're all under contract—whether you're on the road or at home—you're expected to represent yourselves professionally. And having videos, like the one that's now circling the internet at a speed I'm not comfortable with"—her hand went to the base of her throat—"is not something I want our team to be known for. And it's something I'm certainly not proud of."

The room was already silent, but now you could hear a fucking pin drop.

Our coach would have been red-faced with spit flying out of his mouth had he been the one to just say those words to us. I'd already yelled at these fools, and I hadn't been quiet or kind.

But Jolie was poised, her tone sharp, her message clear.

"Let's remember how much talent is on this team and the hopes and dreams we have for this season." She pushed her hair back. "Please don't lose sight of that, and please keep your focus on hockey." She paused. "Are there any questions?" When no one said anything, Jolie continued, "You can go back to your rooms now. If you're hungry, have food delivered. The hotel manager doesn't want any of you at the pool, so let's respect his wishes. For the rest of the time we're here, I would like you to lie low and don't cause any reason for attention." She nodded toward the door to let us know she was done.

I got up, and as we made our way out of the conference room and hit the hallway on the way to the elevator, there was a mix of comments from the guys.

"Mama's hot as fuck when she's angry," my right wing said.

"Maybe she wishes she were the one getting banged in the pool," someone else said.

"But with a pussy like hers, you wouldn't pull out to come in the water, you'd come in her—"

"Keep it down," I warned them, my fists on the verge of swinging. "Did you guys hear any-fucking-thing she said? We don't need to cause any more attention, which means keeping your mouths shut."

As I hit the button for the elevator, my phone vibrated in my pocket.

> JOLIE
> I'll come to your room in 20 minutes.

When I opened the door to my room, my girl looked defeated, like a balloon deflating of helium, circling right before it fell to the ground. I didn't just see it in her expression. It was her stature too—the way she was almost caving inward, looking exhausted, the doorframe holding her up and practically swallowing her.

I pulled her into my room, letting the door shut behind her, and I wrapped my arms around her. "Talk to me."

Several seconds passed before she said, "Working for an NHL team isn't for the weak."

I pressed my lips on the top of her head, holding them there. "How bad is it?"

Her exhale was hot against my chest. "It's not the absolute worst thing that could have happened. There are far worse situations we wouldn't recover from. But it isn't pretty."

I leaned back, pulling my chest away to look into her eyes, holding her cheeks in the process. "And what about your dad?"

Her eyes closed at the mention of his name, her exhale even louder this time. "He wants to murder me." Her eyes opened. "He's blaming me for this entire thing."

"Hold on a second. Kirk meets a girl in the pool. Decides to fuck her in it. Pulls out and comes in the water. The whole thing is caught on video, the video goes viral ... and all of that is ... *your* fault?"

She nodded. "Dad told me to be at the pool and make sure nothing happened. I left long before the guys"—she paused to rub her lips together, as though admitting this part was tough on her—"because, honestly, I couldn't spend one more minute staring at you. It was becoming too painful to bear."

I gave her a quick smile before I said, "You're not the team's babysitter."

"Which is what I told my father when he first gave me the order."

I held her tighter. "None of this is your fault."

"Except, in his eyes, it is. One, why wasn't I down there to stop this from happening? And two, why couldn't my team get ahold of me that evening or the following morning? What was I doing for all those hours when I wasn't answering my phone? Dad hasn't asked any of those questions, but I promise, those are the questions he has."

She put her hand on top of mine, clinging to it. "Do you know how shitty it is that Celeste had to call my dad and tell him the news? And that she and Joel had to go into full-blown boss mode? Mega shitty, Beck." Her voice was getting quieter with each word. "I don't know what's going to happen."

"I'll tell you what's going to happen." My hands slid down to her neck even though she was still holding one. "The PR crisis team is going to take over from here. Statements will be issued by the team and Kirk. And—"

"Not that. I mean, my future with the team." Emotion was pouring into her eyes. "Dad isn't happy. I'm worried that he thinks he gave me too much responsibility and I can't handle it. We're only on our first away trip—our first one, Beck—and this happens and—"

"Baby, it's going to be okay." I held the back of her head and brought her against my chest again, squeezing her so tight.

She was feeling the pressure—I understood that.

Kirk had been an absolute shit, and I'd laid into him for that.

But I also knew the impending conversation she was going to have with her father about us was weighing heavily on her.

And now this had fucking happened.

Even though the PR crisis team was doing their thing, statements had been released, and a new piece of celebrity drama had hit the press, causing Kirk's story to lose some momentum, Jolie was still stressed as fuck.

I didn't know how to fix things for her. I didn't know how to drain the worry from her body. My tongue worked, but the result was only temporary. Same with my dick. Because once she came and I held her in my arms or carried her to the shower, I could feel the tension slip right back into her muscles. I could hear the anxiety in her voice.

There was only one thing I could think to do, one way to get her refocused.

So, when we left Vegas and played New Jersey and had a two-night stopover before we flew to Calgary, I planned an evening that was all about us. I didn't want us to leave for dinner and run into any of the guys in the hotel—not before we told them about our relationship—and I definitely didn't want to be seen by any unexpected paparazzi, so I had my assistant organize a date in my suite.

Once Jolie got out of her meetings and the marketing team was free for the night, I told her to come to my suite. When I opened the door for her and she walked into the base of the living room, lit with candlelight from a table in the center, covered in rose petals, the smile on her face was unlike anything I'd seen since the controversy had gone down.

Even if it was just for this moment, I had my Jolie back.

"You did this?" She glanced from the living room to me, still grinning.

"I made it happen."

She laughed. "That's as good as doing it in my book." Her head tilted back a little as she stared at me. "I cannot believe you went through all of this trouble."

I pressed my lips to her cheek. "Why? Aren't you hungry?"

"I just assumed we were going to order room service, like we'd been doing."

"I've had enough cold fries and stale bread." Even though the room was dimly lit, I swore there were tears in her eyes. "What's wrong, baby?"

She flattened her hands against my chest. "I was just thinking ... this is our first date."

It hit me then; she was right.

"I didn't even think of that."

"And in the best possible way, you made it beyond special." She looked past me. "Look at this room. I can't get over it."

I grabbed her hand and led her over to her chair, waiting for her to sit before I pushed it in. "You once told me you loved Charred."

She smiled. "I did say that."

"And it was where your parents took you for your birthday." I moved to the other side of the table and sat.

"I can't believe you remember that."

I lifted each of the metal plate covers—there were a total of four on the table—and I set them on the floor. "Since there isn't a Toro here, which I know you also love, I went the steak route. Walker would probably be extremely disappointed in me with the way I'm about to describe this"—I chuckled—"but what I got you was a filet, cooked medium, sliced, with a mushroom rub and a burgundy sauce on top, accompanied by a salted baked potato, wild mushrooms, and broccolini."

"Also known as heaven on a plate."

I gave her a smile, pleased that she liked what I'd chosen. "And since I had no way of keeping the main course warm, we're going to eat the appetizers at the same time. I ordered a few of my favorites—the shrimp cocktail and the tuna tartare."

"You're not going to give me their descriptions? I'm gutted." She winked.

"You're funny—but I'll play your game." I pointed at the plate of tuna. "Here's our signature tuna tartare, over a bed of avocado, sliced ginger, and crispy tempura flakes with a wasabi aioli drizzled on top. The fried wonton crisps are used for dipping, and the chef recommends you soak those crisps in the ponzu sauce, which you'll see rolling around the plate, as the combination of the savory avocado and tangy sauce is mouth-watering good." I paused. "How'd I do?"

"I think Walker would be very proud. Also, this looks amazing." She lifted her whiskey sour, smiling—I assumed because she knew I'd gone light on the sour mix. "Beck, you can't possibly understand how happy I am right now."

"I can. Because I am too."

"Yeah?" She clinked her glass against my bourbon.

"Fuck yeah." My eyes dipped down her face, the candles flickering a warm glow across her skin. "I got the girl."

She let out an adorable laugh. "You did, for sure."

I took a drink and set my glass down. "Tell me why you're the happiest."

"I'm here. With you." Her eyes were so fucking full of love. "A man I've been completely obsessed with for years. And I get to watch you play in person rather than on the TV, and I can't even express how much I love that. And I get to work with you. Travel with you. Spend each night with you."

Within an instant, the love and happiness completely fell from her face.

Fuck. This was exactly what I hadn't wanted to happen.

"Jolie, stop worrying."

"I can't help it. I have no idea what's waiting for me when I get home. What if I have to make a choice? What if it's you or the Whales—"

"Don't even put your head there until you're faced with that decision, which I don't think you will be." I nodded toward the food, encouraging her to start eating. "I don't want you dwelling on this tonight. That's why I set up this date—to get your mind off things."

"I adore you for that." She gave me a weak smile. "But it's impossible. It's all I think about."

"We don't have to talk about it."

She shrugged. "Even if we try to talk around it, somehow, we'll end up discussing it. It's the kind of topic that's unavoidable."

She was right.

Aside from hockey and The Weston Group, it was the biggest thing in both of our lives.

"Then let's talk about it." I hoped I didn't regret this. "What's going on between you and your dad? What does he say when you talk to him?"

She lifted a shrimp and dipped it into our new version of cocktail sauce—one we recently introduced to all Charred restaurants worldwide. Instead of offering the traditional ketchup and horseradish mix, it was now a tangy sweet and sour sauce with a bit of a kick.

"*Mmm*, delicious," she said behind her hand as she chewed. "Dad's been short with me. We talk when we absolutely have to, and each time, I can hear the disappointment in his voice."

"It's not getting better?"

She huffed, "No."

I picked up a wonton and dipped it into the tuna. "Do you think it's because you two haven't hashed it out yet?"

"I feel like he's waiting for me to get off the road before he questions me. In the past, whenever there was a mishap with one of the accounts I worked on, I was always in the office, so the interrogation started immediately."

"Sounds like he's a face-to-face guy."

"Insert more anxiety." She fanned her face.

I reached across the table, over each plate of food, and put my hand on hers. "We have two more stops after this, and so far, we're undefeated. I want you to celebrate that because you have a huge part in our wins."

"Me?" She shook her head. "I'm not on that ice. I'm the marketing part of the machine. I have no part in anything you guys do during the games."

"Let me tell you why you're wrong." I released her and picked up my fork. "During that meeting in the conference room in Vegas, you could have said a lot of things to the team. You could have fucking shredded us. Morale would have nose-dived, and we would have gone into the New Jersey game feeling like total shit—even worse than we already did. But you didn't do that."

She finished chewing a piece of steak before she said, "Are you kidding? I wanted to look at Kirk and tell him he was the biggest moron and ask him how he could do that in public *annnd* how he could do that without a condom. Hello? Gross. You don't even know that woman." She picked up a mushroom with her fingers and popped it into her mouth. "But we're always the toughest on ourselves. If he felt bad about the situation, I didn't need to make him feel worse. And if he had no regret at all, then nothing I said would have changed his mind, and I didn't want the team to be verbally punished for his mistake."

"Which is funny because I tore his fucking face off before you and your crew walked in."

She smiled. "We'll call that balance."

I laughed. "I need you to eat up."

"Why's that?"

"Because there's a surprise waiting for you in the bedroom."

"*Daaamn*," Jolie moaned. "I had no idea you were so good at this."

I chuckled. "You think eating pussy and playing hockey are the only talents I have?"

She leaned up a little to look at me over her shoulder; the view of her profile and nakedness of her back was a sight even an author couldn't describe. "I certainly never thought that."

"I'm playing with you."

She smiled before she turned back around and lay flat on the massage table.

I added more oil to my hands and ran them down her bare thighs, concentrating on the muscles, rubbing into them, away from them, kneading their center.

This was the other part of the surprise—set up in the bedroom, lit with more candles and rose petals. I didn't know how my assistant had arranged to get a massage table into my suite, nor did I care. Once Jolie and I had finished dinner, I'd had her strip and get on top of it, face down, doing everything I could to ease that mind of hers.

"It's really this simple: I know your body, and I know what you want."

"Sexually, you do, yes." She groaned as I slid up her spine, gently thumbing each groove and disc. "But usually only professionals are this skilled with their hands."

"I get massaged at least once a week. Sometimes more if I'm home. I know what I like, and I know the techniques that are used. Plus, I can feel what you like—the same way I can when I'm fucking you."

"How?"

I moved behind her head and focused on her neck. "I listen to you. I read your body, your reactions. Your breathing. The noises you make. If you tense or tighten up. If you completely relax into my hands." A grin moved over my lips. "Like you're doing right now."

"This is the best night I've had in a really long time. Honestly, like the top three ever."

"Impossible."

"I'm serious. I hope you know how much all of this has meant to me, everything you've done tonight, it's been perfect."

"I'm glad." I pulled my hands back, eyeing her ass and how sexy and slick it looked. "Flip over for me."

She slowly rolled onto her back, and I walked toward the foot of the table, wrapping my hand around one of her feet. There was a spot right at the bridge of my foot's arch that made me fucking groan every time my masseuse grazed it. Once I found Jolie's, I carefully swiped my thumb across it.

"*Yesss.*"

I laughed.

"What are you?" she asked. "Because, for real, this is next-level wildness right now."

"Listen, there are a lot of things I could do, but the most important is showing you just how far I'd go to take care of you."

She leaned up on her elbows while I got to work on her ankle. "I'm feeling all the feels right now."

"I bet you are."

As I glided to her knee, she let out a loud moan and followed that up with, "Tell me something, Beck. If you can read me so well, what is my body saying to you right now?"

"Oh, I hear exactly what it's telling me. I'm just ordering it to be quiet for a little while longer until I finish this massage."

"Yeah?" She smiled. "So, what is it saying?"

My hand skated up the rest of her leg, curving toward the inside of her thigh, and hovered over her pussy, keeping only a few inches between us. "It's saying it wants my mouth right here."

Long, wavy red strands fell into her face. "And what do you want?"

"I want that too."

"Then don't make me wait." She sat up and bent her knees, pushing the heels of her feet into the table. "Please, Beck, give me your mouth."

I was sure she still didn't know how beautiful she was, but what had changed since I'd met her was her sexual confidence.

Her ability to lock that light-blue stare with mine and communicate exactly what she wanted from me.

There was nothing hotter.

And nothing I wanted more.

"Come here," she whispered, and she pointed at her mouth. "Kiss me first."

I moved in from the bottom of the table, kneeling onto the sheet-wrapped cushion, but instead of diving to her mouth, I went straight to her cunt. With my lips positioned over her clit, I said, "I'm going to kiss you. But my lips are going here first."

I slithered my tongue from the base of her pussy all the way to the highest peak, wedging it in and flicking that tender spot.

"*Ahhh!*" she screamed.

I glanced up her body, most of it slick with oil, just like my finger, so when I aimed it at her pussy, it slid right in.

"Dear fucking God," she cried. "I'm about to ... come."

THIRTY-TWO

Jolie

DAD

I assume everything is set for the Calgary game, or should I not assume that?

ME

Everything is set. Ads are running. Sponsorships are in place. Social media is updating on a constant rotation. Signage will be displayed in the locker room and at the press conference. I've got it handled, don't worry.

DAD

I've heard that before.

What about the footage from the New Jersey game? Where are the highlights? Why hasn't any of it been posted?

ME

The footage is being edited as we speak. Last I checked, it was almost done.

DAD

Last you checked? Why aren't you doing it?

ME

I have two assistants who are more than capable of handling tasks like that.

DAD

This is your job.

ME

And I'm doing my job.

I pulled the spoon out of my mouth and chewed the chocolate chip pumpkin bread pudding—which Beck's chef had made for dessert—topped with a massive scoop of caramel ice cream, and I glanced around his living room. Although I hadn't spent a ton of time here, it was starting to feel extra cozy whenever I came.

I turned my face toward him as he sat beside me on the couch, my legs resting over his lap. "It feels really good to be home."

Shit, that was really only partially true.

The other half of me didn't want to be in LA. I wanted to keep running from away game to away game, hiding from whatever fate was waiting for me.

We'd flown back this afternoon, and while we were on the plane, Beck asked me to drop my stuff at my apartment and meet him at his place to spend the night.

Which was a no-brainer.

But since I'd walked through his door, knowing I'd be returning to my office in the morning, my anxiety had me inhaling everything he put in front of me. First the salmon his chef had prepared. Now, this pumpkin whatever it was, along with the old-fashioned he'd made us as an after-dinner drink.

He spooned a mouthful from his dish and said, "I like that you're calling my place home." He rubbed the side of my thigh, stopping near my hip before he worked his way back down. "Could you see yourself moving in here?"

"Now?"

He shrugged. "The timing doesn't matter—now, later, whenever. I'm just wondering if you would ever be comfortable enough to live here."

An outsider, looking in, would probably think we were moving at warp speed. But in my mind, all those years of wanting him counted for time served.

I was positive he felt the same way.

"I could see myself moving in here tomorrow." I licked off some ice cream from the tip of my spoon. "But I kinda think we should wait until my lease is up. Ginger is new to LA. I can't abandon her—even though I did this evening and probably will tomorrow night."

He put his dish on the table in front of the couch. "Only tomorrow night? How about for the next two weeks that we're home until we hit the road again?"

"Well ... we'll see about that. When I get to the office tomorrow, I truly have no idea what I'll be facing."

"When are you and your dad scheduled to talk?" He set his hands on my knees.

"There's nothing on the schedule. I just have this feeling in my gut that the talk is going to happen tomorrow."

"Good. It's time to get it over with."

I nodded, the tightness moving its way into my chest, and each mouthful I fed it, it was getting worse, not better, so my bowl joined Beck's on the table.

"I don't like keeping this secret, Jolie. I don't like that the guys on the team are still making comments about how fucking hot you are. I don't like that tonight, instead of going to Charred or Toro, we're eating here because we can't be photographed together. I want anyone and everyone to know you're mine."

There was a boulder in the back of my throat, only allowing me to say softly, "I want that too."

But ...

Oh God, there were so many buts.

I just had a feeling that when it came to us, I was going to have to sacrifice something. A balance of sorts. And what that something was made me so anxious.

I needed a subject change, so I asked, "What time is practice tomorrow?"

"We have weight training at nine. That means we'll probably hit the ice around eleven. I'm sure we'll have some meetings after. Coach is going to want to talk about the Vancouver game since we haven't yet." He put his hand behind my head, his hazel eyes focused on mine. "What time do you plan on getting there?"

I drew in a big breath. "Probably really early. I'm sure my desk looks like a tornado hit it, and my email certainly needs some TLC, which will take me hours to get through. I want to review the footage that was shot while we were away and see what we can use for promos. Rather than being there all night, I prefer to just start before the sun rises."

His fingers spread out, covering almost half of my head. "Promise me something?"

I nodded. "Sure."

"No matter what is said between you and your father, you'll tell me the truth. You won't hold anything back from me. And whatever happens, it's not going to affect us."

My stomach flipped, and I wished I hadn't eaten all that food because now I was nauseous. "Those are some big promises, Beck."

He rested his head on the back cushion. "How much do you care about me?"

The word *love* could easily slip through my lips. That was how much I cared.

But for some reason, "More than anything," was what came out.

His hand moved to my chin. "Then promise."

My eyes closed, the tears building and burning behind them as I whispered, "I promise."

I couldn't sleep.

There was absolutely nothing worse than tossing and turning in Beck's bed, staring at walls, the ceiling, my mind a racecourse that never stopped circling, fearing that I was keeping him awake.

Instead of hoping I would at some point fall asleep and finally get some much-needed rest, I climbed out of bed at around five in the morning and quietly took a shower and got ready for work.

Before I left, I went over to his side of the bed and nuzzled my face in his neck, whispering, "I'll see you at the arena."

He reached his arm back since he was facing the opposite direction from where I was standing, and he put his hand on my cheek and groaned, "I'll see you later."

I kissed his fingers as I removed them from my face, and I let myself out of his house and drove to the arena. I gripped the strap of my bag as I headed inside, taking the elevator to the executive-level floor.

As I was walking down the hallway toward my office, nearing my father's, which I had to pass on the way to mine, I heard, "Jolene, come in."

I stilled from the sound of my father's voice.

"And shut the door."

THIRTY-THREE

Beck

> MARK
> When you get to the arena, come to my office. I want to speak to you.

That was the first thing I saw on my phone when I opened my eyes and reached for my cell on the nightstand and looked through the notifications that had come in overnight.

Boss man wanted to talk.

I could only guess what this conversation was going to be about.

Since Jolie had left just a few minutes ago and I couldn't really fall back asleep, I saw no reason to drag out this impending conversation any further. If Mark wanted to speak to me, he was going to get me bright and early.

I threw on some workout clothes, took a premade protein shake to go, and drove to the arena, parking directly behind Jolie's Wrangler. I sipped the shake while I took the elevator to the top floor and walked down the hallway that led to the executive offices. The arena was silent, only one overhead light was on, and it shone directly over the ice. And aside from Jolie and, I was assuming, her father, only a few other people were here—the engineers who maintained the building and the rink and a couple of security guards.

As I got deeper down the hallway, I heard Mark's voice, and the closer I got to his office, the louder he became. From the midway point between the elevator and the office at the end, I could see Jolie's closed door, and there wasn't any light coming out from beneath it. Which told me the conversation, which I figured they were having now, was in his office.

I stopped outside his door and listened.

"Jolene, I do not understand why you didn't stay at that pool. I specifically asked you to watch over the team and make sure nothing happened. Do you want to know why I gave you that order? Because my gut told me something was going to take place and I was right. Which raises the question, where were you when the incident with Kirk occurred?"

"I'm sorry I wasn't there."

"That doesn't answer my question."

"Dad, I went up to my room. What more is there to say?"

"But why? When I asked you to stay down there? If it was to use the restroom, there are restrooms at the pool. Something isn't adding up here."

"I needed a real moment. That's why."

"What the hell is a real moment, Jolene?" He paused and then continued, "The incident took place at six in the evening. According to the few people I asked—and you know I check my sources when I conduct any kind of investigation—the last time you were seen at the pool was at three. You never returned, so what were you doing in your room that kept you so occupied that no one heard from you until the next morning?"

Through the wall that separated us, I could feel her anxiety.

I could feel her worry, knowing whatever she said could potentially jeopardize her future with the Whales.

But I had a part in this.

I was the reason she had gone to her room. I was the reason she had never checked her phone that night and still hadn't until the morning.

I wasn't going to let her tackle this alone and take all the blame.

Even if that meant putting myself directly in front of the goal without a single piece of equipment on.

I knocked on the door and heard, "Come back."

Instead of following that order, I turned the handle and popped my head through the crack, earning a very intense glare from Mark.

"Beck, I'm speaking to my daughter. Would you mind returning in about thirty minutes when I'm done—"

"Jolie was with me." I opened the door wider and stood in the entrance. "That's why she wasn't at the pool when Kirk's incident happened." I closed the door behind me, and I took a seat next to her in front of his desk.

"Beck—"

I cut Jolie off and said, "That's also why she didn't answer her phone that evening."

I glanced at her, knowing we hadn't discussed coming clean like this to her father, hoping she wouldn't be upset with me for airing our laundry. But if Mark was going to understand what had gone down in Vegas, he had to hear it from every side.

"And that's why she was unreachable until the next morning."

My gaze shifted to Mark. "I got your text. I don't know what you planned on discussing with me today, but it was my intention to have a conversation with you about Jolie. I got to the arena early, I came up here to have that talk, and when I heard what you were saying from outside your door, I couldn't let her take all the blame. This is on me too."

Mark leaned his arms on his desk. "Jolene is an employee of mine. She works for the team. That means when I call her or her colleagues call her, regardless of what time it is, she answers her phone. When she's given an order—like the one I gave her in Vegas—she must follow it. So, no, this isn't your fault." He was turning a silver pen in his hand, the movement halting. "This is her fault, Beck." His head pointed down, and he looked at me dead-on. "But do you want to tell me what the fuck you were doing with my daughter, which goes against the code of conduct she signed?" I went to respond, and he added, "Or do you want me to tell you what I know about the two of you?"

My heart was pounding something fierce, and the inside of my palms were getting wet and clammy.

He knows?

"You know?" Jolie said the words I'd been thinking, her hand going against her chest.

"It wasn't hard to piece together."

Jolie shook her head. "But how?"

His thumbs circled as his hands linked. "Let's see ... the first hint was when you called her Jolie right here in this office." He nodded at me. "The second was when we made the announcement in front of the team that the purchase had gone through. Your mother was in for the week and wanted you to join us for dinner. She called you, and when you didn't answer, she tracked your location." He was now looking at his daughter. "Guess where you were."

"At my house," I replied.

"Your HR file provided your address, and within minutes, I

had my answer. And three, I happened to be walking by the locker room when one of the guys made a comment about Jolene, and you gave that man a real earful." He leaned back in his chair, his arms crossing. "Let it be known, nothing happens within my organization that I don't know about. Even if it involves my daughter."

I gripped both armrests. "Except there's a large piece of this that you don't know."

"And that is?" he questioned.

I gave her a quick peek. I could tell that all of this was eating her up inside.

"Jolie and I didn't meet when she came to work for the Whales. We had met when she was a sophomore at BU. That's how long she's been in my life."

"Is that true?" he asked his daughter.

"Yes." She nodded.

His eyes narrowed, his head almost bopping while he appeared to put together what I'd just admitted. "That explains why you reacted the way you did when I told you I was purchasing the Whales. In my office that day, you were putting together that you were going to be your boyfriend's new boss. And you didn't know what the hell to do with yourself."

"That's right." Her voice was soft. "But he wasn't my boyfriend then."

"Insignificant," Mark barked.

"But the timeline of this is significant," she countered, holding her stomach with both arms. "Even though I signed a code of conduct, things had already happened between Beck and me before my signature dried on that paper. And for what it's worth, I took that code of conduct seriously. I told myself that once I was in this role, nothing would ever happen between us again. I couldn't do both—I couldn't be with him and work for the Whales at the same time."

"Yet you broke that code of conduct, and you broke the promise you'd made to yourself!" Mark snapped.

"With all due respect, you need to back off of her." I tried to keep my voice down, but the sharpness was clear in my tone. "Even if Jolie had been at the pool—or if I had been—I don't think either of us could have stopped Kirk from doing what he did. Kirk and that woman consensually made that choice. But you're making this Jolie's fault and blaming her for his action when Kirk is a grown-ass man. Do you think you could have convinced a guy like him to keep things PG in the pool?" I waited and got nothing. "Come on, Mark. I know she's your daughter, but you've got to ease up on her a bit."

His brows furrowed while he glared at me, but not a word came out of his mouth.

Jolie broke the silence with a deep breath and, "There's a reason I broke that code of conduct, Dad."

"Are you going to tell me you're the reason? That this is your fault?" Mark addressed those questions at me.

I rubbed my palms over my sweatpants and flipped my hat backward, so not even the brim was in the way when I said, "What I am going to tell you is that I'm in love with your daughter."

Mark stared at me as that news set in.

"Dad ..." She waited for him to glance at her, and that was when I looked at her, a flush moving across her cheeks, telling me she felt every word I'd said. "The reason I broke that promise is because I'm in love with him too."

When she gave me her eyes, they were soft. So was her expression. And mine were gentle and as tender as I could possibly make them.

We couldn't say anything to each other at this moment, but we were showing the effects of both statements and what they meant to us.

His arms unfolded, and his hand hit his desk. "Goddamn it." That same hand gripped the side of his face. "This can't work. There's no way I can allow you to be employed with the Whales and date one of the players. It's unethical. It disrupts the balance of power." He shook his head. "The fucking press would have a field day with that news. Can you imagine? Owner's daughter and star player of the league." He pushed against his temples. "I won't have it. I can't."

"And I'll tell them we've been together for a long time, we've just kept things off the radar." I held the edge of his desk and leaned in closer. "You worry it's going to be a controversy. But it's not, Mark. Everyone wants a love story, and we're giving them one. But whatever you do, don't take her away from the team. We need her." When he said nothing, I continued, "How are ticket sales compared to last year?" I asked the question because I knew the answer. "How's our social media following and engagement? How's the hype surrounding this season as we move into our next stint of travel?" I smiled at my girl. "You know a lot of that has to do with Jolie."

"I'm not underestimating my daughter and her abilities. She's exceptional. That's why she works for me. But I'm trying to consider the logistics of this relationship, and I don't believe it can work in a professional setting."

"But it's already been working, Dad."

"Working?" He chuckled. "How about working against me? Had you two not been holed up in that Vegas suite, Kirk wouldn't have gotten himself in a pickle."

A real fucking pickle all right.

"I can't go back and fix the mistake I made. All I can tell you is that it won't happen again." There was so much emotion in her voice.

"You're damn right it won't!"

"You have to admit, before the Kirk incident, things were running so smoothly," she said.

He ignored her and eyed me. "What happens if you two break up?"

I was still holding his desk, and I released it, sliding back in my chair. "Forgive me when I say this, but if you and your wife get divorced, she's half owner of the team—am I right?" His glare told me I was correct. "What would then happen to the ownership? Would it be yours? Hers?" I raised my hand before he could say anything. "The point I'm trying to make is that we can't predict what's going to happen between us—no one in any relationship can. But I can tell you that if it were up to me, she'd be moving in with me now."

His brows rose extremely high, the grooves in his forehead deepening. "Moving in with you?"

I nodded.

He asked his daughter, "And do you agree?"

"Yes, Dad, I agree."

"Let me get this straight." He ran his hand down the back of his hair. "As a business owner who lives, breathes, sleeps, eats, and dies by his company, you're telling me, Beck, that I should just sit back and assume all is going to be good with you two? And if shit hits the fan, I'm supposed to just deal with it then?"

I put my hand on Jolie's shoulder. I needed the contact, and I assumed she did too. "We're mature adults. We know what's at stake. If things were to end, we would handle it cordially."

Her nod told me she agreed.

"But whether I'm with your daughter or not, I want her to have a place within this team."

His head dropped. "I don't know ..." He let out a loud breath. "I just don't know."

"I can handle this, Dad. I need you to trust me."

As her vulnerability hit me, I squeezed the spot I was holding.

She was showing; she wasn't just telling.

All that did was make me love her more.

He lifted his face to say, "You're saying that, regardless of what happens with you and Beck, you will conduct yourself professionally at all times."

"Of course," she replied.

"And the two of you understand what's at risk here—it's one thing to say you do, it's another to actually calculate that risk and look it square in the face." He pushed his chair several inches away from his desk and crossed his legs. "Remember, the second the media speculates that something is amiss between you two, we're going to have another Vegas situation on our hands, and I will not tolerate that."

"Mark, I've been in the mainstream media for a long time. It started in college, and it's been that way my entire career. I know how it works. I'm no rookie when it comes to the press or paparazzi."

"But my daughter is." He focused on her. "Will you be able to handle the spotlight?"

"For Beck"—she gazed at me—"I'm willing to do anything."

Mark rocked in his chair. "I'm not promising either of you anything. But I'm willing to see how things go on a trial basis." He waved his finger in the air. "I hope I don't regret this decision." He took a deep breath. "The second I feel like things aren't working the way I want them to, I'm pulling the plug, and Jolene is getting reassigned to a different account."

She moved to the end of her chair. "Dad, I've worked so hard to get this job. But I can't be the best version of me if I'm constantly walking on eggshells, knowing at any moment, you can take it all away from me." She tucked her hair behind her ear, even though it didn't stay. "I've already taken full responsibility for Vegas. I told you that on the phone when we spoke. I told you that again today before Beck even walked into your office. But the thing is, I'm going to make more mistakes. I'm going to screw up again. I'm human, I'm not perfect. Sometimes, real moments happen in life, and they're out of my control." She was keeping her emotion down, but I could see it; I could feel it. "Just because I have imperfections and I don't do everything the way you want me to doesn't mean I deserve to lose everything."

Fuck.

I was so proud of her.

This was the first time I saw a break in Mark's face. It wasn't a smile, but it wasn't the frown he'd been sporting since I had walked in.

"You have a point ... and I can't disagree with it."

"What are you saying?" she inquired.

He licked his lips and wiped them with his hand. "You conduct yourself with professionalism, and you continue doing what you've been doing, and I think things will be okay —assuming you keep your phone on you at all times." He cleared his throat. "However, I reserve the right to change my mind."

"Fair enough," she said softly.

Smiling for my girl, I asked, "Does that mean we have your blessing?"

"My what?"

I held the top of my hat and said, "I never wanted you to find out this way. I wanted to be the one to tell you. And I realize things have already moved forward, and we went about this in an untraditional way, but I would still like to have your blessing to be with your daughter." I glanced at Jolie. "For one, because it means you trust me with her. And two"—I shifted my gaze at him—"because you're my boss."

His head slowly shook for the second time during this chat. "This isn't easy for me, Beck."

"One day, I'm going to have a daughter—I hope—and I'm going to be in the same position. Well, maybe not the exact same, but you know what I mean."

"I do."

"You have my word, I will not hurt her, and I wouldn't be sitting here, saying any of this, if I didn't see my future with her." I reached for Jolie's hand.

He pointed at me. "If that future involves a ring, your ass had better be right back in this chair, asking for a whole different type of blessing."

I smiled. "Understood."

"Good." He tapped his desk. "Now that you both have gotten what you want today, you can let yourselves out. I need to get some work done." His tone was gentle even if his words weren't.

I waited for Jolie to get up first, and I followed her into the hallway, shutting her father's door behind me. I immediately pulled her into my arms, holding her against me. My mouth pressed into her hair, and I breathed her in. "I'm so fucking happy that's behind us."

"You have no idea," she sighed. "I cannot believe you came into Dad's office. That you had my back like that. That you tried to take the blame." She looked up at me. "You were there for me in ways I hadn't expected."

"I will always have your back in every way."

I finally got a smile out of her. "You told my father you're in love with me."

"So did you."

She wrapped her arms around my neck. "Say it to me."

"I love you, Jolie." I grinned, stabbing my bottom lip with my teeth. "And that's just what I'm going to tell the guys today at practice—before threatening their lives if they ever utter another word about you."

Her eyes went wide. "You're telling them today?"

I chuckled. "That's not the important part."

"What is?"

"You saying you love me back."

She slid her fingers through my hair. "I'm completely, fully, and wildly in love with you."

"Sit down," I said to the team once everyone finally returned to the locker room after practice.

"*Ohhh*, the captain has something to say. Listen up, you guys!" Kirk shouted. When the room turned silent, he added, "Whatcha got for us?"

I tossed my gloves and crossed my sweaty arms over my chest. "There will be no more comments from any of you about Jolene Jameson. Not even a fucking hint of a comment. That also includes looking at her for longer than a few seconds. Smiling too fucking large at her. Or getting close enough to her that you get even the faintest hint of her perfume." I paused. "Have I made myself clear?"

"Someone's in love." One of the guys snickered.

I didn't correct him.

Because he was right.

And everyone in this room knew it.

"It's been almost three years in the making, and she's finally mine." When each of the guys nodded, my arms dropped. "I'm glad you all understand."

THIRTY-FOUR

Jolie

As I was walking toward the entrance of the locker room, taking the back way to the ice, Landon was on his way out, smiling as soon as he saw me, releasing the door from his fingertips. I gave him a wave, stopping mid-hallway to speak to him.

"Hi." I studied his face, which was still flushed from practice, drips from his wet hair running down it. "You look tired. Are you feeling okay?"

"Hey, Jolene." He adjusted the strap of his bag as it dangled on his shoulder. "I'm good. Just exhausted. Sore. And really looking forward to our day off tomorrow before we hit the road."

Kirk, along with two of our wings, came out of the locker room, each one greeting me cordially as they passed. Their smiles not too big, their tones even, their eyes staying above my neck.

"My, how things have changed." My lips were pulled into a toothless smile as I shook my head at Beck's best friend.

"Their lives were threatened."

I laughed. "I'm not even a little surprised."

He pointed toward the door behind him. "Beck is almost done. I know he wants to talk to you, so don't go anywhere."

"You got it."

"See you on the plane in two days." He patted me on the shoulder.

As he was walking away, I took my phone out to shoot my team a text. Just as I was hitting Send, I smelled Beck, the spiciness filling my nose, causing my eyes to slowly gaze up from my screen. He was dressed in a pair of gray sweats, his T-shirt tight enough to show the outline of his pecs, with his sweatshirt unzipped and hanging open, a backward hat on his head. His beard was now a heavy shadow across his cheeks, whiskers long enough that I could just clasp it between my fingers.

Butterflies instantly exploded in my stomach.

It had only been a few hours since I'd seen him ... would I ever stop feeling this way?

"Hey, you." He stopped in front of me, keeping a professional distance, but he held the base of my neck, his thumb stroking my skin.

"Hey, you." I knew my smile was obnoxiously big, and I didn't care. Even if I tried to hide it from anyone walking by—although there was no reason to because everyone knew we were in a relationship—I couldn't.

"I was going to go to your office to find you. What are you doing down here?"

I checked my watch. "My team shot some footage of your practice while I was in a meeting. I came this way to find them. I was thinking I'd edit some of it so I can add it to the campaign we're starting tomorrow to promote the Colorado and Nashville away games you have coming up in a few days."

His hand rose to my jaw. "Do you have to edit the footage or can someone else do it?"

My hands went to my hips. "Why?"

"Because I have tomorrow off."

"And?"

He pulled his hand back and stroked his lips with the pad of his finger. "I planned something."

I laughed. "So, because you have this afternoon and all day tomorrow off, you think I can just ditch work and hang with you?"

He nodded, grinning. "That's exactly what I think."

"Beck ..."

"Run away with me, Jolie."

He made everything enticing. A five-word sentence felt like the most exhilarating one I'd ever heard.

The truth was, I didn't have to be at the arena. I had the capabilities to work from home since my laptop could access every task I needed to accomplish. Plus, my assistants would much rather be working from the comfort of their couches as well.

I came to the arena to see Beck.

"Where would we be running to?" I asked.

He took a step closer. "You either say yes and we leave right now. Or you say no and you never find out what I had planned."

My hands lifted from my waist, my arms crossing over my chest. "Now that's just mean."

"What's your answer, gorgeous?"

"I mean ..." I glanced down my body. I had on jeans and a Whales sweatshirt. A pair of cute sneakers. And my hair, it was in a high ponytail—today wasn't a wash day. "Look at me. I'm dressed for a game, not to go out anywhere. Shouldn't I change? Or ..."

"You look perfect." He held my chin. "Stop looking for reasons, Jolie. Just say yes."

I gazed into those beautiful hazel eyes. Eyes that could get me to agree to almost anything. "Yes."

He held out his hand for me to grab. "Come on."

"You're not going to tell me where we're going?" My fingers clasped his, and as we neared the exit of the arena, I added, "What about my laptop? It's in my office. I need to get it so I can get some work done."

"Work your assistants will cover while you're gone." He gave me a long stare. "Where I'm taking you, you're not going to be needing anything but me."

While I'm gone?

"And my Jeep, Beck. It's in the parking lot. Are you going to bring me back here later so I can grab it? I'm assuming we're taking your car?"

He laughed. "So many questions."

"I feel like I'm getting kidnapped. On a random Tuesday. Sue me for wanting to know things." I winked at him.

"Here's all you're getting: a driver is picking us up, and my assistant will have your Jeep taken to my house. Where's your fob?"

What is even happening right now?

"It's in the top drawer of my desk."

"Is your office unlocked?"

"Yes."

He took out his phone, holding it in his palm while he typed with his thumb, appearing to send a text before his cell went back into his pocket. "Done."

"You make everything look so easy."

He smiled at me as we walked through the door of the

arena, an SUV waiting for us directly outside. "Because it is, baby."

When I stepped onto Beck's private plane, I had no idea where we were flying to. Five hours later, as we were getting ready to land, I still didn't know. The monitors inside were dark. The flight attendant had given absolutely no hints at all. The two captains had provided updates, but without the mention of a destination or where we were flying over.

But what had been waiting for me on one of the seats when we boarded was a bag that Beck's assistant had packed for me—the only clue that, wherever we were going, we were staying overnight. Inside were four outfits, shoes, accessories, cosmetics, and makeup. One day, I would meet CC—the woman who had worked for the Weston family for years—and get to thank her in person for having such incredible taste, taste that had only improved from the clothes she'd bought me in college. For now, I just used Beck's phone to text her, sending her my appreciation that way.

"We're about to land," Beck said from the seat beside me. We'd just finished nibbling on a charcuterie board, seated on a couch together, our food and drinks on a table in front of us. "Do you have any idea where we are?"

"No." I huffed. "I don't know if we went east or west, north or south. Every time I look out the window, nothing below gives it away."

His hand fanned over my cheek. "Surprising you might be my second favorite thing."

"Yeah? What's your first?"

He smiled as the plane landed on the tarmac, wrapping his arm around my shoulders and pressing his lips against the side of my head. He held me like that until the plane stopped and the flight attendant opened the door, releasing the stairs to the ground.

He took me by the hand to the exit, whispering in my ear as we stood together in the doorway, "Bringing you home."

Home.

I glanced around the runway, looking for signs, a distinguishable mark—anything. And I took a long, deep breath. Oh God, it smelled just like Boston—a scent only a person from the city would be able to detect and appreciate.

I looked at the man I loved and whispered, "Why?"

Out of all places, here.

There had to be a reason. I was dying to know what it was.

Still holding my hand, he led me down the stairs toward the SUV that was waiting just beside the jet. The driver had the door already open for us, and we climbed into the back seat. One of the crew members packed our bags into the trunk, and the driver steered us away from the runway.

"Why Boston?" he clarified.

I nodded.

"I have the smallest break in my schedule, and since we won't be playing here until later in the season, I thought you could use a little taste of the Northeast. It's been a bit since you were here. I know you've missed it."

"How do you know that?"

"No matter how hard I've tried, I've never been able to fuck the Boston off you." His eyes dipped to my lap. "And we both know I've really fucking tried."

I laughed. "You have."

"But for real, whenever I travel, LA is where I crave to return to. I'm sure you feel the same way about your city." He kissed my cheek. "I don't want you to miss it so hard that you want to move back."

"That's not going to happen."

"You're sure about that?"

I moved my arm around his neck. "Beck, it doesn't matter where I live as long as I'm with you. You're my home."

"*Mmm*." He kissed me hard. "I like that answer."

I unraveled from his neck and linked our fingers. "How long are we here for?"

"We have all of tonight and most of tomorrow. Our plane leaves at eleven p.m., so we get back in time to fly with the team to Colorado at ten the next morning. We'll sleep on my jet, and we can nap on the team's plane if we need to. But seeing your smile right now makes the impending tiredness well worth it."

"I still can't believe you brought me here. Do you have things planned for us?" I snuggled under his arm.

"I didn't want to take anything away from you—a spot you wanted to visit, a restaurant you wanted to eat at. The time we spend here is all in your hands, baby."

"Where are we staying?"

"Miss Questions today." He laughed. "When I spoke to your father about this trip, he told me we should stay at their place."

My brows rose. "You told my father you were bringing me here?"

"I did."

"And he offered for us to stay there?"

"He sure did."

"Are you trying to score brownie points?"

He laughed again. "I don't think that's needed. Your father knows at this point that I'm very much in love with his daughter." He grazed my lips with his.

"Just so you know, we wouldn't only be in separate bedrooms, we'd be on different floors."

"I figured, but that's not the reason I declined his offer."

The SUV was navigating the city traffic. I tried to pay attention to which direction we were going, but there was something so intriguing about this conversation; I was having a hard time keeping my eyes off Beck.

"What was the reason?"

He set his hand on top of my head. "Well, from what I understand, your parents live in Beacon Hill."

"They do."

"But that's not your favorite part of the city."

I stared into his eyes, trying to look past them, to see the words Beck wasn't speaking. "My favorite part of the city ... how do you even know where that is?"

"You told me. The night I met you, when we were in the car on the way to my hotel."

The conversation was barely coming back to me, but within those tiny specks of memories, I recalled saying something about South Boston.

"How do you remember that?"

"I remember everything about you, Jolie. I've said that to you many times before. So, when I was looking for a place here, I only searched in South Boston."

I shook my head, in awe of him, stilling to say, "You looked? Not your assistant?"

"I got no help with this one." He smiled. "It was all me."

"I'm suddenly very impressed."

"Just wait ... it gets better."

The SUV pulled up in front of a high-rise, the driver opening our door. Beck got out first and helped me to the ground. A valet attendant grabbed our bags while Beck led me inside the building.

I looked around the lobby, one that resembled where Ginger and I lived in LA, but this was far nicer. "This isn't a hotel."

Beck escorted me to the elevator, the doors instantly opening, and he waved a fob in front of the reader before pressing the PH button. "No. It's not a hotel."

"Did you rent an apartment for the night?"

"More questions."

"I can't help it. I'm so fascinated with everything that's happening—at the arena, on the plane, here, now."

He chuckled, and once the elevator climbed to the top floor and the doors opened, he brought me out. It took a moment before I realized we weren't in a hallway. We were already inside a condo that was fully decorated with art and furniture. An entire wall of windows in the living room showed the most incredible view of the city.

"Holy shit," I whispered as I walked toward the glass wall.

Beck moved in behind me, his hands on my stomach, his face in my neck while I stared out at Boston. "Welcome home, Jolie."

"What?" I felt myself jump. "Home?" I turned around to face him.

"You love this city. I know it was hard for you to leave it. Of course, you can always stay at your parents', but I can't—at least not in your bed, and I don't like sleeping without you. So, I bought us this place, and when we come to visit, we'll stay here. And if you come back without me, you have a choice of being here or in Beacon Hill."

The only reason I knew my head was shaking was because I started to get dizzy. "Hold on a second. Did I hear you right? You said you *bought* this condo for us? This is ... *ours*?"

"Our first of many homes."

I surrounded his neck with my arms, a sound of complete awe and semi-deliriousness and laughter coming from me. "What are you?"

"I told you ... a man in love with you." He kissed me, softly at first and then with a little more urgency.

With his lips on mine, I not only heard those words.

I felt them.

And he showed them to me in so many ways, this being one.

When he pulled back, he said, "I had your parents come look at the space to make sure it was as perfect as it appeared in the pictures."

"Were they shocked you were doing this for me?"

"You mean, because I'm a wild one when it comes to you?"

I poked his chest. "Not just when it comes to me."

He smiled. "I think your dad was happy I was bringing his baby home."

THIRTY-FIVE

Beck

I knew our winning streak would eventually end. There was no way we could have an undefeated season, but losing to Nashville had not been on my fucking bingo card. The blow was devastating. The morale during the flight home was plain old ugly.

My team wasn't happy, and there wasn't a goddamn thing I could say to cheer them up. Even though we'd won our first game on the road, destroying Colorado in a shutout, Nashville had outplayed us—there was no way around it.

And once we landed back in LA, I couldn't even go home and rest my body because I had an obligation this evening to The Weston Group. From where the team's plane landed, Jolie and I walked right across the tarmac and boarded my jet, flying to San Antonio for the opening night of Horned.

We changed during the flight, and once we touched down in Texas, we got into the SUV that was waiting for us on the runway to take us straight to the restaurant.

I was holding Jolie's hand in the back seat, feeling how sweaty it was becoming.

"Are you nervous?"

She looked at me while she messed with her curls. She pushed them up, she slid them back, and she brought them to the front of her shoulder again. "How can you tell?"

"Where are the nerves coming from?"

Her chest rose and stayed high, even as she said, "I have this strange feeling the paparazzi is going to be there."

"Oh, they'll be there all right. Hart will have made sure of that. He wants every bit of press he can get for this opening. The more cameras, the more celebrity shots, the more buzz, the more reservations."

She rubbed her lips together, her eyes so wide that I worried they were going to burst. "This is the first time we'll be photographed as a couple. Which means, before the night is over, our picture is going to be blasted across the internet."

"And that's a bad thing?"

She shook her head. "I'm just ... anxious."

"Don't be. You're mine. The only person's opinion that matters is this guy right here." I tapped my chest. "And you look so fucking gorgeous tonight."

My stare drifted down her body. She had on a jumpsuit that was black, but the V-neck was cut low, showing a small amount of tit. The material hugged her hips and ass. I hadn't been able to keep my hands off her when we landed.

"You shot me down on the plane—I get it, you didn't want to look 'fucked,' as you called it. But the second we get back on that plane tonight, you are going to get fucked."

She smiled without showing any teeth, shaking her head. "How do you do that?"

"Do what?"

"Make everything perfect."

I leaned into her neck, inhaling her vanilla-amber aroma that I'd never seen her put on once tonight, but it smelled as though she'd just sprayed it over her skin. "I cannot wait to show you off."

"Show me off?"

"Yes. As mine." My lips lingered on her cheek before I pulled back. "The team knows, the staff knows, our families know. Ginger too. All the important people have been covered. Now it's everyone else's turn."

"You mean the women who get all hot and bothered by your stretching memes?" She rolled her eyes. "I can't wait to see how they're going to react to the news."

"The longer you're with me, which I intend to be forever, you're going to learn one thing that's extremely important."

"And that is?"

"We don't give a fuck what any of those people think. They don't matter, Jolie. What matters is us."

She put her hand over the side of my beard and whispered, "You're right."

The SUV pulled up in front of the restaurant, and there were several paparazzi stationed by the stairs near the entrance. Since the property was directly on River Walk, with a pedestrian sidewalk that sandwiched the water and our eatery, I assumed there were more paparazzi stationed there.

Which meant, tonight, we would be surrounded by cameras.

Jolie wasn't just wading in; she was going face-first into the middle of the ocean.

"Are you ready?" I asked.

"As ready as I'll ever be."

"Remember, it's just us. No one else matters."

She nodded.

I got out of the SUV first, and the flashes from the cameras immediately hit my eyes. I held out my hand, and Jolie clasped my fingers, and I helped her climb from the back seat. Once her heels were on the ground, I didn't let her go.

"Tough loss today, Beck," one of them said. "How do you feel about going into the Detroit game in a couple of days? Think the Whales will restart their winning streak?"

"The Whales will be in the finals this year—mark my words," I replied.

"What about those rumors that Landon is getting traded to Philadelphia?" another one asked.

I repositioned my hand over the small of Jolie's back and led her toward the stairs. "That's a rumor I haven't heard."

And that was all it was—a rumor. Mark wasn't trading Landon; he was the best goddamn goalie in the league.

"Do you want to tell us who's on your arm?" I was asked next.

I stopped at the top of the stairs and turned around to face the small crowd. "You mean who the love of my life is?" I rejoined our fingers, and she squeezed them so tightly. "This is Jolene Jameson, the head of marketing for the Whales."

"The owner's daughter?" one of them asked.

There was no reason to hide her identity. The second these photos were posted, the speculation would start. It was best to put out the fire with my own voice rather than someone else's.

"Yes," I responded. "And she finally agreed to date me after almost three years of begging her."

"Three years?" one of them yelled. "That's a long time to make someone wait."

Jolie gave the camera a smile. "He had to earn me."

I chuckled at her perfect response and brought her inside, the doors closing behind us, and I could tell Jolie was finally breathing again.

"You did great."

"I'm so glad that's over with."

"Don't get too comfortable. I'm sure there are some lingering in the back of the restaurant." Still holding her hand, I walked her into the bar, where my entire family, minus Walker, was standing.

"Uncle Beck!"

Colson's daughter, Ellie, was running to me, and I picked her up.

"How's my girl?"

She rested her tiny hand against my shoulder. "I'm the best!"

"Yes, you are." I laughed and kissed her cheek. "Do you remember Jolie?"

Ellie had met Jolie at one of our home games, but my niece didn't always recall the people she was introduced to.

Ellie reached for Jolie's hair and began to twirl it. "*Mmm*, I remember!"

"It's so nice to see you again, Ellie." Jolie was rubbing my niece's back.

"You have the best hair in the whole wide world."

"Maybe if you're good tonight, Jolie will let you braid it."

Ellie's eyes went wide. "You will?"

"After she has a very stiff whiskey with a splash of sour mix, which you're going to help her get."

Jolie playfully slapped my arm. "You're not sending your niece on a drink run, are you?"

I set Ellie down and said to her, "See that woman over there?" I pointed toward Ginger. "Once she hugs Jolie—and that's going to happen at any second—take her by the hand and bring her to the bar. I bet she'll get you the best Shirley Temple you've ever had."

"Ginger!" Jolie yelled once she followed my finger.

Ellie smiled at me. "I'm on it, Uncle Beck. I love Shirley Temples."

"Oh my God, what are you doing here?" Jolie squealed as she ran into Ginger's arms.

"Apparently, I have to come all the way to Texas to see my best friend." While Ginger hugged my girl, she gave me a smile and mouthed, *Thank you.*

Since she couldn't make the time that our corporate jet was taking off, I'd bought her a first-class ticket and arranged transportation to the hotel I'd booked for her.

I grinned back and joined my siblings.

"I can't believe you're here on a game day," Eden said after she hugged me.

"That's one of the perks of playing an early afternoon game," I said to her.

Colson gave me a pound. "You must be beat?"

"I will be, I'm sure." I gripped the back of my neck after man-hugging Hart. "I'm still seething over the loss."

"What would you tell me?" Hart asked.

I let out a long, loud breath. "That you can't win them all ..."

Hart shook my shoulder. "Exactly."

I glanced around the bar, the part of the dining room I could see from here, the open kitchen, where there was no sign of my brother. "Place looks incredible."

"Doesn't it?" Eden said. "We were down to the wire. Hart almost murdered the contractor. But it all pulled together, and everyone is still alive, and our guests won't notice the small imperfections that the contractor's crew will fix tonight once the restaurant closes to the public."

"Jesus," I groaned. "It was like that?"

The anger flashed across Hart's face before his girl, Sadie, joined him. "You have no idea," he said.

Sadie leaned across the space in which we were standing, and we kissed cheeks. "So happy you could make it, Beck."

"Good to see you, Sadie." I took another look around the restaurant. "Guys, where's Walker?"

They all took deep breaths and stared at each other and eventually at me.

"He's ... not here," Colson said.

"What the fuck do you mean, he's not here?" I pressed.

Eden grabbed my arm, her eyes giving me a warning. "We have a lot to tell you."

"Then tell me."

Hart shook his head. "Not here, Beck. Not now."

What the fuck does that mean?

Jolie and Ginger, holding hands with Ellie, joined our circle, my girl sipping on a drink as she moved in next to me.

I kissed the side of her head, and while I listened to my family speak to her—a group who adored her—my mind was on Walker.

This restaurant, like all the others we owned, was my brother's baby.

His love.

So, why the fuck wasn't he here?

THIRTY-SIX

Jolie

"*I like the quiet before the storm.*"

That was the way Beck had once described the arena. When almost all the lights were out and the employees were gone and silence filled the large, echoing space. Now that the situations were similar—everyone had left for the night and I was the last person in the building—I understood exactly what he'd meant. Only the spotlight above the rink was on, the scoreboards black, the stands empty, making Beck's description resonate even more.

After spending countless hours here, week after week, I had learned there was something special about the silence. The quietness spoke to me; it hummed inside my stomach. It gave me little bolts of excitement as my brain spiraled, thinking about the loudness of tomorrow's game.

We were going to play Boston. I was in knots about it.

Since it was my home team against my new home team, I'd spent some extra time editing. I'd studied the numbers. I'd reviewed our preparations for the game. And when my eyes felt like they couldn't look at my computer screen for another second, I locked my office door, and I took the elevator to the first floor.

With my keys in my hand, I approached the exit that would dump me out at the employee lot. But I stayed right there, in front of the glass, completely still. I didn't even raise the fob to the reader.

Because I heard a noise.

And it was ... the sound of skates slicing through fresh ice.

Someone's here?

But in order for them to be here, they would have to get through security and have their own set of keys.

That meant ...

I headed down the hallway, past the locker room, and once I entered the short tunnel, the sight made my stomach explode with those familiar butterflies.

It didn't matter what that man did; he looked beautiful doing it.

"What are you doing?" My hands went to my hips.

Beck wasn't even holding a stick as he circled the ice. He didn't have on any equipment. He was wearing a pair of gray sweatpants and a Whales sweatshirt, a backward hat on his head, a smile beaming from his face.

"Having fun." He skated toward me. "What are *you* doing?"

"I was going home for the night."

He halted at the opening of the rink and held out his hand. "Put on a pair of skates and join me."

"I don't know how to skate."

"What? How did I not know this about you?" He towered over me, the wall of the rink dividing us, the size of his body looking even more massive and muscular. "You're from New

England. It's freezing there. Don't all you Bostonians know how to skate?"

I laughed. "I'm from the city, Beck. Sure, there were rinks. But the only skating I did was with shoes while I was slipping on black ice."

"Not the same."

"Obviously."

His hand was still out, and he pulled at the air. "Come here."

"On the ice? Without skates?"

"Yes, Jolie. On the ice. And without skates."

I held his fingers tightly, knowing I was bound to slip, and stepped onto the raised rink, feeling the coldness seep through the soles of my shoes and go right up my dress. But I wasn't on the ice for long because once I was standing directly in front of Beck, he lifted me into his arms and wrapped me around his body.

"Now, let's go for a little skate."

I hugged his shoulders, begging, "Please don't fall."

"I'm better on blades than I am in sneakers." He gave me a kiss. "Trust me."

"If I didn't, we wouldn't be doing this right now."

Roller-skating had never been my thing. Neither had rollerblading. The only time I'd ever felt the air move past me this fast was on a bike. But that felt nothing like this.

Maybe it was being in Beck's arms that made it different. Maybe it was being on our ice.

Maybe it was that hockey had been what brought us together at the same place and at the same time, and now, as I hugged his body against mine, it felt like we'd come full circle.

Whatever this feeling was, I loved it.

And when he positioned his face in front of mine and the

wind was blowing my hair around us and he whispered, "Kiss me," I didn't hesitate.

Nor did I question how he knew where he was going if his eyes were closed.

I didn't tell him to slow down.

Or stop.

I just fit my lips to his. I took in the warmth of his tongue as it slid into my mouth, and I felt the hardness of his body as it pressed into mine.

We were speeding around turns, going from backward to forward, the change of direction and airflow hitting my stomach each time, and his mouth never left me.

But with each pass around the rink, his kiss changed.

So did the placement of his hands. The deepness of his breath. The way he wasn't just holding me, but drawing me in against him.

Signs that told me this moment wasn't just for kissing.

It was for far more.

"Are there cameras on us?"

I knew it.

My eyes opened, and I loosened my arms the slightest bit so I could lean back and really take in his face. "You're kidding me, right?"

He chuckled, picking up a little speed since he'd slowed. "I'm far from kidding."

"You want to do this here? On the ice? While skating?"

"I can't think of a more perfect spot." He ground the tip of his hard-on against me and nibbled on my bottom lip. "Look what you've done to me."

"Beck..."

"Are there cameras on us?" he repeated.

I was hesitant to give him that answer. The second I did, I knew what was going to happen.

"I can tell by your silence that there aren't." He smiled, and it was devilish and devastatingly sexy. "And you're thinking of all the ways to tell me this is a horrible idea."

"Actually, I was going to remind you that isn't exactly the professionalism my father was talking about."

"But your father wouldn't know." He kissed me, gently this time, and moaned when he separated us. "No one would know. We're not on a live feed. We're not being recorded. No one is here. Security is outside." He came to a fast stop and moved me toward the wall behind the goalpost. "Which means, technically, I can do anything I want to you right now." By putting me against the glass, he could finally lift his hand from where he was holding my butt and place it on my face.

"Technically, yes."

"And nothing is stopping me ... besides you." His brows rose even though his forehead was mostly hidden by the back of the hat. "What do you say, baby? Are you going to give me your pussy while we're on this ice?"

THIRTY-SEVEN

Beck

"What do you say, baby? Are you going to give me your pussy while we're on this ice?"

As I stared at Jolie, waiting for her to respond, I was positive I'd never wanted anything as badly as I wanted her right now.

Having her here, in my arms, in this rink—it was making my dick throb in a way I couldn't control.

She was making me ache.

Pulse.

My thoughts were consumed with only one thing: pounding her cunt until we were both screaming.

All premeditated, of course. I had known she would be working late, and we'd be the only ones here at this hour. So, the entire drive to the arena, I had been teased with the idea of what I could do to her on this ice. Each red light goading me, fucking jerking my cock, my mind a wild mix of what I wanted and what she would give me.

With my arm positioned under her ass, my other hand on her face, she began to wiggle. At first, I thought she was trying to get me to put her down. Then I realized she was lifting her dress, moving it in a way to invite me in.

My girl was giving me everything I wanted.

And the look in her eyes told me that everything I was feeling, she was feeling too.

"Are you wearing panties?"

I knew her pussy was wet. Her smile told me that. The way her lips didn't close, but stayed open, and she panted through them. How her pupils were dilated.

"Don't I always?"

My hand left her face and slid down her chest, my thumb grazing her nipple, and I maneuvered my way under her dress until my fingertips met silk. With one hard pull, I had them ripped off and shoved into the pocket of my sweatshirt.

"You know, you could have just moved them to the side." The way she shook her head told me she'd expected nothing less out of me.

"I could have." Like a yo-yo, my hand was pulled right back to her pussy, tracing the outside, giving her a bit of the teasing I'd experienced during my commute. "But this was more fun."

"*Mmm.*" Her eyes closed. Her fingers sank into the whiskers of my beard, and when that wasn't enough, they went to my head and began to pull those strands. "Beck ..."

"Feels good, doesn't it?"

I traced my finger down her clit. Her wetness reached all the way to the top, getting thicker as I lowered to the base of her pussy. But I couldn't taunt that spot like I could with the rest of her.

Because it fucking owned me.

Because I needed it.

Because she needed it.

And as my finger slowly circled and dipped, her pussy took me right in.

All the way in.

Slick against my skin, contracting around me.

"Fuck!"

"Yes," I groaned. "I can feel how much you want my dick."

Her palms went to the sides of my face, locking our gazes as she begged, "Give it to me. Please."

"You want it, then you take it." I sucked the desire off her bottom lip. "Pull my dick out and put it inside you."

There was no hesitation. Not even a one-second stall before she slid beneath the fabric at my waist, fisted my crown, and aimed me toward her. A slight shift of her hips, and my tip was in.

Just that little bit, and a burst of heat came over my body.

A wave of warmth that jolted me awake.

A tightness that was strong enough to send me to my knees.

A level of wetness that reconfirmed what I'd already known.

This woman was going to be my fucking wife.

"Ah!" Her head banged the glass, the same noise that was made during a game, a sound I was as familiar with as her moans. And a movement she had done on purpose, her body's way of reacting to pleasure. "My God, you have the most perfect dick."

"And it's all yours."

She placed her thumb across the center of my lips. "I want more."

"Take it."

I repositioned us, now holding her with both arms, and once she was settled, she began to bounce, each bob sending me deeper into her cunt.

"That feels so good," she exhaled.

This felt better than fucking good.

This felt incredible.

Because with each plunge, she was becoming narrower. All that did was add more friction. And all that did was make my orgasm build.

"Harder." I gave her ass a slap. "Come on. Fucking ride me, baby."

She listened.

She gave.

And when I back and thrust forward, she took it.

"Hell yes," I roared.

But if we kept up this pace, I was going to come, and she was too, and I didn't want that to happen yet.

"Let's go for a skate."

Her eyes flicked open, her hands pushing my face back so she could get a better look at me. "Now? Like this?"

"Just like this."

My back was facing the rink, so I turned us around and began to glide across the surface of the ice, holding her weight with my arms, using each push off to drive into her. A few quick glances gave me my location. But I didn't really need it. I knew the rink, the distance between each net, how many sweeps of my skates it took to get from one to the other.

"You're going faster," she gasped. "Beck!"

I didn't know if she was talking about my speed or the way I was fucking her—but both were true.

I slowed as I neared the opposite end, circling the net, my skates crossing over each other before I could build up momentum and charge toward the center.

"Fuck me, Jolie!"

There was so much movement.

Pressure.

She was gripping my shoulders as I rocked her up and

down, and she was exhaling across my face each time I was fully inside her.

There was something so goddamn exhilarating about this.

"Baby!" I bent my knees a little and stroked upward, knowing that arch was hitting her G-spot, fully expecting her reaction when she let out a scream. "You like that, don't you?"

"*Yesss.*" Her nails bit into me like teeth. "More!"

I was taking another lap, nearing the opponent's bench, speeding past it, but as I approached our bench, something about it enticed me. I squeezed my fingers into her ass to ensure she was secure, and as I got a little closer, to the spot where I wanted us, I turned one skate, and I made a hockey stop—a quick, immediate halt that sent ice shooting into the air.

"Shit!" she screamed. "Beck, what the hell?!"

"Sorry, I should have warned you."

I chuckled as I set her on the edge of the half wall that separated our bench from the rink. Once she was balanced on top, I could lean her back and use my momentum to drive into her. So, I unraveled her legs from around me, bending her knees and setting her feet against the lip of the wall.

Before I thrust back into her, I took a second to glance down her body.

Jesus Christ.

This was all one big fucking dream.

My gorgeous Jolie.

Her bare, beautiful pussy.

While I was surrounded by hockey.

"I love you," I whispered against her mouth while I stroked into her.

I held her face while I kissed her. I wasn't gentle. Not with her tongue, not with her lips, roughing up the sides of her mouth with the edges of my beard. And as I pummeled her cunt, her breathing getting heavier, her pussy contracting around me, my hand trickled down her body, stopping at each nipple to give them a squeeze through her bra.

"Agh!" She was sucking in air every time she released it. "More!"

Her sounds were only getting louder.

Because she knew I was on my way to her clit.

And she knew within a few seconds of me touching it, she was going to come.

"Fuck." I couldn't handle the way she was milking me, demanding the cum from me. "I can feel how close you're getting."

When she put her hands on my abs, her eyes locked with mine.

Her mouth parted.

But that didn't last because her teeth found her bottom lip; she bit down, and she didn't let it go. Within a few strokes, that was all it took; she was screaming, "I'm going to come!"

Fuck, I was too.

My balls were already tightening, tingles flickering—I'd just been holding them off, waiting for her to join me.

"I cannot fucking wait to come inside you."

Her hand lowered, her fingers closing in around the base of my cock, and they stayed like that for a few drives before she moved to my sac, palming them, tickling them. The words, "Oh my God," rumbling through her throat.

I massaged her clit, rubbing circles over it, swiping from every direction. And it was that fast movement, combined with some hard, relentless fucking, that sent my girl over the edge.

"Ah!" She inhaled, the air quivering through her lungs. "Fuck me!"

As I watched her shudder, my orgasm was coming in right behind her. I reared back and bucked forward, each plunge sending my cum deeper into her pussy.

"Jolie!" Even though my body was a battle of sensitivity, my power increased, and my speed picked up. "Hell yes!"

Her hands slid toward my chest and held the sides of my face, pulling me to her mouth. The moment our lips touched, I emptied the rest of myself inside her, my body overtaken with spasms, matching hers.

We screamed together.

We clutched each other.

And when we moved past our peak and we were ready for stillness, I killed the pace just like it was a hockey stop.

"My God." Her lips hovered over mine. "I did not think I was going to love ice sex."

I smiled. I couldn't fucking help it. "And now?"

"I've been converted."

I nuzzled my lips against her cheek. "You know what you're also going to love?"

"What?"

I rubbed my thumb over her mouth, dragging it across her bottom lip since that was my favorite. "When I eat your pussy in the shower of our locker room."

EPILOGUE

Beck

The Stanley Cup Playoffs

Game seven. We were tied with Tampa, the series three to three. The winner of tonight's game would take home the Cup.

And there were twenty-three fucking seconds left on the clock.

My right wing and I were on each side of Tampa's net, my center at the point.

Positioned.

Ready.

And we were passing the puck between us, looking for an in. Only a couple of inches would be enough, but their goalie was good, and so were their defensemen.

This was going to be hard—we knew that.

I didn't want the game to go into overtime. We were tired.

The level of play was so much more intense during the finals, and each period, although only twenty minutes long, had felt like they were double that.

But with the score two to two, we either had to make this goal, or overtime was happening.

I could hear Coach yelling from the bench. Words that triggered schematics and certain plays—things we had learned during practice when we studied Tampa's lines and their style of attack.

Except it didn't matter how much time I'd spent in the league, or how many shots on goal I'd taken throughout the years, or what we had covered during practice and watching film; nothing could have prepared me for a situation like this.

This was part luck, part skill, and part timing.

The puck went to my center, his arm rising, his skates pointed toward the ice to ground him, but he didn't shoot toward the goal; he passed it to me instead.

Ten seconds.

I didn't look up at the clock. The crowd gave me the countdown.

Time was the only thing I heard from them. Everything else—their chanting, screaming, cheering—never came close to hitting my ears.

If I shot and it was deflected or caught by the goalie, we'd lose our chance. I couldn't take that risk. The only way the puck could get in that goal was if there was a clear opening.

And I didn't have one.

Fuck me.

I skated toward the left, hoping the new angle would create one.

Eight seconds.

Seven.

I returned the puck to my center, who immediately

directed it to my right wing. The slightest nod of his head told me his plan. He was going to fake a pass to the center, which meant it would come to me; the goalie would be too focused on the middle, and I could hook it into the corner of the net.

I just couldn't miss.

Five seconds.

It was either now or never.

The small disk flew toward me across the ice, taking about as much time as a blink. Rather than capturing it with my stick, aiming, shooting, I met the puck as it was still in motion, repositioning my body to rear my arm back, and I connected with the bottom of the rubber.

The placement had to be just right to send it into the air. The intensity in which my stick hit it had to be perfect. The goalie had to leave the smallest hole uncovered, allowing it into the net.

So many factors.

But when they worked together, the puck would soar across the zone, through the crease, and hit the net.

Like it just did.

The puck sank into the top pocket, hitting the back of the goal and falling behind the line.

My stick lifted, my mouth opened, and I froze, waiting for the red light behind the boards to go off, for the goal horn to blow—signals that indicated the goal was fair, unless the refs challenged the play.

And then I heard it—the blow of the horn—and all I saw was a glow of red.

Then, "Goal," screamed out of my mouth.

Not just from me.

From the crowd.

From my center and right wing, the three of us charging

each other as the buzzer for the game went off. Time had run out.

We won.

We fucking won!

The entire team came out onto the ice, including Coach, the trainers, and the staff, and I was suddenly picked up by two players and held in the air while my entire team below shouted, "Beck! Beck!"

This was the first time all night that I glanced into the stands. I saw my family's box; everyone was in there, standing and pointing toward me, so I lifted my stick and gave them some love. The owner's box was center ice, and that was where I looked next. There were several people inside, but none had the beautiful red hair I was searching for.

Since I knew she wasn't on our bench, I turned my head toward the tunnel—an entrance covered in glass—and there she was. Arms raised high, hands clapping, with a smile on her gorgeous face.

"Put me down," I told my teammates.

Once my skates hit the ice, I hugged the players that I passed on my way to her, and as I got closer, she opened the door to the rink, stepping over the lip on the floor, and I grabbed her, hauling her into my arms.

"Baby!" She hugged me so tightly. "Oh my God! I can't believe it! You scored the winning goal! You won!"

My gloves and helmet were still on, but that didn't stop me from squeezing her. "I love you."

"I love you more."

When I pulled back, the only thing I wanted was her lips, so I removed my helmet and set it on the ice and tossed my gloves, and I put both hands on her face, her smile getting bigger as I led her toward me.

"Every camera is on us right now," she said softly.

"Then we'd better make sure we give them a show."

Our mouths smashed together, and I breathed her in, holding her, ravishing her lips, and when I finally separated us, I grabbed her hand. "Come on. You're going to celebrate with the guys on the ice."

As she walked and I skated, I lifted her hand to kiss her wrist, and something shiny on her skin caught my attention. It was like she'd rubbed lotion on the spot just below her palm. And right in the center of all that gleam was a tattoo.

A tiny, thin black B.

There was a smirk on my face when I voiced, "I thought you were one and done with tattoos? Isn't that what you said to me?"

"That was before I met the wildest one." She let out a small laugh.

"I love that we're having a real moment right now." I kissed all around the small letter. "It's perfect."

"You know, I've told you I love you a thousand times. I sometimes change up the words, or I scream them or whisper them, but ultimately, it all means the same. This is my way of showing it."

"Baby, you have."

To my Tampa Bay Lightning:
Don't hate me. I'll always be a lifelong fan.
But for The Wildest One, *the Whales had to win the Cup.*
XOXO,
Marni

Interested in reading books about some of the characters mentioned in *The Wildest One*?
Hart Weston's Book: *The Arrogant One*
Walker Weston's Book: *The Mysterious One*

ACKNOWLEDGMENTS

Nina Grinstead, whenever I get to this point in the book, I reminisce over the last few months and what's happened. Most things I can't even wrap my head around. I think back to where we started, how things were then and what they look like now. The goals we've set. The dreams we've conquered and the ones that are well on their way. The conversations we've had and, as always, the ledges you've talked me off. All I can say is, we're one hell of a team. To more moments, Nina. Moments where I ugly-cry over Zoom. Moments that I can frame on the wall in my office. Moments where I get to hug you the tightest. I love you so much.

Jovana Shirley, it's hard to find words that I haven't already used when describing you. We've been at this for so many years, and we're going to be at it for so many more. This job is an endless puzzle, and you're one of the biggest pieces. A piece I simply can't live without. I've said this a million times before, and I'll never stop saying it because I mean it with my whole heart: I can't be me without you. Love you so, so hard.

Ratula Roy, there are very few people who know the real me. Who I can be the rawest version of myself in front of. But with you, I can strip off every layer of hardness and happiness and reveal the vulnerability that lives inside me. You know what I need, even before I need it. You know what I need to hear, even when I don't want to listen. There isn't an emotion you haven't seen from me, and yet you still love me. Plus, you never stop feeding my love language. <3 I owe you everything, and I love you forever.

Hang Le, my unicorn, you are just incredible in every way.

Judy Zweifel, as always, thank you for all that you do and for being so wonderful in every way. I adore you. <3

Christine Estevez, when I said last time that you are such a light in my life, I could not have meant that more. There's no one who makes me smile like you. LOVE YOU.

Vicki Valente, you're the best—I hope you know that. Thank you for everything.

Nikki Terrill, my soul sister. Every tear, vent, virtual hug, life chaos, workout—you've been there through it all. I could never do this without you, and I would never want to. I've been saying this for years, and I ALWAYS will: Love you.

Pang, grateful doesn't even come close to cutting it. Neither does thank you. Just know, I love you. So much.

Kim Cermak, Kelley Beckham, Sarah Norris, Christine Miller, Valentine Grinstead, and Daisy—I love y'all so much.

Erin O'Donnell, my audio goddess, I love your ears, your heart, and your soul. Forever.

Brittney Sahin, I'll never be able to thank you for everything you do for me. Just know, I could never do this without you. Love you, B.

Kimmi Street, my sister from another mister. Thank you from the bottom of my heart. You saved me. You inspired me. You kept me standing in so many different ways. I love you more than love.

To my ARC team—To the moon and back, I appreciate you all. <3

Mom and Dad, thanks for your unwavering belief in me and your constant encouragement. It means more than you'll ever know.

Brian, my words could never dent the love I feel for you. Trust me when I say, I love you more.

My Midnighters, you are such a supportive, loving, motivating group. Thanks for being such an inspiration, for holding my hand when I need it, and for always begging for more words. I love you all.

To all the influencers who read, review, share, post, TikTok—Thank you, thank you, thank you will never be enough. You do so much for our writing community, and we're so appreciative.

To my readers—I cherish each and every one of you. I'm so grateful for all the love you show my books, for taking the time to reach out to me, and for your passion and enthusiasm when it comes to my stories. I love, love, love you.

ABOUT THE AUTHOR

Audie® Award–winning and *USA Today* best-selling author Marni Mann knew she was going to be a writer since middle school. While other girls her age were daydreaming about teenage pop stars, Marni was fantasizing about penning her first novel. She crafts unique stories that weave together her love of flawed beauty, mystery, intense passion, and the depths of human emotion. A New Englander at heart, she now resides with her husband in Sarasota, Florida. When she's not nose deep in writing, crafting her next tale, she's fulfilling her wanderlust heart, sipping wine, boating in the Gulf, or devouring fabulous books.

Want to get in touch? Visit Marni at ...
www.marnismann.com
MarniMannBooks@gmail.com

ALSO BY MARNI MANN

THE WESTON GROUP SERIES—EROTIC ROMANCE

The Arrogant One

The Wildest One

The Mysterious One

The Irresistible One (2026)

The Forbidden One (2026)

SPADE HOTEL SERIES—EROTIC ROMANCE

The Playboy

The Rebel

The Sinner

The Heartbreaker

The One

THE DALTON FAMILY SERIES—EROTIC ROMANCE

The Lawyer

The Billionaire

The Single Dad

The Intern

The Bachelor

THE BILLIONAIRES OF BOSTON SERIES—EROTIC ROMANCE

A Million Times, Yes

HOOKED SERIES—CONTEMPORARY ROMANCE

Mr. Hook-up

Mr. Wicked

THE AGENCY SERIES—EROTIC ROMANCE

Signed

Endorsed

Contracted

Negotiated

Dominated

STAND-ALONE NOVELS

Even If It Hurts (Contemporary Romance)

Before You (Contemporary Romance)

The Better Version of Me (Psychological Thriller)

Lover (Erotic Romance)

THE BEARDED SAVAGES SERIES—EROTIC ROMANCE

The Unblocked Collection

Wild Aces

MOMENTS IN BOSTON SERIES—CONTEMPORARY ROMANCE

When Ashes Fall

When Darkness Ends

When We Met

THE PRISONED SERIES—DARK EROTIC THRILLER

Prisoned

Animal

Monster

THE SHADOWS DUET—EROTIC ROMANCE

Seductive Shadows

Seductive Secrecy

THE BAR HARBOR DUET—NEW ADULT

Pulled Beneath

<u>Pulled Within</u>

THE MEMOIR SERIES—DARK MAINSTREAM FICTION

Memoirs Aren't Fairytales

Scars from a Memoir

SNEAK PEEK OF THE MYSTERIOUS ONE

The Mysterious One, the third book in the Weston Group Series, features Walker Weston. It's a sizzling age gap, billionaire, enemies-to-lovers romance that's releasing this winter.

Here's a sneak peek ...

Walker

"Fuck this!" I flung the fry pan, like it was a Frisbee, across the kitchen of my family's restaurant. The mushrooms that I'd been sautéing splattered everywhere, even covering my chef's whites. The stainless-steel pan hit the counter across from me as though it were a bowling ball, taking out the rack of spices like they were pins, the hot metal continuing down the line until it was stopped by my sous chef, his shout filling the silence as he burned his hand. I didn't have an apology in me. All I had was, "I'm fucking out of here."

I stormed off past my sister, Eden, and brother, Colson, who had arrived a few minutes ago to speak to me, and headed

SNEAK PEEK OF THE MYSTERIOUS ONE

to my office in the back. I pushed the door open with so much force, the wood threatened to snap from its hinges. I flipped on the light and went over to my chair, my bag sitting on top of it, and I grabbed the strap and tossed it over my shoulder, kicking the chair into my desk when I was done. As I turned around to leave, Eden and Colson were standing in the doorway.

"Sit down," Eden ordered.

My top lip curled. "I know you're not talking to me."

"Sit." She even pointed at my chair.

The thought of putting my anger in a seated position made the blood inside me boil to the brim. I backed up until I hit the wall behind my desk, sandwiching the framed awards and photos, giving zero fucks if the weight of my body caused them to fall or shattered their frames.

"What the hell do you want?" I roared across the small space.

"I want you to relax for a second," Colson demanded, his stare piercing when it was normally so calm. "I want you to take a deep fucking breath before you explode."

"I'm beyond exploding."

My younger brother came closer and put his hands on the edge of my desk. "I understand you're crashing out—"

"You understand nothing. You're not in my shoes, and you're not even close to slipping your feet into them. So don't you dare say those words to me." I shoved my hands into my pockets before I did something with them—something I regretted. "If you want to add more cooked dishes to Toro's menu then you fucking create them. I'm done."

Our seafood and raw bar, now with three locations, had made quite a splash in the LA food scene. The wait to get in was almost two months long. And Eden and Colson had the fucking nerve to come into the kitchen of Charred tonight and attempt to kindly ask if we have could have a quick meeting over Toro's menu.

A menu that hadn't even been broken in yet, the LA location was still too goddamn new.

"Just hear me out, Walker. We want to capture a larger audience than just sushi and seafood eaters." Colson's voice was so low and calm, I wanted to throw my shoe at his throat. "If there isn't an adequate selection of cooked items, giving them a solid choice, they're not going to come—"

"There's four cooked dishes. Each are different. How many more do they fucking want?"

"We need a chicken option—"

"Take your fucking chicken, Colson, and shove it up your ass."

"Stop!" Eden took several deep breaths. "We didn't come here to argue or upset you, which we've clearly done. And, shit, your poor sous chef is probably on his way to the hospital as we speak."

"I've reached my limit, Eden." I tore at my hair.

Now standing at Colson's side, she crossed her arms over her chest. "I know, so here's what's going to happen ... you're not coming to the San Antonio opening of Horned. You're going to stay here, in LA, and take a week off, maybe two, to get your head straight. After the two weeks, you come back to work, and we'll attempt to discuss things again. You know, once the Fry Pan Incident has died down a little."

The opening of our latest restaurant, Horned, was a carrot that had been dangling in front of me. Once the new Charred menu was strategized—an update that had been a long time coming—I mentally told myself I could go to San Antonio. But then several of the new dishes I'd created were tested, and perfecting those had become my incentive to attend. The logistics of getting those food items to our locations nationwide proved to be harder than I thought, and once that was worked out, I promised myself I'd get on the plane.

Every fucking day, it was something else.

And every fucking time I glanced up at that carrot, it was becoming more rotten, prompting the question: why am I still looking at it?

This—this feeling that was happening within me—wasn't about Horned.

It wasn't about Charred.

Or Toro.

And two weeks off wasn't going to fix me.

And it certainly wasn't going to mend me.

How do you put something back together when the pieces no longer fit?

"If you think a vacation is going to heal me then you haven't listened to a fucking thing I've said to you."

Colson's head dropped.

But Eden, she stayed focused on me, her hands moving to her sides. "I've listened. I just don't know what other choice we have, Walker. The Weston Group needs you. We can't operate without you. We've built our entire company around you."

Three restaurant brands. Clubs. Hundreds of locations around the world.

All on me.

Me.

And more fucking me.

"Don't you realize that therein lies the problem?" My voice was rising with each word. "Everyone needs me. But what about me? What about what I need? Do any of you ever consider that?"

"You need a vacation." Eden flattened her hands against my desk and leaned toward me. "One that's away from us. Away from this restaurant. Away from all the demands we place on you every day. Where you can completely unplug and escape and—"

"Breathe," Colson added. "When the hell was the last time you did that?"

Not since we'd launched our company.

While my four siblings went into our pretty corporate office every day—or played in the NHL, in my younger brother Beck's case—and had their fluffy meetings about expansion and menu colors and HR bullshit, I was the one carrying the weight.

I was the one who bore the mounting pressure.

I was the talent.

"When was the last time you let me breathe?" I picked up the stapler—a sight that was too calm for my liking—and I tossed it toward the wall beside me, the plastic device going right through it. When that gave me no relief, I barked, "I can tell you right now, a vacation isn't what I fucking need." I stared at my sister, my eyelids narrowing. "You, out of all people, know what the darkness feels like. So you, out of all people, should know exactly what I'm going through right now."

"Jesus Christ," Colson groaned. "Walker, you're hitting way below the belt right now. You need to back off."

Eden filled her lungs, her chest staying high as she rubbed her lips together. "I do know ... and that's why I'm giving you a timeout."

"To do what? Sit in my goddamn living room and stare at my kitchen that I can't stand the sight of? Or drink until I can't take another sip? What the hell is a break going to do for me aside from make me angrier? I don't want to sit home." I pounded my fist against the wall. "I want to love my fucking life again."

"Walker ..." Eden whispered.

"This family took away my love of cooking." I paused. "Somehow, you need to give it back to me."

Eden stared at me silently, the emotion thick in her eyes even though there wasn't a tear present. "Give me your phone."

"What?" I challenged.

"Your phone, Walker. Hand it over." Her fingers extended toward me.

I couldn't imagine why she wanted my cell, but I didn't have the patience to question her, so I set it on her palm.

"What's your password?" she asked.

I rattled off the six numbers, and she tapped the screen multiple times. Colson watched from beside her, his face full of shock, even more so when she gave the phone back to me and said, "I just installed the Hooked app on your phone."

The Hooked app?

Some used it to find their wife. Others just for fucking.

But if you were open to dating or marriage or just sex, this was more than likely the app you used.

I didn't have time for any of that bullshit.

"Why the fuck did you do that? The last thing I want on my phone is a hookup app—"

"Because what you don't need is to sit at home, alone, draining your wet bar and staring at a kitchen that you'll probably end up blowing up. You want to get out of the darkness, then I'm putting you toward the light." Her expression softened. "Since I highly doubt you want to spend that time with me, I'm encouraging you to spend it with someone else. Go make a profile and bury yourself in someone for the next week. Or two. I promise, Walker ... it'll help." Her voice had turned haunting toward the end of her last statement.

"Some mindless sex isn't going to hurt." Colson smirked.

"It isn't going to help either," I countered.

"You'd be surprised, brother," Colson shot back.

Before I could process any of this, Eden continued, "I'm going to book you a suite at the Beverly Hills Spade and Cole Hotel. Check in, get pampered, order in every meal—I don't want you anywhere near a kitchen."

"And fuck away your anger," Colson said.

I couldn't believe what I was hearing.

"I'll check on you in the morning when we board the jet." Eden released my desk. "Do not turn your phone off or I'll send one of the Spade brothers up to your room for a wellness check and I don't think you want that."

The owners were close family friends we'd done business with for years since our restaurants were in many of the lobbies of their hotels.

"Don't you dare threaten me." I lifted my middle finger. "I don't need anyone to check on me."

"Tough. I'm doing this for your own good and because I love you." Eden moved to the doorway, and Colson followed. "Please take our advice. And please, please stay away from any and all kitchens."

My brother gave me a look—one I didn't recognize. "You haven't been you in a long time, Walker."

He shut the door, and they were gone.

The silence was so startling, the shaking I felt earlier, before the handle of the pan had left my fingers, was back.

But instead of throwing something within reach, I was frozen, with Colson's words repeating in my head.

You haven't been you in a long time, Walker.

The issue with that statement was that I agreed.

As I stood in my office, halfway between the wall and my desk, I loaded the app, creating a profile, and I went through the questionnaire, forcing myself to really read each prompt and taking the time to answer every one truthfully rather than skimming the words and choosing random answers. This part was important, given that the results would pair me with someone who had the same sexual demands as me.

Once I finished, my thumb hovered over the button at the bottom that would make my account live.

Fuck, do I really want to do this?
Do I really want to bury myself in someone?
For a whole week?

I pressed the button.

The app informed me that every time I logged in, the accounts would show in order of compatibility, which meant the first photo to appear was who the app thought I should be hooked with most.

The woman who was most like-minded as me.

And the picture I was looking at was ... of *her*.

Click HERE to pre-order The Mysterious One.